MEANT FOR
you

A NOVEL

MEANT FOR you

A NOVEL

RANEÉ S. CLARK

SWEETLY US
PRESS

Cover design by Sweetly Us Press

Cover Photo Credit: "2 People Sitting With View of Yellow Flowers during Daytime" picjumbo.com | pexels.com

Editors:

Stacey Turner

Jenny Proctor | www.jennyproctor.com

Published by Sweetly Us Press

www.sweetlyuspress.com

❀ Created with Vellum

To those of you who crushed on Anthony,
Who thought David was the sweetest,
Who believed in Sean's loyalty
Who read and asked for more.
You make my day every time you turn a page.
Thank you, Readers.
♥

ACKNOWLEDGMENTS

It feels like a long time ago that I wrote a story about a quarterback and the girl who loved him. After my mom read it, she texted back and asked me, "What about David?" And so I gave him a story. And then if David got a story, then Sean and DJ also needed one. Thank you, thank you, Mom. Three novels wouldn't be here if you hadn't asked for more.

Once again, thank you to my family members who lent their names all that time ago and got roped into being characters in novels. So to my brother DJ, thank you so much. Not only did you help me write about a football player, but you weathered your namesake being known as the least serious of the roommates. To my dad, Doug, who read like the wind to make sure my firefighters were all up to par. Any mistakes there are totally mine. Thanks, Dad!

To my writing group, my Suite Sisters who always support and help where they can. To Kaylee Baldwin, Kate White, Gina Denny, and the many others who read and gave ideas for how to polish this story up. To my editor, Stacey Turner, it means more than I can say to have you be a part of this project. To Jenny Proctor, who not only beta read and helped me through a tough revision, but also did editing work as well.

To my family, my husband who supports most of my crazy ideas and my boys who have survived so far with a creative person as a parent.

CHAPTER ONE

"You love spaghetti, remember?" Chelsea lifted her two-year-old son's plastic fork, full of pasta and the special sauce she'd made to hide something like a million vegetables. She tried to tempt Austin by gently tapping his sealed lips, but he shook his head and reeled back, shouting, "No! No, sketti!"

A second later he banged his head against the back of his high chair. His screaming increased by several decibels, and he smacked the bowl away, sending it and three-fourths of the spaghetti still inside flying across the kitchen floor. Chelsea also got her fair share down her shirt. She dropped her head onto the table in total defeat— right into a pile of spaghetti.

It didn't surprise her. Of all the bites she'd tried to get into Austin's mouth over the last half hour, she hadn't succeeded with even one noodle. Of course, there was always the possibility some had *accidentally* gotten into his mouth while he flung it all over her and the kitchen.

"You okay?" she asked, reaching for a nearby rag and dabbing it over his tear-stained face. No sauce that she could see. Funny how it could cover her and the kitchen, yet he'd escaped unscathed.

"No!" he yelled, pushing her hand away.

Of course. His favorite word. Sure, he used to love words like *Mommy* and *pease*. A year ago, his babbling and increasing vocabulary had made her sure he'd be speaking full sentences by now, but ever since Brady had left, it seemed like the only word that passed Austin's lips was *no* and always in the same high-pitched yell.

The French door leading from the backyard into the kitchen opened and closed, making Chelsea turn to see who'd entered. Her mom had come in, wearing a pair of dark-colored jeans and a T-shirt emblazoned with the logo of Chelsea's cousin's bakery, Cutie Pies.

"Mmm, lunch, little man?" her mom asked. Denise Gardener laid a light hand on Chelsea's shoulder but quickly lifted it back up. When Chelsea turned to look, her mom was eyeing spaghetti on her fingers. Denise put down a box with the same logo as her t-shirt on the table. She picked up a napkin from the shabby-chic napkin holder to wipe off her hand.

"Want me to try?" she asked, laughing.

Chelsea shook her head. "With what?" She stood to clean up the spaghetti around the high chair. It almost blended in with the warm, red-brown of the hardwood floor.

Denise glanced at the stove. "I'll make him up some more and give it a try. What do you say?"

"I can do it, Mom," Chelsea said from the floor. She swept wide underneath the high chair with the rag, gathering up most of the spaghetti in one swipe.

"Gamma! Gamma!" Austin had forgotten his temper tantrum as he reached for her, but Denise only planted a careful kiss on his cheeks.

"I know you can," she said to Chelsea, "but you never let me feed him. Give me some grandmotherly duties. I bet I could tempt him to enjoy some spaghetti. Mmmm!" She stepped over to the stove and dished some more pasta, dipping her finger into the sauce and trying it. "What's in this?" she asked with a smile, dipping her finger in for another taste before adding some to the bowl. "It's good."

"Why are you so surprised?" Chelsea teased. "It's a recipe from that new cookbook I got. Tomatoes, obviously, sweet potatoes, carrots, cauliflower, zucchini, and some spinach. Can you taste it all?" Chelsea frowned as she scooted across the floor to scrub streaks of spaghetti from the white cabinets next to the stove. She'd waited a long time to be a mother and had expected the trials that would come with it. But doing it without Brady was a different kind of hard than she'd anticipated. "I thought it tasted like regular spaghetti sauce."

Denise smiled and helped her off the floor. "There's a hint that it's not normal sauce but not in a bad way. I love the way you used the seasonings to perfect it. Don't let it get you down. Babies always have super taste buds. Not your fault."

"He used to eat vegetables without me having to trick him into it. Now I'm lucky if he'll eat peanut butter and jelly."

Denise crossed back to the kitchen table, where she set down Austin's bowl, then went back to the counter to prepare her own lunch. She dished up some of the pasta, added sauce, and headed to the fridge, where she pulled out the parmesan. She sprinkled some cheese on top of Austin's food and her own and then sat down.

"He'll get better if you keep trying, sweetheart. Don't give up."

Chelsea picked up Austin's fork again and held it toward him. "Look, Gramma got you cheese," she said in a bright voice, but Austin started shouting "No!" again, so she gave up. "How was the bakery this morning?" she shouted over Austin's tantrum.

"Busy. As always. Wendy said to ask if you could come in a little early to help her get ahead on the afternoon baking."

Chelsea sighed as she looked at the big clock on the kitchen wall. "If Austin goes down for a nap earlier. Which he might. He didn't sleep well again last night. I'll text Wendy." She had hoped to spend some time that morning looking at the shop's books but hadn't gotten to it yet. When she worked at the counter at Cutie Pies, going back and forth between that and her computer always left her feeling frazzled. But Wendy needed her to do double duty, and small as it was, Chelsea didn't want to turn down the pay.

With the child support Brady paid and her meager paycheck, she could probably afford to move out on her own, but she appreciated more than just her parents' financial support and wasn't ready to give it up quite yet. There was a small house a block away for sale, and if she saved up carefully and got a few more freelance clients, she'd be able to afford it.

Denise waved her off. "She said not to stress about it if you couldn't." Denise pointed to the box she'd brought in earlier—sugar cookies by the looks of it. "Nabbed these from the day-old stash. Couldn't believe that someone hadn't already bought them. You should have one."

"Maybe later."

"You too, Austin," Denise said with a grin. "Finish up your lunch." He screamed louder.

The door banged open again. "What's all the hubbub for?" Chelsea's dad shouted, making a beeline for Austin. Even though Max Gardener was just a few inches taller than his wife and Chelsea, he had the broad, muscular build of a farmer. Before Chelsea realized what he was doing, Max handed Austin a cookie from the box on the table and lifted him out of the high chair.

"Max," Denise scolded at the same time Chelsea cried, "Dad!"

He stared between the two of them, bewildered. "What?" Austin, meanwhile, shoved most of the cookie in his mouth.

Chelsea gestured toward the spaghetti-splattered high chair. "He hasn't eaten lunch yet. You can't give him a cookie because he's screaming."

Max sniffed some of the glop on Austin's shirt—what hadn't trans-ferred to Max's oil-stained work shirt. "You don't like spaghetti now, little monkey?" He scowled mockingly at Austin before turning back to Chelsea with the same sad-puppy look he always gave her after spoiling his grandson. "And I can give him a cookie, Chels. I'm his grandpa."

"Max, we talked about this." Denise offered the box to Chelsea, and since denying one to set an example for Austin was a moot point now, she took two. "It was one thing for you to spoil him when he was visiting, but they live with us now."

Max's jaw worked to clamp his lips together. He tried hard to keep his criticism of his former son-in-law to himself. Eight years ago, he'd asked Chelsea to consider giving her first baby up for adoption. She and Brady were so young. But once they'd chosen to get married, he'd kept his peace and mourned with her and her mother when she lost the baby. She respected her father for that, and she respected him even more now, when he had ample reasons to spout I-told-you-so's. He'd been right about it being a mistake to marry Brady at eighteen just because she was pregnant, but he'd never say so.

"Doesn't seem quite fair that Brady's the one that gets to swoop in and spoil him now." Max walked with Austin toward the apron sink to wash him up, muttering, "When he even comes at all." Chelsea noticed red streaks on the sink's usually sparkling, porcelain-white surface. She sighed again but didn't move to clean it up.

"Max." Denise's voice held a warning tone.

"It's okay, Mom." Chelsea waved her off. Brady hadn't been to visit for a while, using his job as an excuse. She'd remind him on their next video call how long it had been. She joined Max at the sink, grabbing a new rag from the drawer and helping her dad wipe up Austin before she used it on herself. "He's been busy since he started with the new firm. I'll talk to him."

Max dropped an arm on her shoulder. His unique machinery/cow manure smell was comforting instead of off-putting since she'd grown up smelling it on him. "He'll figure out how important time with Austin is . . . eventually."

"Thanks." She understood Brady's job took a lot of time—a new lawyer at the firm doing all the grunt work—but his job would *always* take a lot of time. He had to figure out how to balance that. Her ex-husband was notorious for getting wrapped up in projects and not balancing the other priorities in his life. He'd gotten better in the year since their divorce, but he still had learning to do.

She kicked away the nagging feeling she should move back to Salt Lake. It would make it a lot easier for Brady to make time if they lived in the same city; she could *encourage* him a lot more. She'd come back to her hometown to regroup after her divorce and lean on her parents for emotional support, but she had to admit, it wasn't what tied her down anymore. Selfishly, she knew staying in Wyoming meant she could spend at least part of the day at home with Austin. She'd longed for a baby for so long, she fought against giving up what she had now —working for her cousin during nap time and spending most of the day with her son.

When she'd first found out she was pregnant at the end of her senior year, she had been terrified, but losing the baby two months later had devastated her more than she'd expected. Brady's obvious relief hadn't helped. She'd struggled with her and Brady's decision to wait to have children until he was done with school, approaching him every year or so about changing his mind, but she'd anticipated blessings because they'd waited: Brady would finish school debt free, and she could fulfill her longing to stay home once she had kids. She didn't want to give up on that idea just because they were divorced. She'd worked for it. She'd earned it.

But would Brady ever figure out how much he needed his son if he was effectively out of sight, out of mind? She sighed and shoved the thoughts away. She definitely didn't need to make that decision today.

———

CHELSEA ROLLED over and glared at the neon-green numbers of her bedside clock. Had she gone into Austin's room just four minutes ago? Maybe his constant screaming made time run slower. The parts of the sleep book she'd read so far said something about letting him cry for ten to fifteen minutes, but he was waking everyone in the house. Heck, everyone in the neighborhood. She threw her legs off the bed and hurried out of her room and down the hallway. She'd give in— again—and let Austin sleep with her, if he'd sleep at all. She'd reached the door when Denise emerged from the master bedroom kitty-corner from Austin's room. Chelsea's insides tightened.

"Sorry, Mom," she whispered.

Denise waved her hand. "I heard your door open and wanted to see if you'd let me take a shift while you got some rest."

"I'm okay," Chelsea said. "Did he wake Dad up too?"

Denise shook her head and came toward her, one hand on the wooden railing of the stairwell, letting her eyes adjust to the dark.

"He's sound asleep. Has his earplugs in and playing that sleep machine with rain or ocean waves or something."

"Good." Chelsea forced a smile.

Denise reached for her hand, rubbing the top of it. "Let me help, sweetie. Letting me help doesn't mean you can't do it by yourself."

Chelsea gripped her mom's hand, grateful for her support. "I know it's not a big deal for you to help. But Austin . . . at some point he needs to get back to something more normal, and I'm his mom. It's best for me to do this." They wouldn't live there forever, she hoped, and she wanted to disrupt his life as little as possible. He'd already been through so much.

"Even before, you had help, Chels. It's not going to spoil Austin to let his grandma calm him." Denise leaned forward toward Austin's door, where they could both hear him wailing at the top of his lungs.

"He didn't sleep bad before." Chelsea moved to go into the room and cut off the discussion. Denise caught her hint and laid a hand on her back before padding back to her room.

Austin's screams calmed to hopeful whimpers when he saw Chelsea. She should lay him back down in the crib. He wouldn't learn to sleep there again if Chelsea picked him up and took him back to bed with her, but she couldn't argue with the fat tears rolling down his cheeks and the anxious way he stretched his arms over the railing toward her. She gathered him in her arms, letting the tension in her shoulders relax when he nestled his head on her shoulder, his small body jerking with hiccups.

"It's still bedtime, little man. Can you go back to sleep in your crib?" she whispered.

Austin's cries picked up again. "No, Mama, no!"

She couldn't do it. She couldn't put him back when he was so upset. "Okay, okay." She swayed as she walked down the hall to her room, tears stinging the insides of her eyes. She entered her room and slowly rocked her way across the short distance from the door to her bed, hoping that exhaustion would overtake Austin before they got there. Having Mom lying beside him didn't always equal sleep for him. She tried to joke with herself as she lowered both of their bodies to the bed, telling herself that since Austin had slept through the night at only two months old, he was making up now for the sleep she hadn't lost then. The knot in her chest tightened. It wasn't a joke. Austin's good sleeping habits had dissolved right along with her marriage.

She let out a relieved breath as he settled next to her and closed his eyes. Carefully she reached to tug the blanket up to cover them. Already her own consciousness started slipping.

She was jerked out of her almost-sleep by a loud scream, now right in her ear. Austin arched his back and howled, resisting her efforts to hold him against her. She rolled over with him on her chest, standing and rocking. He calmed but looked around, now wide awake. Two nights ago, the car had worked to put him to sleep. Chelsea was too tired to figure anything else out. Plus, Austin couldn't keep her parents awake from the car. She stopped by Austin's room to grab him a blanket before trooping down the stairs and out to her Honda Civic. Austin had the nerve to giggle as she put him in his car seat, but even sleep deprived and upset, she couldn't resist his toothy smile.

"Yeah, yeah. Real funny, bud."

She slipped into the driver's seat and started the car. As she pulled out of the driveway, she noticed Denise waving from the window above the garage. Chelsea waved back, even though she didn't think her mom could see her. She turned on the lullabies she'd been using to lull Austin to sleep and settled in to drive the deserted, late-night streets of Clay for a few hours.

———

DJ HAD BEEN THINKING about football when the fire alarm went off. Five months after becoming a fireman, some things were already automatic; falling asleep in his bunk at the firehouse no matter what time of day and instantly waking up when he heard the fire bell, sliding down the pole to the garage and trying to beat ten or so other guys into the truck, even when his brain was on other things. It was possible sliding down the pole was still more of a little boy's dream come true than anything. But DJ would never admit as much out loud.

As he pulled on his bunker gear, he calculated the number of days until the college football season started (one hundred and thirteen) and how many more of David's baseball games he'd have to endure (too many) before that time came. He hopped into the first truck headed out of the station, proud of himself for making it.

It wasn't until he was on the scene—an accident on Highway 14— and Assistant Chief Will Zollinger arrived that he took notice of the fact that this turnout pants fit a little snug and rode a little high up his ankle.

"Kaiser!" Zollinger shouted loud and with enough of an edge that everyone near DJ looked up.

"Yeah?" he asked. The anger in Zollinger's expression made DJ take note that his turnout jacket *also* felt tight across his chest. Or maybe it was the fact that the head of their crew's jacket looked a few sizes too big.

Zollinger stalked through the dry sagebrush that lined the highway and came to stand next to where DJ stood directing traffic. The highway patrolman who'd responded first took down a statement from the victim. The accident had involved one vehicle, an old but sturdy Ford truck that had run off the road and rolled over once. The driver, the only passenger in the truck, had climbed out on his own. He had some bumps and bruises, possibly a concussion, but more likely than not, the Clay Fire Department would be dismissed from the scene before too long.

"Next time you wash the bunker gear," Zollinger said, holding out his arm to demonstrate how the sleeve of his jacket draped over the end of his hand, "don't switch your gear with mine."

DJ swallowed. He glanced around, noting one of the paramedics, Abbey, talking to Sister Rasmussen. Sister Rasmussen was in DJ's ward and had been driving behind the truck when it rolled. She had called 911. She and Abbey avoided his gaze, probably trying to at least look like they weren't listening to Zollinger's lecture, but both of them covered smiles with their hands. It bothered him most to have Abbey witness the scolding. He'd asked her out once after he'd been back in town a couple months and encountered her at a few call-outs. She'd laughed and told him that he didn't date girls like her. But didn't he get to decide that?

"Add it to the list," he muttered to himself. Another bullet point on the list of things he'd gotten wrong since moving back to his home-town of Clay, Wyoming. At least this wasn't worse than the time he caught his own house on fire or when he'd backed into the chief's truck when he'd pulled one of the fire trucks out to clean it. He'd thought he was finally getting the hang of something, that maybe he'd even found a job he could be good at. But maybe not.

Originally, after his plans to play in the NFL had fallen through, he'd come home to work while he figured out where to go from there —but now, more than ever, he wanted to stay. He'd witnessed how many kids went off to college and never came back, how the town needed reviving, and he could be part of that. *Not* failing had become part of his need to conquer.

"What was that?" Zollinger snapped. Will Zollinger was a few years older than DJ. They'd played sports together in high school and grown up in the same ward. He was normally a pretty calm guy— that's what made him good at leading their crew—but DJ suspected having to take charge of an accident scene in turnout gear that had him tripping over himself didn't sit too well.

"Nothing, Cap. Sorry." DJ sighed.

"Give me that," Zollinger hissed, yanking at the turnout jacket. "You're gonna bust mine wide open."

DJ ripped the Velcro attachment open and unzipped the jacket, shoving it at Zollinger without even so much as a glance at Abbey.

Zollinger muttered to himself as he stalked away. More than a few snickers were directed at him too. He wouldn't forgive DJ for a few days. DJ let out another sigh and waved through a car approaching the scene slowly.

As he suspected, the firemen were sent home after a local tow truck came to retrieve the banged up old Ford from the ditch. DJ was straightening up the gear—double and triple checking that he'd put everyone's gear back in the right place—when Abbey walked through the open garage door.

"Making the rookie do the housekeeping?" she asked and held out a box from Cutie Pie's bakery. "Raided Wendy's day-old stash. Try that brownie." The fringes on Abbey's out-of-style, padded cowboy jacket swayed with her movement. Abbey's outfits never ceased to surprise him. After over five years of trendy Provo, it was kind of a relief. One of DJ's best friends, David, was engaged to a high-maintenance girl who'd never approve of any of Abbey's fashion choices. The thought of Sophie's reaction to Abbey's outfit made DJ smile. And he liked Abbey all the more for it.

He opened the box and reached for the giant brownie smothered in peanut butter cups and caramel. "How in the world did something like this last ten *minutes* at Wendy's bakery, let alone a couple days?" DJ hadn't even finished talking before he shoved a bite into his mouth. Before her bakery had taken off, Wendy Gardener had worked nights as a dispatcher, and most of the policemen, paramedics, and firemen in town knew her voice well—and her baking. She'd tried out more than a few recipes on them as she prepared to open her shop. She usually dropped off whatever hadn't sold at the station.

"With all the delicious stuff she makes, I'm sure some things don't sell right off. There were a couple pieces of fudge . . ." Abbey rolled her eyes back and sighed. "I really wanted to save one for you, but I couldn't, like *physically* could not stop myself from eating both."

"Thanks." He chuckled then devoured another bite of the brownie. Wow, Wendy had outdone herself with this creation. Hopefully it made regular appearances in her lineup.

Abbey backed out of the garage door. It was just like her to drop by for nothing else than to give him a brownie and brighten his day. "Have a good night, DJ."

"When do you work tomorrow? Still swing?" he asked before she got away. With the fireman's schedules of three days on then two days off, it wasn't always easy to sync up with Abbey's schedule. Paramedics worked crazy hours too. "We could do something."

She shrugged and headed out into the dimming light without

answering him. Color rose in his face, heating the back of his neck. He ducked his head and hurried back toward the bunker gear, going through it one last time before heading upstairs to join the rest of his crew. His insides pinched with discomfort and wariness. At least the guys had all gone upstairs and hadn't seen Abbey shut him down again.

She hadn't been the first girl to turn down a date with him, but it'd seemed a lot more trivial when he'd lived with Anthony, David, and Sean. Anthony Rogers had been BYU's star quarterback, and DJ had dated plenty of girls that had dated Anthony first and then settled for him. In fact, both DJ and David had. He'd never cared about that.

A part of DJ had grown used to girls wanting to date him because he'd played football in college with some pretty famous guys. Anthony played quarterback for the Broncos now, and David's baseball career with the Atlanta Braves was taking off. But in Clay it was different. He wanted things to be different.

DJ had come home because life in Provo had felt shallow—*he* felt shallow. He wanted to amount to something more than a hometown hero constantly reliving his BYU glory days. He wouldn't be some guy who sat around moaning about how he'd been *this close* to playing in the NFL. So he'd come back to Clay hoping he'd find a way to make a difference to the community. To matter.

When DJ got back upstairs, most of the guys on his crew were lounging in the rec room, watching the last of David's baseball game. DJ had scheduled his own DVR to record it so he could watch it when he got off in the morning, so he headed for his bunk instead. The hour or so of sleep he'd gotten in between calls didn't feel like enough.

"Hey, Kaiser," Xander Leavitt stopped him before he got too far. DJ knew what was coming based on the smirk on his coworker's face.

DJ squared his shoulders, ready to take whatever these guys doled out. He was used to living with guys who made fun of each other so well they could've gone pro in it. He could take it from a few amateurs.

"Just so you know, high-waters are not the way to go in turnout gear. I know styles are different in Utah, but we don't do the tight shirt, skinny jeans thing here in Clay," Xander said. DJ had actually seen one of Xander's nephews wearing that exact outfit a few days earlier, but he refrained from pointing that out. The sooner his conversation with Xander was over, the better.

"Ha. Ha." But DJ made sure none of the guys knew that the teasing actually needled him. In fact, the *teasing* didn't get to him. What got to him was the way it reminded him of how big a failure he was.

"Ease up, guys, he'll find a way to get back into Zollinger's good graces," Miles Hansen broke in. "Like convincing David Savage to come play on our softball team for a game or two."

DJ leaned up against one of the couches. "David's usually pretty busy during the summer, guys. You know, playing baseball."

"You might want to call in a favor." Miles laughed. "So you have good news for Zollinger next time you talk to him."

"Yeah, don't get your hopes up." DJ made a break for the sleeping quarters and grabbed his phone and headphones from the nightstand next to his bed. He shoved the bright blue headphones on, turning up the volume on his old warm-up music. The familiar songs always had a way of turning his mood, reminding him of the confidence he'd once had. Helped him remember some of his greatest plays, like the time he and Anthony kept lateral passing after the clock had run out in order to score one last time to win the game. Nobody had forgotten that for a long time.

Not that DJ needed his glory days of football to be happy or that he even wanted people to only remember him by that, but life had been good then. He'd been happy. On the football field he'd known exactly who he was and what he was meant to do. All he needed to do was figure out how to get that feeling back.

CHAPTER TWO

Wendy's bakery smelled magnificent, as always. When Chelsea wasn't worrying about what Austin had eaten or if he'd take a good nap while she worked, the heady chocolate smells drifting together with the lightest touch of almond and vanilla lightened her mood and made her job part heaven.

It was a busy day. People hadn't stopped coming in since Chelsea had arrived in the middle of the lunch rush; they'd sold dozens and dozens of doughnuts, muffins, scones, and Wendy's killer brownies.

Things finally slowed late-afternoon, but a handful of people still ebbed and flowed, buying pastries to go or sitting to chat in one of the half-dozen café style tables crowded into the tiny front portion of the shop. Chelsea noticed a particular person entering the store and grimaced.

DJ Kaiser. The Kaisers had lived next door to Brady's family and were co-owners of the small grocery store in town. DJ and Brady had grown up playing football together. Chelsea knew the countless hours the boys had spent in their enjoined backyards practicing—running drills, playing catch, whatever. They'd grown up more like brothers than just friends or neighbors.

Truthfully, he was just another entry on a long list of people

Chelsea tried to avoid in this small town. It particularly stung to avoid him though, considering the friendship they'd shared over the years. When she and Brady had started dating junior year, Brady's parents had encouraged DJ to tag along on a lot of their dates. Dating Brady had meant gaining a new best friend in DJ. He'd honed the flirting skills he'd later become known for on Chelsea, making her laugh at his silly lines and earning a good-natured punch or two from Brady. He knew their story. And the ending too. DJ and Brady were close, so she had no doubt Brady had discussed every move in his marriage—and its downfall—with his lifelong best friend. If she hadn't been certain of that, she might have called him herself for a few words of advice on how to navigate this new relationship with Brady. How could she and DJ stay close friends without the common denominator? Another unfair thing that had happened in the wake of their split: since DJ had come with Brady in their relationship, Brady got him in the divorce.

She looked around for Wendy, but her cousin was busy in the back.. Of course she was. That was the whole reason Chelsea worked afternoons, to mind the counter while Wendy kept up with the baking. She had come out from the kitchen a few times during the busy lunch, helping customers while things baked, but now that it had slowed down, she hadn't emerged from the kitchen in well over an hour.

"Good afternoon." DJ stepped up to where Chelsea stood behind the register, waiting while some people browsed the glass cases of the counter, trying to choose between all of Wendy's delectable treats. He was tall, much taller than Brady, at least six-four or five. Brady always said that made him a great receiver—it was easy to grab the ball over the defender's head. Standing so close to the bakery case, he seemed to loom over her, his whole face and especially his hazel eyes dancing with playfulness. She had always thought DJ was attractive, but thinking it now brought a blush to her face. Maybe more out of surprise than anything else. She hadn't really considered dating in the year since she and Brady divorced. Not that thinking DJ was attractive meant—

She put a quick stop to the crazy course her train of thought had just taken. "Hey, what can I get you?" She tried to sound casual and even managed a smile for her old friend. The easy way he leaned against the counter and stared at the food said discomfort didn't twist in his chest like it did in hers. Since moving back, she hadn't seen him that often. He lived in the other Clay ward, and with his work schedule, he wasn't always up and around town at normal hours anyway. And he obviously hadn't ogled her when he came in the way she had him.

"Do you work here a lot?" DJ asked, looking up from his perusal of the food.

"Every afternoon," she said, wishing he'd figure out what he wanted. She didn't know what Brady had said about her. Had he told DJ he didn't love Chelsea? What had DJ thought of that?

"Ahhh." DJ nodded. "I usually come by in the morning. Explains why I never see you here." He cast her a smile and went back to perusing, thankfully. The part of her that wasn't anxious over how their relationship would change was grateful that he at least acted like nothing had changed. One less thing different in her upside-down world.

"Who watches Austin?" He glanced up at her curiously before leaning over to examine the back row of treats.

"Normally my mom, but she wasn't feeling well today so he's at Madison's house." Chelsea's ex-sister-in-law was always encouraging Chelsea to bring Austin over more so he could play with his cousins.

"Austin's probably gotten so big since I last saw him. Guess I know where I'm going when I leave here. And with an extra brownie too."

"You can't feed him a brownie with that much sugar!" Then Chelsea forced a laugh to cover her burst of bossiness. But she worried enough about what Madison fed him. She needed Austin to start eating vegetables again, but more often than not the containers of homemade food she left for Madison to feed Austin came home untouched. Of course, that wasn't necessarily Madison's fault. Most of the food Chelsea made for him *period* ended up untouched.

DJ straightened and put on a mock stern face. "Right. Of course. I'll get two and save one for later. And also a dozen raspberry scones."

Inwardly Chelsea groaned. The scones tasted as to-die-for as the caramel smothered brownies—and were full of just as much sugar, right down to the homemade raspberry filling Wendy used.

"I could refuse to sell them to you without a written statement that my son won't come home filled with refined white sugar and flour and . . . well . . ." She tried to make it sound like a joke but stopped when DJ's eyebrows started rising higher and higher. She plastered an I-don't-actually-care-that-much expression on her face, trying to hide that her shoulders were tensed with real anxiety. DJ leaned closer and peered at her. They weren't talking about Brady, but the conversation unnerved her just as much.

DJ nodded slowly as he studied her. "I see." His smile returned. Another thing she knew about DJ. He didn't stay serious for long. She remembered the times they would all hang out in high school and how DJ was always good for a joke—usually a flirtatious one. Or the times DJ came up to Rexburg or Salt Lake after she and Brady were married. The two men would spend their entire time together recounting hilarious stories of their childhood and teenage years. DJ could always make Austin giggle, even when he was a baby. Since Brady wasn't a very hands-on dad, it always surprised Chelsea that more often than not, DJ would hold Austin on his lap when he visited.

"I promise only one scone," DJ said. "Better than the brownie. I'll even lick all the icing off for him. I'm a conscientious guy."

A real laugh escaped Chelsea. "Fine." She reached for one of Wendy's heart-speckled brown bags, *Cutie Pies* written in swirly letters on the front.

"Hey, you know I could watch Austin for you sometimes. I don't have anything else to do on my days off."

Chelsea peeked over the counter. DJ looked serious about his offer —and chagrined too. Nothing else to do? Not that there were a lot of single women in Clay and the two surrounding towns that made up the Bellemont Wyoming Stake, but Chelsea knew they had all swooned over the BYU football star when he'd returned home. He'd been in the shop only a minute before *her* mind had gone there and she was well past the young and swoony single stage of life.

"I doubt that." She turned to put the final scone inside the white box before putting the box inside the bag. She grabbed another box and shuffled to the side to get his two brownies. "And don't worry." She stood up to ring up his purchases. "There are plenty of people I can call on to watch Austin."

DJ handed over the cash before she finished ringing it up. "Put the rest in the tip jar." He pointed before putting the wallet back in his pocket. "How about when it's not just for you to work? Do you take anyone up on those offers then?" He raised his eyebrows.

Heat pooled in Chelsea's cheeks. Madison had told her plenty of times to bring Austin over. She was anxious to do her share, but she was Austin's aunt, not his father. She didn't *have* a share she was responsible for. Besides, Chelsea could do this. Part of her believed she could give Austin the same Mom + Dad + Austin life she'd always planned on, just without the Dad part of the equation for now. Letting his grandma and aunt spoil him in place of that normality didn't fit in with her plan. It was hard enough to leave him every afternoon for her job. With all the upheaval in his world, evidenced by the drastic change in his eating and sleeping habits, she didn't need to add regular visits to Madison's.

The bell above the door rang, and Mr. and Mrs. Morales, a couple that frequented the bakery often, came in. Relief settled over her. She would have to help them, and DJ would leave.

"Sure," Chelsea said in a hurry. "I know I should take him to Madison's more, though. I will. And Patty's." Chelsea closed up the register and stuffed his change into the cutesy, turquoise-painted Mason jar that Wendy used for tips. Brady's mom, Patty, wasn't in good health, so she couldn't watch Austin. Her husband, Dale, spent a lot of time busy on the farm, but guilt crept up on Chelsea for not taking Austin out to their house—a few miles outside of Clay—more often.

She cleared her throat, hoping the Moraleses picked out something quickly, but by the casual way they browsed the case on the other side of the L-shaped counter, that didn't seem likely.

"Let me babysit some morning so you can get some things done or take a nap or something." DJ leaned back on the counter, even though she'd finished with his order. If she had a couple mornings a week free, that would mean she could pick up more freelance accounting clients, but it would also mean more mornings away from Austin. When she looked around to make sure the Moraleses didn't need anything, DJ straightened. "And I won't even feed him refined sugar."

"Excuse me, Chelsea, can we get a half-dozen of the apple-cinnamon muffins?" Mrs. Morales asked from the other side of the counter before Chelsea could reply to DJ.

"Of course," she said, then cast him an apologetic shrug, even though she was grateful their interaction would have to end. He waved and headed out of the shop. Chelsea crossed her fingers that Madison would stay strong and only allow a bite or two of the scones. She knew how Chelsea felt about how Austin ate, even if she thought she knew better how to raise him.

Still, she was pretty sure she'd find Austin covered in raspberry filling when she went to pick him up. But a girl could dream.

An hour later, with no customers to serve or keep an eye on in the main room, Chelsea wandered to the door that separated the kitchen from the front of the shop. She propped it open and headed to the desk where Wendy kept her laptop. She reached for the folder of receipts and invoices, then pulled up a web browser to check the accounts. Wendy was usually pretty dutiful about printing out invoices from things she purchased online, but she'd hired Chelsea to make sure nothing slipped through the cracks.

"What're you baking?" Chelsea asked as she sat down. She swirled the office chair to face the middle of Wendy's large wooden baking table.

"The best lemon bars you've ever had in your life." Snatching a spoon from the bowl, Wendy dipped it into the bright yellow filling and came toward Chelsea, holding it out.

Chelsea took it and licked the filling off the spoon, savoring the mix of tart and sweet that Wendy did so well. "Yes. Definitely the best. It must be since this bakery's so darn successful."

"About time," Wendy said proudly, pouring the filling over what was probably a light and perfectly crumbly crust. "How's it going out front?"

"Quiet, for now. About a half hour until the school lets out and we get another rush. Anything you need help baking to get ready?" She could always do some of the accounting from home, after Austin was asleep.

"Nope." Wendy scraped the last of the filling out, dripped it into the pan, and then licked her spatula before tossing it behind her into the sink. "The latest batch of bread is all out of the oven for sandwiches. Wait . . . are the chocolate muffins all stocked up? That's a popular one with the high school crowd."

"Yeah, I did that a few minutes ago."

Wendy slid the tray of lemon bars into the oven before turning to Chelsea. "You're the best. You ever think about trading your mom for a couple hours here? You know she doesn't do it for the money—and it would be a blast to have you here more. I know you take home work without telling me." She pointed a stern finger.

Chelsea shrugged. She knew the books. Even though she worked for Wendy for a much lower hourly wage than she charged her other freelance clients, her cousin couldn't afford to pay her for any extra hours. Not more than she was already.. "You know I can't. I've got Austin." She did enjoy working with Wendy. She was the closest thing Chelsea had to a best friend and with Wendy's busy schedule at the bakery and Austin's demands on Chelsea, there was never much time for hanging out.

"Your mom wouldn't mind watching him. Or Madison." She gave Chelsea a smirk. They'd discussed Madison's passive-aggressive hints about Chelsea's mothering plenty of times.

"Ha. I know. But I'm not a working mom. At least I'm trying to be one as little as I can."

"Well, coming over to help more wouldn't kill you. Or getting out of the house to have a life of your own." Wendy pulled another mixing bowl from a stack and went to work on something else.

"The same way *you* leave the bakery from time to time?" Chelsea challenged with a smile.

"Fair enough."

The bell above the door rang, and Chelsea glanced out to see a couple guys in slacks and button-up shirts from the print shop down the street. She popped up from her chair, grabbed a loaf of bread, and headed to the counter.

"Let me know if you need help," Wendy said.

"Of course." Chelsea reached the counter the same time as the men and tucked the light, fluffy loaf of bread into the case. "How can I help you?"

———

DJ KNOCKED on the back door of Brady's little sister Madison's house, calling "Hey, it's me," as he came in. Maddi was in the kitchen with Austin and two of her older children. On the other side of the room was a large closet space that Maddi's husband, Jason, had converted into an office so he could run his online business from home. How he ever got anything done with four kids under the age of five running around was beyond DJ. Jason waved at DJ, but then went back to his computer.

"Where are Olivia and Charlotte?" he asked, about Maddi's youngest two, ages two and a few months.

"Naps," Maddi answered as she cut up sandwiches at the dated, cream-colored laminate counter. "What are you up to?"

"Saw Chelsea at the bakery. She said Austin was here. I brought treats." He rattled the bag, and the three boys sitting at the table squealed with delight. Maddi's oldest, Noah, was five, and Austin sat next to her three-year-old, Will.

She chuckled. "You couldn't have waited five more minutes until I had sandwiches in them? You know what Chelsea will say." She shook her head at him as she distributed the sandwiches on three small plates and turned to take them to the table.

"I have permission to feed him one scone." DJ set the bag on the table and pulled out the box. "As long as I lick the icing off."

Maddi scowled. "Disgusting."

"Fine. I won't lick it off. But if you tell Chelsea, you're going to have to take the heat." He handed Austin one of the smallest scones then put one each on Noah's and Will's plates before he headed for the cupboard to grab a glass for milk. He figured he'd have to settle for a scone for his breakfast instead of the brownie he planned on. If he opened up the brownie box in front of the boys, they'd want some too. Madison wouldn't care about Noah and Will eating them, but after DJ caught the hint of desperation in Chelsea's eyes, he couldn't in good conscience give Austin a scone, *and* a brownie. Chances were Chelsea would never find out, but DJ wouldn't risk disappointing her. Brady had already done enough of that.

"You talked to Brady lately?" DJ sat down next to Austin..

Maddi turned back to the counter and grabbed the cups she'd already filled up. "Not in the last few weeks—not really. I've called him, but he only talks for a few minutes before he says he has to go. Probably worried I'm going to give him some lecture about not visiting enough."

DJ smiled down into his glass of milk. He had no hope of Maddi missing the look, but he tried anyway. He'd been lucky growing up to have another sister in Maddi. He was especially grateful now since most of his family lived in Utah. His parents had moved last year to be closer to DJ's siblings and their kids. With all of his nieces and nephews several hours away, it was nice to be welcome at Maddi's to spoil the kids and babysit when he could. The more he thought back on it, the more he realized he hadn't done that like he should have for Brady and Chelsea. They hadn't lived that far away while they were in Salt Lake. Maybe if DJ had taken the time to watch Austin for them a time or two, they would've had more time together to keep their marriage on track. He'd used the fact that all of them were busy as an excuse, but he could have done better. He *should* have done better.

"We both know that's exactly what you would do if he gave you the chance," he said, rousing himself from his thoughts and teasing Maddi as he would his own sister.

Maddi shook her head but not with any real seriousness. "I know. He seems to think that sending a check every few weeks covers his parental duties. Mom raised him better than that."

"Everyone knows that, even Chelsea." He picked out the scone dripping with the most icing and offered it to her.

"No, thanks." She turned toward the sink, starting to load dishes into the dishwasher. She shook her head. "Poor kid. Chelsea says he hardly eats anything, and it's no wonder considering what she sends over." She pointed to an opened container of off-colored rice mixed with small squares of carrots and another vegetable he didn't recognize.

"Doesn't look so bad . . ."

Maddi scoffed. "You should smell it. She makes everything from scratch so Austin gets the best." She rolled her eyes, and DJ wondered what annoyed her most: that with only one child, Chelsea had the time for that or that Maddi didn't even try.

The way Chelsea had forced her indifference and looked so anxious over Austin having a scone came back to DJ. "I'm sure she just wants to be a good mom," he said, the need to defend her rising inside him.

"I know." Maddi sighed, sounding as defeated as Chelsea had looked. DJ ate the rest of his scone and reached for another. Brady sure had done a number on some of the women in Clay. Maddi worried about him as much as Patty and Dale did.

"Mo?" Austin interrupted the discussion to point to the box.

Sharing a smile with Maddi, DJ lifted Austin out of the chair. "Who wants to go outside and play with me?" He pointed to the window. Austin grinned and bounced in his arms, pointing with DJ and chanting *yes* along with the other two boys. DJ left his uneaten second scone on the table and headed outside, thinking about Chelsea and the tired rings under her eyes. Brady wasn't around to help lift the load, but DJ was. He would find a way to help Chelsea out.

When Chelsea and Brady had gotten engaged so young, he'd done his share of trying to convince Brady to wait. Didn't he want to go to college, play football, and date a bunch of girls like they'd always planned? DJ hadn't known about the baby until later, after they got married—and it had surprised him. He and Brady usually talked about everything. When they lost the baby, Brady refused to talk about it except to admit that he felt guilty for being a little relieved. Years later, when DJ had long assumed Brady and Chelsea were in it for the long haul, Brady hadn't even hinted that something was wrong with his marriage. It had shocked DJ to learn—from Maddi, no less—about Chelsea moving back to Clay and the divorce that followed. He should have been there for them, for *both* of them. Maybe if he'd done more to help, to ease the stress of Brady's new, demanding job and of having Austin, they'd still be together.

DJ set Austin on the trampoline and then climbed up carefully next to him. How could he know if anything would have helped? Brady wouldn't talk about it, and DJ suspected that since he wasn't married himself, he wasn't qualified in Brady's eyes to give marital advice. The fact that he hadn't even had a serious girlfriend in a few years probably didn't help.

Sure Chelsea had plenty of family and friends here in town, all willing to help, but something about her expression in the bakery had said she still needed something. Someone to make her accept that help? He wasn't sure. He couldn't deny the tug to do something. He may have grown up with Brady, but he'd spent a lot of time with Chelsea over the years. It was time for him to live up to the friendship he claimed to have with her.

CHAPTER THREE

Even though she'd grown up in her parents' house, after only a few years away, it didn't really feel like home anymore, especially when Austin screamed for what felt like hours on end. It made her feel like the worst kind of house guest. Like an intruder that kept waking her parents up, ruining any chance of them having a good night's sleep. She'd lain awake through her brothers' kids screaming when they were all home for holidays or something, and she had never cared, but being on this side of it made her stomach churn with guilt. Usually she loved being able to live with her parents, but in the midst of Austin's late-night fits, she longed to have her own home again. She clenched her fingers and then took a slow breath in.

She rolled over and eyed her clock. Seven minutes. She should go in. She got up and hurried down the hall, promising herself she'd pat him on the back and lay him down.

"Mommy, Mommy!" He stretched as far as he could over the railing, reaching for her. Though it broke her heart to see the tears rolling down his face and the anxious way he begged for her, she couldn't keep giving in. She ran her fingers over his silky blond hair and situated him back in a laying position. He whimpered at her, but she held strong, tucking the blanket back around him and giving him the stuffed bear Brady had gotten him before they'd left Salt Lake.

"I love you, sweat pea," she murmured, brushing her fingers over his head a few times before she left the room. Austin screeched louder when she closed the door. She slumped against it, remembering how that simple routine used to calm him if he ever woke in the middle of the night. How he would cry softly for a few seconds and then fall back asleep. He probably felt safer then. She couldn't imagine how he interpreted the fact that his daddy only came to see him once in a while and that most of their interaction took place via video chats.

She padded back to her room. If she stayed in the hallway, she'd go back in. She plopped back down in the bed, Austin's crying ringing through the house. She stuffed her face into her pillow and let out a whisper-yell of frustration for all the junk she could no longer control. No, she hadn't been mom of the year before she moved back to Clay, but things had been so much better. Austin had eaten regular, healthy meals. He'd slept well during bedtime and naps. Brady hadn't really been an attentive dad—starting out at a law firm took a lot of time—so she'd done a lot on her own, and it had all worked out. Why did the divorce make everything fall apart? Why couldn't she raise her son by herself when she'd basically been doing that anyway? She pounded her fist into the pillow then collapsed against it, too tired to even cry in frustration.

Ten more minutes ticked by, and still Austin screamed. Chelsea returned to his room and gave up, picking him up and holding his shuddering body against her. Though his cries lowered in volume, he didn't calm down, even when she went to her bedroom and rocked with him beside the bed.

"Another driving night?" she whispered, her shoulders slumping. How had it come to this? When successful nights were the ones that Austin slept fitfully in bed next to her. She slipped her feet into a pair of flip-flops, wrapped Austin's blanket around him, and headed to the car. The night was warm, and the thick scent of lilacs from her mom's prize bush carried on the ever so slight breeze. Even just a couple deep breaths as she walked to the car soothed her.

She made her circuit through some of the older parts of town. Sometimes she liked driving by the newer houses, thinking about how she and Brady had planned to come home and live in one of those houses someday. But tonight, she wanted familiarity. Maybe it was a subconscious rebellion of the plans she'd made with Brady, but she found herself more and more drawn to the sprawling ranch-style houses built in the fifties and sixties, even with their dated, cream-colored brick and deep-red trim.

She had started up Second Avenue when she noticed a figure jogging along the side of the road. It startled her so much she let out an involuntary yelp and tapped the breaks. Austin's wail filled the car. If he'd been anywhere close to sleep, that was gone now. She pulled the car off the road a little and turned toward her son, reaching back.

"It's okay, buddy," she said soothingly. She leaned as close as she could to him and gently rubbed his head. His cries calmed after a moment. They'd be driving for longer than she'd planned now.

She willed her heart rate back down after the surprise of seeing the outline of a person on the road (what were they doing jogging at two a.m. anyway?) and was almost calm enough to start driving again when someone tapped on the window. She screamed again and then turned to see DJ staring through the glass at her, his expression chagrined. As she rolled down the window, Austin's wails returned, increasing in volume.

"Uh, hey. Sorry. For scaring you," DJ said, panting.

Chelsea reached back for Austin, unbuckling him and pulling him into her arms before she answered. She took a deep breath and let it out. "Yeah. No . . . problem. What are you doing?"

"Jogging."

She arched an eyebrow at him. He flashed her a devil-may-care grin that didn't help calm her heart. She turned her face into Austin's hair for a moment, kissing the top of his head as he took a shuddering breath.

"What? It's not normal for people to go on runs in the middle of the night?" DJ teased.

"Well, it's not really . . . safe," but the last of her sentence trailed off as she turned back and eyed DJ's toned arms.

His grin widened, his cheerful expression making her heart thump.

What. Was. Going. On? She took another deep, but subtle, breath to smooth her nerves. Probably just still on edge from him startling her.

"With my schedule, my sleep clock is off. It's either this or watching baseball, and since I finished off the last of the games in my queue last night, tonight I jog. The question is, what are you up to?" he asked.

"Just soothing Austin. He likes riding around in the car. Usually, it'll lull him back to sleep."

"Makes sense." DJ bent further over to peer at Austin in her lap. "Hey, little punk."

"Dada?" Austin leaned forward putting a hand out. He squinted against the darkness, probably trying to get a better view.

DJ's eyes flashed to Chelsea before he shook his head. "Nope. Uncle DJ." That's what Brady had always taught Austin to call him.

Austin started crying again, this time a soft, sad, heartbreaking cry that made tears prick in Chelsea's eyes. She blamed it on total exhaustion.

"Daddy," Austin whimpered.

"Sorry," DJ whispered, letting his hand rest on Chelsea's shoulder. The sympathy in his expression startled Chelsea. She'd never known DJ to act serious enough for something like that. Brady couldn't even comfort her without making some kind of joke about it, and DJ was even less serious than him.

"It's not your fault." She forced a laugh. Maybe she could be the one making the joke, if only to avoid the discomfort of his pity.

DJ straightened. "You look exhausted. Why don't you let me drive you around tonight?"

She raised her eyebrows. "No. That's okay. I don't want to keep you from your workout . . . or anything, because you have to stay fit for your job, you know." She clamped her lips shut and concentrated on stroking Austin's back to calm him. The lack of sleep must be catching up with her. What a stupid bunch of nonsense to ramble about. She didn't want to admit that it might be because she was nervous around a guy she'd practically grown up with who happened to be really good-looking and super sweet.

He laughed. "Don't worry about it. I'm happy to interrupt my jogging."

"I can't ask you to do that."

He folded his arms across his broad chest, the muscles made more obvious by the fact that sweat drenched the front of his shirt and it clung to his skin. "You didn't."

"It's okay. I mean, he'll fall asleep in a few minutes, and we'll go back to my mom's." He wouldn't be asleep though. It usually took a good half hour to get him to that point, and she'd have to start all over since her screaming had startled him wide awake.. "It's good of you to offer," she said, discomfort squirming through her.

He leaned over into the window. "Let me help."

Why did he have a longing look in his hazel eyes? And why did that look make Chelsea nod her head and say, "Okay"? It almost felt as if letting him drive them around would be doing *him* a favor.

His expression showed relief. "Perfect. Scoot over."

———

DJ HAD SEEN Chelsea's panic—her hesitance to accept help and inconvenience someone else. He was glad she'd given in anyway. His smile widened when she opened her car door, buckled Austin back into his car seat in the back, then walked around to the passenger side, throwing him a confused smile of her own.

He slid into the driver's seat and pulled on his seat belt. "Okay. Do we have any specific route to take?" he asked when Chelsea had shut the passenger side door.

She shook her head, still smiling. "No. Just drive until Austin falls into a deep sleep. Then we go home, and strangely enough, he stays asleep when I put him back in his crib."

"Whatever works, huh?" He glanced over at her as he started forward down the street.

She leaned back against the seat, and before she turned her head toward the window, he caught a glimpse of hopelessness in her expression. Her soft-looking blonde hair fell out of a messy bun on top of her head. One strand kinked at an odd angle, giving her a bedraggled appearance; an attractive bedraggled appearance, but still. Poor Chelsea.

"Yeah. I guess. Seems like I'm applying that to a lot of things lately."

"I want to tell you that things will get better, but your son is half Lewis, so . . ." He waited, hoping to coax a laugh out of her.

She looked back at him, and to his relief, the corners of her mouth had turned up. "So reassuring."

"I've heard Patty say, 'Thank heavens for Alyssa and Maddi' more times than I can count. Apparently, Brady's sisters saved their mom's sanity. I'm sure it didn't help to have me and Charlie encouraging Brady into all sorts of mischief."

Chelsea rested her face against the seat rest. "I used to tell people I knew exactly who Brady was when I married him, so I couldn't complain about how much he goofed off or how he joked about everything. He used to make me laugh so much. I liked that . . ." She whispered the last and turned her gaze down, cheeks blooming with pink. Chelsea was a petite girl, short and lithe, and she looked even smaller curled up in the passenger seat of the small car.

"Until he left," DJ said without thinking. "Sorry." He eyed her and sighed. "I shouldn't have said that."

She shook her head. "You're like a brother to him. I'm sure you have opinions."

"Ha, yeah." DJ focused on the road, turning onto one of the lesser-used dirt roads on the edge of town. He had guessed that something was up with Brady when he'd started calling less and less. And when he did call, and DJ asked about Chelsea and Austin, Brady's responses had been short and shallow. *Doing great.* DJ couldn't count the number of times he'd asked Brady to fill him in, knowing that something was off, but Brady always rebuffed the attempts. Then he'd dropped the bomb that he'd moved out and he and Chelsea were getting a divorce —which DJ already knew anyway. After that, Brady's calls had dwindled to almost never. Same with his responses to text messages. The distance left DJ feeling empty and helpless. Helpless to understand what his best friend was going through; helpless to do anything for him.

"It's hard to form a good one when he won't tell anyone what's going on," DJ said. He glanced over his shoulder at Austin, who stared out the window, though his eyes did look glazed, much like his mom's.

"Really?" Chelsea turned to him, her astonishment clear on her face. "I figured—"

"That he'd told me everything, like he used to? No. Not so much anymore."

She frowned, her expression pained. "Deej," she said softly, using a nickname from their high school days. "I'm sorry."

He chuckled, shaking his head. "*You're* sorry? He divorced you."

"I'm good with it. Honestly, things are way better for us now. We can actually talk instead of being afraid we'll say too much."

It was DJ's turn to stare, surprised. "I thought . . . ?"

She laughed at his befuddlement. "We'd been together since I was seventeen, so I must be devastated, right?"

"Something like that."

She turned to stare out the windshield. "We got married because I was pregnant. I don't know if I ever actually loved him enough to marry him." She shook her head quickly. "That must sound horrible, right? We made it work because we thought we had too, but when he told me he didn't love me, that he couldn't keep going on like we were, when we were both so unhappy . . . all I felt was relief." She chewed on her lip. "I feel so guilty for that."

Keeping his eyes on the road now, DJ let what she'd said sink in. Maybe that's why he wanted to take part of the responsibility. Brady *had* always told him everything. DJ was the first to know when their high school coach made Brady starting safety. The night he proposed, Brady had called DJ with the news before he'd even told his own parents. Sure, he'd left out some hard details, which was maybe a pattern DJ hadn't picked up on, but who was Brady turning to if not to DJ?

"You don't have anything to feel guilty for," he said, firmly.

"I can't shake the feeling that I didn't try hard enough to love him —that *we* didn't try hard enough—even though it's like a weight is gone, not having to try so much. We're so much better as friends. I wish I'd seen that in high school before it was too late." She cleared her throat and turned away from him. Even in the dim light, he caught her cheeks turning pink.

"Chels." He reached over to squeeze her hand. He hated the idea of her feeling embarrassed or guilty for what had happened. She and Brady had been sealed, so their mistakes in high school had been taken care of. "You got scared and rushed into something. Forgive yourself, okay?" It surprised him that she squeezed his hand back, even though she looked away.

They drove in silence, his hand still wrapped around hers, her staring out the side window. Until he noticed that her grip had slackened. Did it mean she felt awkward now? After sharing something so personal and then holding hands with him? He hadn't meant more than to comfort her, to comfort her because he couldn't shake the idea that if Brady had confided in him—when they found out she was pregnant or when he'd realized he didn't love her—maybe he could have done something to save her from the heartache of a nine-year, loveless marriage and then divorce. To save *them* from what had happened.

Then he noticed her head tipped forward against the window, eyes closed, shoulders moving up and down in a steady rhythm. She'd fallen asleep.

DJ pulled his hand away and looked back at Austin. Yep. Still awake, though his eyelids looked heavier than the last time DJ checked on him. "Just you and me now, Austin," he whispered. Then his smile spread more. Chelsea must still trust him to tell him the things she did, enough to fall asleep and not feel obligated to stay up and keep him company.

It felt good to have helped someone, to have actually done something right. That familiar burst of accomplishment settled over him, just like when he'd pulled in a difficult pass. The feeling was just as great as he remembered.

———

"Chelsea?"

She opened her eyes and scowled, trying to place her surroundings.

The car.

Had she fallen asleep at the wheel? She sat up, panic racing through her. "Austin?" She murmured, trying to turn to check on him. Her tired limbs resisted moving.

"Shhh," the voice commanded. "He's sound asleep. You don't want to wake him up."

Chelsea blinked a few times and looked toward the voice, shaking her head in the darkness. "Oh," she whispered when her vision cleared. Not Brady. DJ. He'd driven them. For how long? She looked at the clock. Only about a half hour since she last remembered looking at the clock.

"We're stopped," she said, looking around.

DJ chuckled. "Yeah," he whispered. "We're at your parents' house. I figured you'd want to get Austin into his bed. And get yourself into bed. You didn't look that comfortable."

She reached over to squeeze his arm, grateful that he'd thought to stop and wake her instead of continuing to drive around to let her sleep. Austin would sleep better in his bed, now that he was finally asleep.

"Thanks." She stretched her arms over her head and then quietly opened the door. When she opened the backseat car door, DJ had reached back and carefully unbuckled Austin, then he slipped Austin's arms out of the harness. "Thanks," she whispered again, lifting Austin out. DJ grabbed the blanket that had fallen to the floor and got out of the car, shutting his door softly. He hurried around and draped the blanket over Austin then dropped the keys into the pocket of her sweatshirt. "Night," he said.

She nodded, unwilling to risk another quiet whisper with Austin asleep on her shoulder. She was already in her son's room when she realized DJ would have to run home, almost two miles from her parents' house. She laid Austin down and waited a couple seconds to make sure he was settled before she rushed to the window that overlooked the driveway. DJ was gone.

Something electric shot through her chest. When she'd told DJ she wished she could have figured out in high school that she and Brady were better as friends, it had reminded her of the night of their senior prom.

Her parents had asked her to go with someone other than Brady, so DJ had asked her. Max and Denise had likely seen right through the charade—Brady and Chelsea had spent the entire dance together. But in the early morning hours of the next day, after the late-night party they'd all gone to together, Brady took his date home and DJ did the same. She and DJ had sat in front of her house for over an hour, tiredly laughing and talking. When she'd gone up to her room after he left, her brain refused to turn off, and she'd lain in bed for another hour going over the conversation. When had she and Brady ever talked like that? Confiding in each other things about their worries about graduating, even though they were excited. How she'd admitted to DJ that she didn't know if she and Brady would make it through college. A deeper conversation than she'd ever had with her boyfriend.

She hadn't been able to get that night out of her brain for nearly two weeks. Something scared her more than her and Brady growing apart in college.

The fact that maybe they'd never grown together in the first place.

The fact that she might have feelings for his best friend.

But then she found out she was pregnant and the night with DJ was forgotten. She'd never really even thought of it over the past nine years. But when she'd said those words to DJ— *I wish I'd seen that in high school before it was too late*—she'd remembered.

What if she'd seen it six months before the prom? What if she'd noticed the shallowness of her relationship with Brady? How it was mostly physical? How they hadn't been good at talking about things, even then? What course would her life have taken, and would that course have led her to DJ?

She shook the thoughts away. No use lingering over the what-ifs.

As she walked back to her room, she couldn't keep a tiny, tired smile from forming. She thought of the calm that had trickled through her when DJ put his hand over hers. He hadn't tried to make a joke, to lighten the awkwardness when she admitted why she and Brady had gotten divorced. The comfort in his reaching out to her had allowed her to give in to exhaustion, to sleep, even though she should have stayed awake with him.

Even though her life hadn't taken this course then . . . was it possible it could take this course now? Her insides wriggled with an excitement she hadn't felt in a long time, but she forced herself to laugh it off. This was DJ she was thinking about. Her ex-husband's *best friend.*

Still, the security of the moment remained with her even after she'd settled into her bed. It usually took her a while, despite her exhaustion from waking up multiple times a night, to fall asleep. Driving around, the solitude, and the thoughts that drummed in her mind sometimes kept her up until she finally managed to shoo everything away. But not that night. She closed her eyes, holding on to the comfort DJ's warm hand had instilled in her, and drifted off immediately.

CHAPTER FOUR

When she awoke the next morning, Chelsea reached across the bed, catching the edge of the mattress and an armful of empty space, instead of Brady. Longing swelled up inside her, but she banished it quickly. She'd dreamed of him the night before. She hadn't dreamed about him in months, and she knew that riding around and holding DJ's hand had brought it on. Though she was happier now that they'd divorced, she'd still spent over ten years with him, and a tiny part of her still missed the comfort of having a *someone* in the bed beside her.

Shortly after she'd had Austin, Brady had joined a city league basketball team. Most of the guys on the team were single. He'd go over to their apartments after their games to watch television or play video games. He'd said he just needed chill time, but Chelsea blamed it on the way things had changed since they'd had Austin. They'd been struggling, figuring out his new job and a baby. When he'd started staying out later, she would sometimes wake up at two or three in the morning and reach across for him. Most nights she reached into empty space. Then one day he came home and told her it had been a mistake for them to get married. That they should have listened to everyone that tried to stop them, that tried to tell them to consider adoption rather than getting married. That he didn't love her and how could he ever make her happy if *he* wasn't happy?

Chelsea settled back into her covers and tried to remember the warmth and comfort she'd felt the night before, the way it spread through her when DJ took her hand. But dreaming of Brady, then waking up without him overshadowed any peace she'd felt, and made her loneliness feel even sharper. She glanced at the clock and did a double take. Eight forty-five? Austin hadn't slept this late for months. She hopped out of bed, racing past his room and down the stairs to the kitchen, where her mom must have him, feeding him pancakes drowning in syrup since Chelsea wasn't awake to stop her. She skidded to a stop on the landing after galloping down the first four stairs and looked behind her.

Austin's door was still closed.

Her mom might have pulled it shut after getting him up. She tiptoed down the stairs just in case. She'd catch her mom red-handed.

Denise hummed softly to herself as she moved around the kitchen it had taken her years to perfect. She'd started with a picture from a magazine when Chelsea was little, and even that vision had evolved with time. Denise still tinkered with the little stuff from time to time, getting the wall decorations right—some kitschy paintings, a wooden pallet sign that said *Money can't buy happiness, but it CAN buy chocolate,* and some vintage plates in bright orange, red, and blue—or sometimes changing out the centerpiece on the rustic-looking table. Right now, a golden-yellow vase filled with fresh, red daisies brightened the room from the middle of the table.

Still silent, Chelsea peeked around the corner to find that Denise was the only other person in the kitchen.

"Why are you skulking around like that, Chels?"

She jumped and turned to her mom guiltily. "I figured Austin had to be up already and you just didn't wake me."

Denise sighed. "It'd do you good to let me help out, but I know you like to get him up. Don't you trust me?" She went back to chopping at the counter next to the sink.

"Of course, Mom." Chelsea walked across the kitchen and leaned her chin on her mom's shoulder, snatching one of the quartered cucumbers from the cutting board. "I just can't believe he's still sleeping."

"You both could use it. Maybe it's finally catching up with him."

"Maybe. If only it would last."

Denise reached up to pat her cheek. "I know it doesn't seem like it, but this too shall pass, sweetie. Eventually."

"I know." Chelsea kept telling herself that. This phase would last a few more months at most. With sunlight streaming in through the windows, it was easy to believe again, but come tonight, it'd feel never-ending.

"Why don't you go grab a shower while you can? What should I feed him if he wakes up?"

Chelsea wrapped her arms around Denise's narrow shoulders, squeezing her eyes to keep back sudden tears of gratitude—and guilt. Of course she wouldn't have fed Austin syrupy pancakes. "There's some mango puree in the fridge from yesterday. I mixed it with oatmeal, and he seemed to like it."

"Sure thing." Denise leaned her head against Chelsea's for a moment before shooing her out of the kitchen.

Chelsea let herself relax and linger in the steamy shower. What had DJ asked her the other day? How often did she take people up on their offers to help? Not often. Austin's life had changed enough, she didn't need to step out of the routine every time she didn't get a decent night's sleep—especially since that was every night. But it couldn't hurt to take a nice, long shower every once in a while either. And letting DJ drive last night had helped her, had soothed her soul.

The lift in her mood lasted through the morning. What a difference a couple more hours of sleep and a good, long shower could give.

Her phone rang at eleven thirty with a FaceTime call from Brady. She picked Austin up and settled in a chair, holding the phone level with her son's face before she answered.

"Daddy!" Austin squealed, pointing to the screen.

"Hey, little man," Brady replied. "How's it going?"

Austin startled babbling, interspersed with comments from Brady to keep him going. Chelsea leaned her head against the chair, keeping the phone far enough away from Austin so he wouldn't hang up on his dad. It only took four or five minutes before Austin started wiggling around, trying to climb off her lap. Chelsea struggled to keep him in the chair, talking to Brady.

Finally, Brady sighed. "I should get back to work anyway. Bye-bye, little man. I love you."

"Bye-bye," Austin said, sliding off Chelsea's knees.

She grabbed him before he could get far. "Tell Daddy, I love you," she whispered.

"Bye-bye," he said, struggling more. "Wuv you."

Brady grimaced when Austin had finally gotten away. "How can I get him to stay on, Chels?" he asked.

"He hasn't seen you in two months. It's hard for him to connect that the guy on the screen is Daddy in real life." She made sure her voice was gentle. Though they communicated far better now, she didn't want Brady to put up a defensive wall.

"Two months?" he scoffed. "No way."

"I came for a couple days at the end of March, remember?" She shrugged. "Two months."

He sighed again, this one heavier. "I've got so much work. I can't get away."

"I know."

He shook his head, rapping his fingers on the desk. "But you don't agree."

"I know your job is stressful and takes up a lot of time. I promise— I get that."

"But . . ." he prodded.

"Your son has to be a priority, or you'll never find time." She cringed inwardly, but Brady needed to hear the hard things too. Opening up and being honest had been the biggest thing to make their relationship work since the divorce.

"He's definitely a priority," Brady insisted. "He's right up there with tacos. Maybe even more than tacos."

Chelsea granted him a laugh and let the serious part of the conversation go. "Good to know." She'd said her piece, now she'd drop it and let him think about it.

"I'll call again in a couple days," he said, then they said their goodbyes.

Fifteen minutes later she was thinking about cheating for Austin's lunch and giving him a peanut butter sandwich, when the doorbell rang.

She hurried through the kitchen and the large, open space of the family room to the front door. She halted when she saw DJ through the wide front window. Her mom loved how much light the floor-to-ceiling window allowed in, especially in the summer, so she hadn't hung curtains and rarely let down the white, wide-slatted plantation blinds. It gave Chelsea a perfect view of DJ standing on the wooden porch that ran the front length of her parents' house. Her thoughts turned to the memory from last night and the way he'd held her hand and how, even though last night had been easy, it would be awkward now, in the light of day. *It doesn't have to be a big deal*, she told herself. He'd done it in a friendly, best-friend-like way. The same way he would have hugged her before, like the night Brady got a concussion in a football game and DJ was the first one out of the locker room to calm her.

A second ring of the doorbell snapped her out of her thoughts. She glanced out the window. DJ had turned to her and waved. Oh, wow. What an idiot he must think she was, standing there staring at the door in full view. Thanks to the window, he had the same great view she had, and he'd even shifted sideways a little. She jumped forward and yanked the door open.

"Hey."

"Hey. You look a little dazed—did Austin wake up again last night?" He frowned in concern, and her stomach tumbled, in a good way, like when she walked into Wendy's shop and the first, sweet scents washed over her. "I could take him for an hour or two after lunch," DJ offered.

Chelsea waved him off and opened the door wider. "Come in—and uh, no, he slept great. So did I. Thanks again for driving."

A grin, which looked far more natural on his face than the frown, reappeared. "Good. Good." He held up a plastic bag from the local grocery store. "Look what I found at the store."

Since she couldn't see through the opaque-white bag, Chelsea arched an eyebrow. "Groceries?"

He laughed. "No. All-natural baby food in these cool pouches. Leavitt's kid is always eating them, so I thought maybe Austin would like them. I know he's a little old for baby food, but it's worth a try, right? The squeezy pouches are fun. Maybe he'd eat his vegetables a little better." He held open the bag for Chelsea to inspect.

She swallowed, reached into the bag, and pulled out a pear/brown rice/spinach blend. She turned it over to read the back, even though she'd seen pouches like this at the store and had already inspected their ingredients. All the same stuff she put in his meals at home but in premade—and expensive—squeeze pouches. She didn't just make his food to make sure Austin got the best but because her mom paid for groceries. Making it herself cost a lot less. She forced a smile anyway. DJ looked so proud of himself, and she couldn't shoot him down. He wanted to help.

"Perfect," she said. "It's lunchtime anyway. Come on, we'll go try it out." She led DJ back toward the family room, where she'd left Austin playing. He looked up from the blocks and eyed DJ.

He gave DJ a wide grin. "Hewo."

Chelsea's heart skipped. Austin didn't talk a lot, especially not to people he didn't know well. She and her parents could hardly coax the necessary words out of him. Madison was always frustrated with his pointing and grunting instead of using his words. For him to talk to DJ without any prompting and grin at him like that? Did he remember more about DJ than she realized? Austin had been about a year old when Chelsea moved back to Clay, and he hadn't seen DJ except for occasionally around town. Maybe all the times DJ had held and played with Austin when he visited had stuck with the toddler.

DJ handed the bag to Chelsea and plopped down in front of Austin on the thick, cream-colored carpet. "Hey, kiddo. Remember my name?"

"He doesn't usually talk much," Chelsea said as a warning. She hovered over them with the bag at her side, unsure if she should join them on the floor.

Austin squinted and gave DJ a contemplative look that had both Chelsea and DJ laughing. Austin giggled too. "Daddy?" he guessed, but his voice had a teasing tone, as though he knew this would get a reaction.

"Deeee-Jay," DJ said.

"Daddy?" Austin clapped his hand over his mouth and laughed again. That contentment—the one that had helped Chelsea get to sleep last night—came back, lighting up her insides as a part of her playful little boy showed himself again the way it sometimes did with Brady. Maybe Austin had inherited his Dad's love for DJ. What else could explain it? Although Brady and DJ acted like brothers, they didn't look anything alike. Both were tall with lean, toned bodies, but DJ had dark hair where Brady's was sandy blond—the color that Austin's darkened to bit by bit with every passing week. She didn't actually believe Austin was confusing DJ with Brady, but she liked that he was pretending, *playing* with DJ.

"Let's try again. Deeeee?" DJ prompted.

"Daddy." This time Austin threw up his hands as he shouted it.

"I give up." DJ scooped Austin into his arms and strode back across the family room and into the kitchen. He clipped Austin into his high-chair while Chelsea rummaged through the baby food. She pulled out the pear/brown rice/spinach blend again. If she could get Austin over his spinach aversion, it might be worth shelling out almost two dollars a pouch for them.

"Let's try this one." She handed it to DJ.

He unscrewed the lid and gave it to Austin. Austin held it by the sides, staring at DJ and waiting. Chelsea moved forward to help, but DJ beat her to it, lifting the pouch toward Austin's mouth and squeezing gently. To Chelsea's surprise Austin swallowed.

"He never eats spinach," she said under her breath.

DJ turned and beamed at her—just in time for Austin to spew the next mouthful all over the side of DJ's face. His expression changed to shock. Chelsea clapped her hands over her mouth, trying not to laugh. Austin would think it was a game, but the breaths pushed past her hands anyway. It didn't matter; Austin had already dissolved into giggles.

"I'm—so—sorry," she gasped at DJ. She hurried to the drawer next to the sink and fished out a dishtowel for him, almost running back across the wide kitchen space to hand it to him.

"Maybe we should try another one," he said, wiping the green blobs off his face. She noticed he'd already taken the pouch from Austin and screwed the lid back on.

Chelsea pushed through the half-dozen pouches DJ had bought, finding one with carrots and sweet potatoes she figured Austin would like. DJ held out his hand.

"Are you sure?" she asked.

"This tastes way better than sweaty linemen, trust me." He gestured with the green-goop-covered dishtowel. "I'm not afraid of whatever Austin can dish out." He growled and turned to Austin, who growled right back.

Chelsea chuckled. "He can dish out way more disgusting stuff than spewing baby-food everywhere, but I'm afraid I would scare you off if I talked about that kind of stuff."

DJ handed the other pouch to Austin. "I'm not—never mind." His face flushed, and he concentrated on helping Austin again.

For some reason, Chelsea laughed. The last couple times she'd been with DJ, he had made her feel so . . . comfortable, even in the moments that seemed almost domestic. It felt like old times, the way he could lift her mood. It made her wonder if she should've sought him out sooner, hung out with him more. Up until last night, she'd assumed Brady had confided in him and that she'd be stepping on toes.

"Yeah, uh, the one time Austin puked on Brady, he almost melted, so . . ."

DJ chuckled. "He's always been sort of a princess." Still, he kept his eye on Austin, who sucked down the food, squeezing the sides with both hands. She couldn't remember the last time a mealtime with

Austin didn't include a tantrum or food-throwing. Maybe it came from more than the cool pouches. Maybe it was the company.

"A little bit, yeah," Chelsea admitted. Every time Austin had a dirty diaper, Brady had carried him under the armpits, holding his son away from his body as he rushed him to Chelsea. She'd always laughed, and after Austin was a few months old, she knew Brady did it just to entertain her. "Sometimes he was a really good dad," she said, then wished she hadn't voiced that thought out loud, especially since her voice cracked.

"Brady?" DJ arched an eyebrow, but she saw by his grin that he was teasing.

She smiled back. "Imagine that. He and Austin had a routine at night before he started staying out late. They'd read *The Going to Bed Book* two or three times, and then Brady would sing to him. Bedtime was their thing."

"Sing?"

"He has a terrible voice."

DJ laughed and turned to Austin. "Well, it's safe to say he likes this one." Chelsea looked up to see him holding the pouch up, sucked flat.

Though she should have been happy that Austin ate his vegetables for once, her shoulders still sagged with defeat. Stupid, since she'd been having a good time with DJ.

"Now if only I could figure out how to get the cheaper baby food I make into one of those pouches."

DJ nodded. "Yeah, these were kind of pricy, even with the family discount." He chuckled. "I think Leavitt's wife gets them online or something, in bulk, so they're cheaper."

Chelsea leaned forward. "How do you even know that?"

DJ reddened again. "I asked Leavitt." He rolled the empty pouch in his hand for a minute before he looked up. "I wanted to help."

Warmth charged through Chelsea's chest, and the feeling returned that somehow letting him help her helped him. "Thanks. It means a lot." She glanced at Austin, whose head bobbed in the highchair, his eyes half-closed already. "Oh, wow. Being full must have worn him out." She went forward to scoop him out. He wrapped an arm around her neck but reached for DJ with the other one.

"Dee."

DJ looked over at Chelsea, and they shared a smile. For all his teasing, Austin had listened to DJ trying to teach him his name. Chelsea didn't know what to think of this bond between them. Austin had always bounced around with joy and reached for DJ when he came to visit. She couldn't help but be glad her son remembered that.

DJ leaned toward Austin and kissed him on the forehead. The close proximity meant Chelsea could smell his cologne—something sporty. It reminded her of dates with Brady after football games. Without thinking, she took a step back.

DJ straightened and met her gaze, confusion filling his eyes. She wanted to apologize, but what for? He looked away a second later.

"Deeeee-jaaaaay," he said softly to Austin.

Austin reached his arm out again. "Dee."

DJ took Austin's hand and slapped his own with it. "Great job, buddy. Dee-jay." He emphasized the syllables again.

"Say night-night to DJ." Chelsea waved Austin's hand at DJ, who waved back, keeping his spot next to the high chair.

"Dee do it, Mommy." Now Austin reached both arms toward DJ, squirming in Chelsea's arms. Chelsea was torn. The fact that he'd spoken a simple sentence elated her, but that he wanted DJ to take over bedtime? It sort of stung.

"You'll see him again soon, okay?"

"Dee do it," he said again, but he leaned his head on Chelsea's shoulder.

"Soon." She patted his back and headed for the stairs, waving over her shoulder at DJ. Five minutes later, after she'd tucked Austin in to bed, she came back downstairs to find DJ sitting at the kitchen table, fiddling with his phone.

"He went down good," he said, pocketing it when she walked in.

"Yeah, nap time hasn't really been a problem." Chelsea picked up a rag by the sink and headed toward the high chair. She needed something to do with her hands now that it was just her and DJ. Why did it feel so awkward? "Thanks for the baby food." She nodded toward the table where the sack rested.

"Yep. Except for the spinach, it seemed to work."

"Yeah." She scrubbed at some dried food from an earlier meal and didn't look up. How long before DJ noticed that she'd developed a little crush on him? "I'll have to do some research and see if I can get them cheaper online. Maybe that's what I need to do. Find some way to make his meals more fun."

"Yeah."

She heard the chair scrape backward and looked up to see DJ standing, hands in his pockets. "So, if you need a babysitter, I'm free a lot. Usually I'm three days on and two days off."

"Thanks, but you'll need to relax on your days off, and where do I have to go? It's Clay."

He chuckled. "Even just down to Wendy's for some dessert? I bet an hour would be nice."

She stopped scrubbing the high chair and tried to look relaxed. "He's napping right now." She glanced at the clock. He'd gone down earlier than usual, maybe still catching up from the rough few nights they'd had? "I have an hour to myself right now before I have to go to work."

A knowing smile spread across DJ's face. "You're right. You could leave him here with me while you go in early for a few extra bucks."

"It's still my mom's shift," Chelsea said, though the excuse sounded lame in her head. Denise didn't work at the bakery for the money, and she only worked mornings because Chelsea didn't. If Chelsea showed up early, Denise would just leave.

DJ raised an eyebrow that said he saw through the excuse too. "You wouldn't even have to worry about what I feed him." He took the rag and started nudging her toward the living room.

"But . . ." She resisted, but it was futile. DJ had played football for BYU, and from the looks of it, he still kept in pretty good shape.

"You don't trust me?" They'd reached the front door.

"Well, of course I do."

"Which means you don't really." He laughed.

"I do."

"Prove it." He folded his arms and eyed her, his expression full of challenge.

Austin could wake up, and what would he do if he found DJ there instead of Denise, like usual? He might be okay with it, or he might freak out. "What if—"

"You have a phone." DJ pointed to the lump in her pocket. "I could call you or your mom if I needed to."

It wasn't the same. Denise always stayed with him while Chelsea worked. He wouldn't understand that being with someone besides her or Madison didn't mean that his mom wasn't coming back.

"It's not that simple," she said.

"Chelsea." DJ put his hands on her shoulders and shook her gently. "Stop freaking out. What's the worst-case scenario? He wakes up, and I pick him up? He cries a little, and it's a few minutes before you or Denise get here. You won't scar him for life by leaving him with someone besides your parents or Madison. Trust me." He gently nudged her toward the door some more.

"You know this how? All the kids you have?"

"I have a nephews and nieces—and Maddi's kids." DJ folded his arms, mimicking her defensive stance.

"Oh, so you spoil a few kids, and suddenly you're an expert?" She tried to sound lighthearted, make the joke that would ease the tension inside of her. DJ was right. This wasn't a big deal. So why did it feel like it?

"People leave their children with babysitters quite frequently, you know. And most of them grow up to be perfectly adjusted adults who don't need therapy or anything." He put his arms back on her shoulders. "If you think it's a bad idea, I understand, but . . . think about it for a second. You leave every afternoon anyway. What's an hour earlier this one time?"

She took in a shuddering breath and looked away, embarrassed. "One day Brady left him and didn't come back. Austin doesn't know I won't do the same. Or his grandma. This is part of his daily routine. He's only two."

DJ dropped his arms from her shoulders but slid one hand into hers. "Which is why you need to show him you will." They stared at each other a few brief moments, and then DJ dropped her hand. Chelsea thought it might catch fire. "There's nothing wrong with loving him and worrying about how he'll react. You're a mom." He gave her a you-decide look and a shrug.

She did keep Austin's circle of caregivers pretty small. But her son did like DJ and had fun with him. "Yeah . . . okay. I'll go." She sighed and stepped out the door, hesitating on the welcome mat. "You will call . . . if anything happens," she asked.

DJ nodded solemnly. "Promise."

She believed him. "Okay. I'll be at the bakery then."

"Have fun." He waved and shut the door on her. She hesitated a second longer before heading for the sidewalk.

Since it was a beautiful day and Chelsea didn't have to be at work yet, she took her time walking. She still reached Cutie Pies in under ten minutes and found her mom bustling around, serving the early lunch crowd.

"What are you doing here?" Denise asked.

"DJ came over with some food pouches to try with Austin. Austin went down early, and DJ offered to babysit so I could come in and get an extra hour." She grabbed her apron from the hook and tied it on, moving to help another customer.

"Must have heard my prayers," Denise said with a chuckle. She tapped her knee when Chelsea glanced at her questioningly. "It's been a little sore this morning. I'll be glad to get off my feet early."

The last of Chelsea's guilt for leaving Austin with DJ dissipated. "I'm glad I let him talk me into it then."

They served a few more customers, until the shop quieted for a moment, and then Denise went back to the kitchen to wash her hands and let Wendy know that Chelsea had come in early. Wendy waved through the open kitchen door as Denise came back out, but Chelsea couldn't go back since Allison Rees, who owned a diner down the street, had come through the door. When the diner was especially busy in the mornings, she sometimes purchased desserts to serve in the afternoon. She bought in bulk and always told her customers the desserts came from Cutie Pies. Wendy was happy to give her a discount in exchange for the free marketing.

"Well, hello there, Chelsea. You're in early today." The middle-aged woman smiled at Chelsea warmly. She glanced over at Denise. "It's good to see Wendy busy enough for two employees. Austin over at Madison's?"

"Uh, no. DJ Kasier is watching him for a few minutes until Mom gets home." Heat flew through Chelsea's face at the startled look on Allison's face that turned into an oh-I-see expression.

"How nice of him," she said.

"Yeah." Chelsea cleared her throat. Of course it was, but it didn't mean what Allison thought it meant. At least not to DJ. DJ and Brady were best friends. The three of them had always been together back in the day. Why would Allison jump to DJ and Chelsea being romantically involved? She didn't *think* it was written on her face that she thought he was attractive and kind and . . . a possibility? Granted, the singles scene in Clay was slim pickings, making DJ one of only about a dozen options. Still.

"I think he just wants to spend time with Austin. He thinks of him as one of his nephews," Chelsea continued, hoping to put a halt to the unnerving train of Allison's thoughts. Her mom's smirk as she lingered near the counter didn't help.

"Sure, sure." Allison straightened, looking like the cat that got the mouse. "What does Wendy have by way of pies today?"

Denise answered, since she had been the one in the bakery all morning, and Chelsea relaxed once Allison changed the subject. Maybe she did have some kind of a teenage crush thing going on, but mostly she hoped that she and DJ could go back to being friends like before, just without Brady; especially since DJ seemed to want to help. Having a friend would be nice. Someone to hang out with and talk to besides her parents. They'd probably like it to. They hadn't exactly had a ton of alone time since she and Austin had moved back in. But would people assume that it meant there was more?

In this town? Of course they would.

But then, was that such a bad thing? Chelsea did kinda want something more. Didn't she?

Regardless, she didn't think she could turn away DJ's help, not without hurting his feelings. And that was something she didn't want to do. They'd enjoyed their time together while feeding Austin, laughing, making jokes, and teasing. And like the night before, she appreciated having someone. She hated to admit it, but she needed the help as much as DJ seemed to need to give it to her. Not just to get Austin eating but to put some fun back into her life.

A few minutes later, Allison held a small box filled with two pies and a couple dozen assorted cookies. "Thank you, dears!" she called as she left, casting another knowing smile in Chelsea's direction. At least if Allison had *said* something about Chelsea and DJ dating, Chelsea could have corrected her, though she didn't know if it would have done any good.

"Have a good afternoon, sweetie," Denise said as she moved to follow Allison out the door. She raised her eyebrows slightly, her expression similar to the one Allison had worn, though her mom's held more teasing.

Chelsea sighed. "Oh, Mom. It's not like that. You know how close DJ and Brady were."

"And you," Denise added, putting her hand on the door. "Sometimes I wasn't sure which one you were dating." She winked.

Chelsea laughed. "That's not true. Except when we purposefully tried to make you think that." She pretended to grimace, and with a laugh herself, Denise left. In a lull of the lunch rush, Chelsea perched on a stool and pulled out her phone, checking up on her Instagram feed. She hadn't expected to come in early, so she'd caught up on the accounting the night before.

Plenty of the posts featured the kids of friends from both Rexburg and Salt Lake. She paused on a picture of a couple of women she'd sometimes done a play group with before she and Austin moved back to Clay. They held their babies on their laps, their toothless grins smiling up at the camera. It had been a long time since she'd done that. Admittedly, the women in her Clay ward invited her to their play group all the time, but they frequently gathered over lunch. It was hard for Chelsea to make it work while she was juggling Austin's care and her shifts at the bakery. She lived in a strange limbo, straddling the world of stay-at-home-mom and working-mom.

She flicked past the pictures, making a mental note to try harder. Spending more time with mom friends and letting Austin have social time would also help get more fun into Austin's life.

She came across a picture of Brady at a Jazz game, a group of people all crowding their heads together to get into a group selfie. The two women in the picture wore Jazz T-shirts, same as the men, but their salon-done hair and French manicures on wedding-band-less fingers stood out. Brady had his arm casually over the shoulders of the man next to him and the brunette woman on his other side.

They'd done a lot of this kind of stuff together before Austin. Chelsea had gotten pregnant shortly after they moved to Salt Lake, but pregnancy hadn't stopped them from hanging out with their couple friends. Two years ago, she'd been one of those women with expensive hair and nails. Brady had a good job, and she'd worked up until the last few weeks before she had Austin.

She stared hard at the picture. Brady still lived that life. Without her. Without Austin. It was as if she'd quietly disappeared to be a mom and he hadn't even noticed. After they'd had Austin, she didn't have time to spend a couple hours at a hair salon or forty-five minutes for her nails. Brady started working even longer hours, and then started hanging out with his new single friends, and not the couple friends they'd done things with before. When he was home, Chelsea did make an effort to spend time with him, to fix the mysterious thing that felt wrong between them. But she didn't make an effort to tag along when he went out with his friends, not once she had Austin in her arms. The fear of missing out on little things nagged at her so much that she could count the number of times she'd called a babysitter on one hand. Three of those times had been when her parents had come to town to visit. Had that been part of the problem?

She shook her head and scrolled on. Their lives *had* changed when they had a baby—everyone's did. Brady hadn't understood that.

The picture right below Brady's made her stop again. The photo showed a group of women she'd done girls' nights with in Salt Lake. All of them had kids near Austin's age, but they'd tried once a month to get dinner together and chat without having to chase kids. If Chelsea went back through her own Instagram posts, she'd find pictures like this one from a year and a half ago where she was leaning into the picture too. A pang of loneliness and jealousy struck in her chest as she stared at the photo. She missed those nights. The kinship. They may not have happened frequently, but they had helped quell the loneliness she'd felt as a new mom.

She clicked the side button on her phone, darkening the screen as she stared out the front window of Cutie Pies. Brady had moved on with his life, but Chelsea had lingered in transition for too long. She'd always insisted she was just being there for Austin, but was there more to it? Fear, maybe. Moving on was *hard*.

But she *was* divorced.

There was no going back to hanging out with Brady at Jazz games or doing girls' nights in Salt Lake with her old group. She could focus a little more energy on finding friends for that here. She didn't want to make out-of-place-single-mom her story. She'd told her mom how Austin had to get back into some kind of routine—but maybe that was true for her too.

CHAPTER FIVE

With Austin sitting quietly on her lap looking at a book, Chelsea scanned the heads in front of her in sacrament meeting. It made sense to start her search for girlfriends in her ward. It would mean a convenient way to contact them and it guaranteed geographic proximity—though, considering they lived in Clay, she had geographic proximity with pretty much everyone. She could walk the entire length of Main Street in under an hour.

Alissa Piper, maybe? Alissa was from California and had moved to Clay with her husband, Josiah. Josiah had known Chelsea in high school. He was a year older and had gotten back from his mission not long before marrying Alissa. They'd met at BYU freshman year or something, and she'd waited for him. Mentally, Chelsea crossed Alissa off the list. It reminded her too much of how her story should have gone.

And how was she supposed to make friends now, anyway? Get up the nerve to talk after the meeting and suggest they get together to hang out sometime? The thought made her anxious, but after seeing pictures of her old group, she knew she *needed* a friend. Wendy didn't have time for the occasional lunch at a McDonald's Play Place. Besides it would be nice to have someone with kids that could relate to that part of Chelsea's life.

There had to be an easier way, a way to find someone like DJ, someone easy to talk to and fun to be around. Someone like him—except a girl. Too bad DJ's sisters were still going to school in Idaho. Chelsea had always liked them.

For sure, she couldn't bring herself to hang out with Madison more. They'd never been close, and the condescending way Madison always gave parenting advice made a genuine friendship difficult.

Chelsea thought of the girls she'd known in high school, but she'd drifted apart from her closest friends when she and Brady started dating, and they'd all but forgotten each other when she and Brady got married. Off the top of her head, she couldn't think of any that had moved back to Clay after college, with or without husbands.

A couple of women with kids around her age seemed like the best possibilities, like Sharae and Valerie. They'd seemed nice enough, and the commonalities between their kids would make it easy to find stuff to talk about. Chelsea resolved to try and set something up.

At the end of the meeting, she spotted DJ standing just outside the door, hands in the pockets of his gray slacks, chatting with Sharae's husband, Jace.

Austin noticed him too. He scooted off Chelsea's lap and went running for him, shouting, "Dee!" Chelsea sighed with relief that he hadn't called him "Daddy" again, even just to tease. DJ nodded in their direction, gave Jace a pat on the back, and met Austin in the aisle. Chelsea hurried out of her seat to follow.

"Hey, buddy." DJ swung Austin into his arms and took a few steps closer to Chelsea than she thought necessary. Not that she didn't like it . . . but she didn't think DJ saw her that way, and getting gossip started in small town Clay would take less than fifteen seconds.

It was Allison Rees's fault, insinuating that if she and DJ hung out, there *must* be Reasons. Of the dating variety. Chelsea bet a lot of single women in the area wanted to date DJ. And she knew, just *knew*, that the eyes of Allison and everyone in that room were on her right then. Speculating. She edged an inch or so away. DJ eyed her, that same confusion in his expression that she'd seen when he'd been helping her feed Austin.

"What are you doing here?" she asked, hoping to dispel the questions in DJ's expression. She worried too much about what Allison might think and not enough about how DJ might feel. It was fine if they were friends. Let people think what they wanted.

"Accidentally slept through my ward's meeting." He put one of his hands back in his pockets and then paused.

"That's what happens when you go jogging at two in the morning," Chelsea said.

"That's probably true." They shared a look that she couldn't translate. Understanding, maybe? But more.

"Can Austin have a Tootsie Roll?" he asked.

"No." She hated turning him down, especially since he'd asked. Some kind of something fluttered in her stomach that he'd thought to. "But not because of the sugar. He's two. He'll choke."

"Hmm. Yeah, safety first. Sorry, buddy." He shrugged apologetically at Austin, who stuffed DJ's yellow tie in his mouth.

"Austin!" Chelsea cried, reaching for him.

But DJ leaned away. "No big." He took the tie from Austin and rolled it up, putting it under his chin and then letting it roll back down.

Austin giggled and bunched it up, trying to shove it back under DJ's chin. "Again."

DJ repeated the game but looked up at Chelsea. "Didn't see you out driving last night."

"Haven't needed to for a couple days, thank heavens. He's been content to crash in my bed." Just thinking about the rest she'd gotten relaxed her.

"Disappointing for me. Good for you."

"If you don't want to run in the middle of the night, you don't have to," she reminded him.

"So you're saying we can hang out any time, and I don't have to use jogging in the middle of the night as an excuse?" He pretended to look thoughtful over this.

She nodded. "Yes. I've come to the conclusion that I do need to get out more. Girls night stuff like manicures and gossipy dinners. You in?"

"Obviously." DJ held up his fingernails, giving a grimace at the extra-short nails.

Chelsea laughed.

Before she could suggest something he might like better, like card games with her parents or something, Bishop Howell came up from behind and clapped a hand on DJ's shoulder. "Wrong ward, Brother Kaiser."

"Now they tell me." He let go of the latest roll-up of his tie and reached to shake the bishop's hand.

Bishop Howell released DJ and turned to Chelsea. "Excuse me, Sister Lewis, do you mind visiting with me for a few minutes before Sunday School?"

Chelsea gulped. In the year since she'd moved to Clay she'd been busy with Austin and exhausted most of the time, so she'd escaped without getting a calling. She suspected her parents had something to do with that, intervening on her behalf. It looked like her time had come. "Okay." She reached for Austin, but DJ didn't move to hand him over.

"I'll take him to nursery." He walked away before she could protest.

"What if he gets upset at you leaving him—?" She hurried after them and made another move to take Austin, but DJ turned sideways to avoid it.

"Then I'll stay with him, and you can come in when you're done meeting with the bishop." He moved forward again, and she couldn't keep chasing him down the hall without looking silly, especially since Bishop Howell was waiting for her.

She saved her breath to take a few calming ones as she hurried back to Bishop Howell. She followed him to his office. The calling couldn't be anything too big. Maybe a Primary teacher or even nursery leader. That wouldn't be too bad. She wouldn't mind hanging out with Austin during the second hour.

She took a seat across from the bishop but couldn't look up. He hadn't been bishop when she and Brady got married but sitting in his office still reminded her of how nervous she'd been when she'd been interviewed before the wedding. Her bishop had been supportive and kind, but the thought of sitting there as a divorced woman still made it intimidating. She didn't know if she'd ever shake the reminder that at eighteen, she'd had to get married because she was pregnant, even if she had repented.

"How are things going, Sister Lewis?"

She rubbed her hands along the smooth wooden arms of the chair and looked at the top of his almost bare desk. "Good. Fine. My parents are taking good care of me." She forced a hollow laugh, though she didn't know why.

"I'm sure they're happy to."

She looked up finally to see the gentle smile on his face. "I hope so." Another stupid laugh.

"We're glad to have you in the ward. How would you feel about accepting a calling?"

She nodded too enthusiastically. "Yeah. Of course." She wrung her hands in her lap, then stopped herself, trying not to appear as on edge as she was.

"We'd like to call you to serve as the second counselor in the Relief Society." The bishop leaned forward over the desk to study her with warm blue eyes, kind of striking now that she noticed.

She cleared her throat. "Excuse me? Did you say second counselor in the Relief Society?"

He dared to let out a short chuckle. "Yes, I did. What do you think?"

She shrugged, dumbfounded. Her. Relief Society presidency. She couldn't make the words fit. "How can that be? I'm a divorced single mother. Not exactly Relief Society counselor material." At least half the sisters in the ward were over twice her age and had much more experience.

The bishop's smile didn't waver, though it clouded a bit. "You served in the Relief Society presidency in your old ward."

She dropped her gaze back to her hands, staring as she nervously rubbed her thumb into the palm of her hand. "That was different." She'd been about the same age as many of the girls. She'd felt comfortable giving advice on adjusting weekly family home evenings for little ones or strengthening their eternal marriages. She'd been sealed to Brady and Austin, and though they struggled, she'd assumed they'd get through it.

"Whether you think it's true or not, you have something to offer the sisters in this ward, young and old. The Lord thinks so too, Chelsea. That's why He's asking you to serve. The structure of our Sunday meetings is shifting, and I think you're a great person to have on board as we go forward with that." The kindness in his voice made her look up at him again. He went on. "Sister Barber said she'd never felt so strongly about serving with someone as she did you. I feel the same about calling you."

Chelsea stared at him, maybe hoping he'd see her desperation and offer to take it back. But of course he wouldn't, so she said, "Yes. I can accept."

"Good. Thank you." Bishop Howell stood up, and she jumped out of her seat. "We'll present your name to the ward next week and then set you apart."

With a quick shake of his hand, she darted from his office. Second counselor in the Relief Society? She rubbed her upper arms. What on earth could she teach the women in this ward? What did she have to offer? How *not* to build your eternal marriage?

She slumped. She didn't get it, but if Sister Barber and Bishop Howell were so convinced about it, who was she to argue? She forced herself forward toward the nursery, knowing that Austin would have been upset with "Dee" leaving him.

Instead she met the nursery leader, Sister Bell—lucky woman—in the hallway as she came out with a pitcher. "How'd Austin do today?" Chelsea asked, pointing to the door. She didn't hear her son crying.

"Perfect. Didn't even look twice at the door and headed right to the table for snack." Sister Bell walked down the hall toward the kitchen in the direction of the chapel, where the Sunday School class met, so Chelsea walked along with her.

"Oh? I thought that since DJ took him and it was different, he might be upset."

"Not at all." Sister Bell leaned over and rested a hand on Chelsea's arms. "Sometimes it's easier when Mommy doesn't do it. Babies are like dogs, dear, they sense fear." The middle-aged sister gave her a gentle pat on the arm along with a commiserating smile and then disappeared into the kitchen.

Sense fear? What did that mean? Sister Bell had almost made it sound like Chelsea was afraid of Austin going to nursery. She narrowed her eyes at the closed kitchen door for a moment before heading to Sunday School. She didn't understand DJ's magical connection to her son, but how else did she explain all the weird things happening since he started spending time with them again?

DJ was sitting next to her parents when she walked in, instead of by Brady's father, Dale, like Chelsea would have expected. A quick glance over the room told her that Dale wasn't in Sunday School. Madison taught in Primary and her husband, Jason, was a ward clerk and usually taking care of other business during this hour. But why had DJ sat *there*? Now she had to sit next to him. It would be obvious if she didn't. At least Allison wasn't there either. Maybe she hadn't told anyone else about her suspicions, and the other members of the ward wouldn't think twice about her ex-husband's best friend sitting with her family. She sat down on DJ's other side. He hadn't even left an empty space between him and her mom for her.

She pinched the bridge of her nose. She was definitely over-thinking things.

DJ leaned over. "Well? Anything good?" He waggled his eyebrows at her.

"You know I can't talk about that." Already his playful expression released the unease that had built inside her since she walked into the bishop's office.

"I'm not even in your ward. But I can tell since you look like you've seen a ghost that it's big. Primary President?"

"We're not talking about this. You can find out next week, along with everyone else."

DJ reached for her hand and squeezed it before letting it go. "You'll do great. Whatever it is."

"Maybe." She held his gaze a moment, grateful for his faith in her. Maybe he was right.

———

DJ TOSSED a football up and down from where he lay sprawled on his couch. He'd lingered for a while at Dale and Patty's after Sunday dinner, but once Madison and Jason took their kids home, Dale had helped Patty to bed early. Sunday meetings, even though an hour shorter now, always exhausted her. And though Chelsea kept sneaking back into his mind, he couldn't come up with a reason to drop by her house.

He picked up his phone, noting that it was after nine, but he texted Sean anyway. *How are your girlfriends?* It was probably unfair to treat his friend's situation so lightly, falling for another woman while his girlfriend, Jane, was on a mission, but he bet that Sean could use the laughter about it.

Sean answered with a GIF of a guy rubbing a hand slowly down his face. His oldest niece had shown him how to use the GIF keyboard on his phone, and he used them to answer texts all the time now. *Can we not talk about any of that, please?* Sean added after the GIF.

Have you e-mailed Jane yet? DJ wished there was a way to add his genuine concern for Sean and his predicament. Well, *mostly* genuine concern. If they were speaking in person, DJ would add something about how difficult it must be to worry about *which* girl to love rather than *if* he'd ever find a girl to love.

Then he'd get pummeled.

Bro. Seriously, I'm not talking about it. Did you ask that girl out yet?

Abbey? Sean had been the only one DJ had told about Abbey. He didn't exactly love telling people he'd asked her out and then gotten shut down.

No. The one with the kid.

DJ imitated the action of the GIF Sean had sent, rubbing his hand down his face. *What? It's not like that with us. We're friends.*

Friends? The way you talk about her, it doesn't sound like that to me.

DJ scowled. *Dude. She was married to my best friend. Do I need to spell out how awkward that would be?*

But you want to. Now Sean sent a *Harry Potter* GIF of Snape saying, "Obviously."

DJ blew out a long breath. Yeah. Maybe he did. Chelsea was attractive, he'd always known that. She was fun and easy to hang around with. Maybe the best part was that he didn't have to try so hard with her. After a little bit of stilted conversation at the bakery, their relationship had reverted to the close, lighthearted relationship they'd had in high school. It had been nice having Chelsea around then. On those rare serious situations, or even the not-so-serious dating conundrums, she'd always given him a thoughtful opinion.

Awkward, he repeated.

You could be throwing away your soulmate because of a little awkwardness. He followed this message with a couple heart emojis. What had possessed his friend? Heart emojis?

I hope Victoria didn't swipe your phone. I'm gonna feel bad about that Jane comment if she did.

What?

Since when do you talk about soulmates and use heart emojis? DJ pointed out.

This conundrum I'm in has me thinking about relationships a lot. Obviously too much. A moment later he added, *But in all seriousness, you should think about this.*

DJ thought about how Chelsea had created distance between them. Moments he hadn't thought that much of but had questioned because of her reaction. He could see how they could have come off as flirty. When they'd hung out when he visited Rexburg or in Salt Lake, it had never even occurred to him to think of her in a romantic context. She was almost as much his best friend as Brady had been—and these days, maybe more since Brady hardly ever spoke to him. There had always been a line he didn't cross, had never even thought about crossing. Though it hadn't disappeared, the line had faded since the night he drove her around Clay.

He shook the thought away. Chelsea *had* been a huge part of his teenage years—as Brady's girlfriend. This had the potential of ruining his relationship with Brady, what little was left of it. He couldn't ask her out like it meant nothing.

I know you didn't hang out with Brady a lot in college, but the guy is like my brother. So I guess I'll just hang tight and take Jane out when she gets home.

Point taken. I guess you're right. I'm sure you have other options anyway, right?

Disappointment pinched in DJ's chest. He realized he'd wanted Sean to tell him to throw caution to the wind and seize the moment. If this could be real with Chelsea, he should take the chance, shouldn't he? Having Sean confirm DJ's fears was a letdown.

Now I definitely know Victoria has your phone. You'd never have such a high opinion of my dating life.

I guess it's true that absence does make the heart grow fonder . . . not that I didn't already have plenty of proof of that.

You'll get over me soon. DJ didn't realize that it sounded like he was referring to Sean moving on and dating someone else while Jane was gone until he'd already sent the text. He cringed and waited for Sean's reaction.

You're the worst friend. Way to make it easy to get over you.

DJ searched through his GIF app for an apology and then added, *I'm nothing if not thoughtful.*

Sean's reply was a laughing face.

———

WHEN AUSTIN WENT to sleep Sunday night, Chelsea texted Wendy. *Hey, do you still do those girls' night get-together things?*

The ones you're always too busy to come to? Wendy responded. She followed it with some emojis rolling their eyes.

Yes. Those ones, smart aleck.

Wendy replied with some laughing emojis and then added, *Actually, I was going to ask you tomorrow if you wanted to come this week. We're going to the diner on Thursday night. I take it you're in?*

"Do you have anything planned for Thursday night?" Chelsea asked her mom, who sat across the family room with Max, watching a documentary on BYUtv.

"I don't think so. Why?" She looked up, her eyes sleepy.

"I'm going to dinner with Wendy and some of the girls she gets together with. Do you mind watching Austin?"

Denise's eyes brightened. "I'd love to, sweetie."

Chelsea rolled her eyes at her mom's obvious glee that Chelsea was going. "Thanks."

Yes, Chelsea typed decisively to Wendy. *I'm in.*

The next morning, during the part of the day Chelsea knew would be slow at Cutie Pies, she and Austin walked over to indulge in some girl talk with her mom and Wendy.

The front part of the shop was empty when she got there, and she called, "It's just us," when the bell rang so Denise wouldn't hurry out expecting a customer. Chelsea pulled Austin up into her arms and walked around the counter to the kitchen. Both women were there, chatting and shaping rolls for the lunch hour.

"What's up?" Wendy asked.

"Not much." Chelsea pulled a stool up to the table for Austin and stood behind him. Wendy handed over a small dollop of dough and a tart shaper sitting on the counter, and Austin went to work walloping his dough to oblivion.

"You don't look like not much is going on," Wendy said.

"She's getting a calling," Denise said.

"Must be big considering the circles under her eyes," Wendy teased.

Chelsea scooted Austin forward a bit on the stool so she could sit on it with him. She shrugged at Wendy. "Big-ish, I guess."

"What's your hang up? I'm sure whatever it is, you'll do great." Wendy carefully shaped a roll before putting it onto the pan.

Chelsea admired the perfectly crafted roundness of it before answering. "Thanks. I shouldn't complain. I've been worried about how much everyone has had to help me out lately. I guess I should welcome the chance to serve someone else." Chelsea's thoughts turned to DJ and how he'd gone out of his way to get those food pouches. Maybe serving in the Relief Society could help her do something like that for someone else and balance out things in her own life.

"I've said this a lot, I know, but there's a time and season for everything, Chelsea," Denise said. "Just because you need a lot of help now —and even if you need a lot of help for a long time to come—there's nothing wrong with that." Chelsea nodded, her eyes focused on the quick way her mom formed the rolls, going twice as fast and finishing with a product as pretty as Wendy's more conscientious effort. Desserts had always been more Wendy's thing. Her breads tasted great, perfectly chewy and light, but it took more from her.

"Your mom's right," Wendy said. "You think I like only paying you guys minimum wage for the help I need to keep me going? And we both know your mom would do it for free if I asked. If I want Cutie Pies to make it, I have to ask you for that right now." Wendy glanced at Denise's quickly filling pan and rolled her eyes at her own. "You know what I need to figure out? How to get more lunch customers. We're closer to the school, but most people still go to Rees' Diner."

"Plenty people come here for dessert afterward," Chelsea argued. "Allison's pies or anything she makes can't compare with what you offer here. Why do you think she buys desserts from you half the time?"

"I know. But the fact of the matter is, if I want to survive, I have to have more than just the dessert customers." Wendy scowled at the rolls, obviously deep in thought. She pushed some more bits of dough to Austin, since he had pounded his into a thousand tiny pieces that littered the table and floor around him.

"What about some trendy kind of drinks or something. Like flavored hot chocolate or Italian sodas," Chelsea suggested.

Wendy's face lit up. "That's actually brilliant, Chels. And it wouldn't cost that much to add. Some good flavorings, the cups. I can put stickers on some generic ones until I can order some with the logo. . ." Wendy continued to mull to herself for a few seconds. "You're a genius, Chels. Someday I'm gonna end up making you partner. *If* we can get you over this sugar aversion you have." Wendy winked at Austin, and even Chelsea had to laugh.

"I know, but when I get so few bites into this kid, it's important that all those bites count." She ran her fingers through the flour on the big island with its plain, cheap countertop and already a million nicks. It'd been all Wendy could afford when she opened the place. Their dads had built the island for her and installed the cabinetry that lined the edges of the room not taken up by the three mismatched ovens, all commercial grade, all bought for a steal from Craigslist.

"You know, though," Chelsea went on. "I kind of like reading some of the healthy food blogs I've found. They're teaching me not just about good, whole foods, but basic cooking techniques. Maybe this food thing runs in the family."

Wendy eyed Denise's rolls pointedly. "Yes. It does. We just don't know where you veered off." The women shared a chuckle, but Wendy's ribbing didn't bother Chelsea as much as Madison's remarks. It sounded a lot like DJ's good-natured comments. That he, like Wendy, got what Chelsea was doing. And maybe even admired her for it?

"Toss me some dough," Chelsea said. She pulled some into her hands, following her mom's example and pinching at the bottom to round the top. Like Wendy, it took her some time to get it shaped right, but rolls, like a lot of things in life, were sometimes worth the extra effort.

CHAPTER SIX

Even with most of the weekend off to catch up on sleep, DJ woke up late on Monday morning. He'd go back on duty the next day, so he liked to sleep in while he could. As he came back from his run, crossing Main Street, he caught sight of Chelsea leaving Cutie Pies. He veered down the block and jogged up beside her as she pushed the stroller.

"This is definitely a *more* normal time for a run, although it's too hot," she said.

"That's why I go at two a.m." He gave an exaggerated shrug. "What are you up to?"

"Actually? Gossipy girl stuff. I was hanging out with Mom and Wendy for a little bit."

"So does that mean we're not doing that girls' night like you promised?" He waved his hand in front of his face. She was right. It was too hot for running.

She grimaced. "Don't hate me, but I'm going to dinner with Wendy and some other ladies from around town. Want to come?" she teased.

"Most of the women Wendy does her dinner dates with are married—except for her and now you—so I'll pass." He'd seen the group at the diner from time to time when he'd dropped in to get dinner after a shift or to pick up food for the guys at the station.

Chelsea's gaze snapped to him for a second before pink tinged her cheeks. "Don't worry. I'm sure you can find a young single adult activity with plenty of single girls," she said.

Her reaction made DJ think about his and Sean's conversation the night before. Had she thought about crossing the line too?

"I'm usually working when they hold activities. And if I'm not working, I'm sleeping. How about you?" he challenged. "How many have *you* been to?"

She laughed and shook her head. "No thanks. That is not a scene I was sad to miss out on. But not going out on the weekends must be pretty different from when you were in Provo?"

He *had* gone on more dates, gone to more parties back then. While he was playing football, there had been no shortage of girls at his house. "I knew things would be slower if I came home. I don't miss that too much, although I wouldn't turn down having a few more options for eating out around here."

"Rees' Diner isn't hip enough for you?" She tilted an eyebrow at him.

"Do you remember that time we all went there for prom, and Sister Rees had it all decked out like a fancy restaurant? Who did I take that year . . .?" He bumped her shoulder playfully as he pretended to think. Her cheeks turned a deep shade of red, and she forced a smile. He couldn't think of why talking about that night embarrassed her.

Until he thought of how they'd ended it. After Brady had married her, DJ had buried that memory in his brain because he couldn't afford to feed the seed that had started that night. Maybe there had been a chance for something—in the future, far in the future—after their talk that night, but not once Brady had married her. Any potential had rightfully disappeared after that, and he had forced himself not to give it a second thought.

"I'm pretty sure my parents saw right through you asking me," she said, and the awkwardness around them eased.

"Especially since all the pictures in the yearbook show you dancing with Brady. Good thing his date was nice." DJ leaned over and took the stroller from her, making car noises as he maneuvered a squealing Austin in circles around his mom. Anything to distract them both from that particular memory.

"Brady only got out of my dog house for asking Gretchen when he told me you made him do it."

DJ looked up to catch Chelsea grinning. Last time they'd talked about Brady, her expression had been wistful, but it was more genuine now. Her focus was on the way Austin was giggling, full belly laughs that were pretty adorable.

Definitely a bad idea. Sean had agreed with him, so DJ tried to put out of his head the way her face lit up. She was pretty and fun; that didn't make her irresistible.

"What was so bad about him asking Gretchen?" DJ said, going forward with the stroller without the car noises now. Austin provided them instead.

Chelsea rolled her eyes. "Oh, I don't know. Gorgeous. Great at everything she did. Really popular."

DJ rolled his eyes right back. "Clearly your total opposite."

Her expression turned contemplative, her hand going to the phone in her pocket. "That's the type of girls he's going out with now. Super successful, gorgeous."

DJ's stomach clenched at the insecurity riddling her drawn expression. "Exactly the type of girl he married," he responded. "The type of girl you still are. Just because your office is in a bakery or behind a stroller, doesn't make you any less successful. And the gorgeous part is obvious."

She turned to study him, chewing on her lip. "You're nice. I don't understand how those girls in Provo let you come back here without one of them."

He stopped the stroller, only realizing a second too late how close they'd come to each other. He really didn't want to listen to Sean—or to himself—right now. She stared right back up at him, blinking in a way that matched his own indecision.

"I . . ." he began, not sure what he planned to follow with. But at the same time, she cleared her throat and took a step back. Even from that distance the electricity crackled between them. His heart hadn't pounded with that much expectation in months.

"Remember my roommates," he said, breaking the heated silence between them. His brain felt fuzzy and full of arguments *in favor of* asking her out. "How good-looking they were? I mean, it takes a lot to overshadow this—" He paused to sweep a hand down his body and give her a duck face, which she snorted at. "—but it happened." It was a relief that his joke landed. The tension, not exactly the bad kind, eased.

"Rocket *is* very good-looking. Is he married?" She gave him a look of fake hope. When he nodded, she turned it into an exaggerated pout.

"Anthony will be glad to know I'm still coming in second to him."

"Third."

He looked over to see her wearing a straight expression. "The one that plays baseball. He's not married, right?"

"Wow. I can't even beat David these days? He's engaged."

"I can work with that."

DJ stopped and put his hands on his hips. "You're stuck with me." The line, meant to be causal, held a lot more insinuation now. He kept up his act though, because if he let on how much he wanted to take their relationship a step further, he wasn't sure he'd be able to stop himself from doing exactly that.

She put a finger to her lips, biting it to keep her smile from overtaking her expression, her cheeks still a little pink.

DJ swallowed.

She. Was. Killing. Him.

"Well, fine," she said, with an exaggerated sigh. "I guess you'll do."

They reached the path that led up to Chelsea's house. "Hmmm," DJ said. "Should I take a walk around the block?" Giving them both the mental picture of exactly how she and Brady used to end their dates might do them both some good. Brady had suggested that DJ walk around the block more often than DJ could count when they'd dropped Chelsea off.

Chelsea burst into laughter, and DJ joined her, relieved—until she reached over and took his hand. "You were such a good friend, DJ," she said. "You still are."

Her hand was soft. He wanted to hold on, to pull her in closer. Instead he gave her fingers a quick squeeze and dropped her hand. "I'm still counting on manicures and dinner, girlfriend."

"Pencil me in!" she called over her shoulder, heading up the sidewalk with the stroller.

DJ turned back to the street and sprinted toward his house. His stomach jittered with excitement and leftover electricity from their interaction, and he had to run it off.

Except, he didn't know if that would do any good. The only way to soothe the energy pounding through him was to do the one thing he couldn't: take Chelsea out on a real date.

———

SINCE IT WAS ONLY the third time anyone on his crew had let him drive one of the fire trucks, DJ figured he'd better focus on the curvy road as he slowly made his way down the mountain and back toward Clay. It was well past one in the morning, and the three other guys in the truck all dozed as they headed back to town. They'd been called out to help with a cabin fire in the mountains that ran along the west side of the county. Clay's fire department was the closest. Of course, the guys had only let him drive because none of them wanted to be at the wheel in the middle of the night.

As he came off the switchbacks and the road straightened, DJ loosened his grip on the wheel and allowed his mind to wander. Since his walk with Chelsea, whenever he had a quiet moment, his thoughts increasingly turned to her. As a full-time fireman with no life outside his job, those moments were piling up.

The level of attraction he felt surprised him and sent his mind reeling. He argued with himself constantly. He was right not to pursue anything because of the Brady thing. Asking out his best friend's ex was too . . . too much like what someone from a big city would expect of a small town like Clay. He couldn't risk ruining his friendship with Brady.

But then he would justify it. What if she was The One? How else would he find out? And he and Brady barely spoke. Plus, the way her face lit up when he was with her made his fingers tingle with excitement. He kept thinking of bigger and better ways he might bring out that soft gaze she'd given him or earn a squeeze on his arm. As he compared his interactions with Chelsea—how conversation came easy, how natural their friendship felt—with the interactions he'd forced with Abbey, he realized she might have been right about her not being his type. She was kind and thoughtful, and anyone would confess to liking Abbey, but the real attraction, the kind he found swirling through him every time he was with Chelsea, wasn't there with Abbey. Before he'd wanted someone—a friend. Abbey had been right not to let him take it further than that. Thinking of Chelsea made that really clear.

But DJ always circled around to how he and Chelsea couldn't be a thing. He hated when that happened.

Tha-thunk. The ever-so-slight jar to the truck brought DJ out of his thoughts in less than a heartbeat. He hit the brakes, praying he hadn't hit something or even someone while his thoughts had centered on Chelsea.

"What's going on?" Leavitt asked, stirring in the seat beside DJ. He didn't answer. He hopped out of the truck, rounding to the back. Fear tightened in his chest so much he couldn't breathe. When he didn't see anything behind the truck, he dropped to his knees to peer into the darkness underneath. What had he done?

His heart sank as he spied a small, unmoving lump midway between the front and rear wheels. He yanked a flashlight from his pocket and shined it over the still form—not a person but a dog. His stomach revolted as he realized it. Backing into the chief's truck was stupid, but *this* made him a horrible person.

And it wasn't just any dog either. It was a small, black, white, and brown corgi anyone in town would know. The mayor, Mrs. Tingey's beloved pet—the one that ran up and down the dirt drive that led to the Tingey's home right outside of Clay like he was some kind of cow dog. The one that Mrs. Tingey spoiled and carried around in her purse.

He rocked back on his heels, sitting on the highway behind him. The guilt grew so heavy in his throat it gagged him. Mrs. Tingey loved this dog. It would break her heart. What was it doing out this late at night?

"What is it?" Leavitt asked from behind him.

"The mayor's dog." DJ's voice was hoarse as he made the admission. His stomach churned even more as the shame mixed with the adrenaline now draining from his system.

Leavitt whistled in response. "Ahhh, man," he sighed.

"Yeah." How he could have let his mind wander so much that he didn't see the dog? The poor thing hadn't stood a chance against this big truck and the idiot behind the wheel.

"Pom-Pom! Pom-pom, where'd you go?"

Things could not get worse. Cringing, DJ reached under the truck as far as he could and pulled the dog out, holding it carefully in his arms as he rounded to the other side of the truck to face Mrs. Tingey hurrying down her dirt drive.

"What are you boys stopped out here for—?" A scream broke off Mrs. Tingey's demand as DJ came into view. She swept her flashlight over him as she rushed forward.

"Pom-Pom!" She moaned her dog's name.

"I'm sorry, Mrs. Tingey. I never saw her," DJ mumbled, handing the dog into its owner's waiting hands. Mrs. Tingey didn't answer. Her wails increased in volume. DJ made out the words, "We should have never fed him that cheese," amidst all the crying. He clenched his fists, wishing he could go back five minutes in time.

Leavitt had followed him around the truck, but the other two guys stayed inside. DJ didn't blame them for not wanting Mrs. Tingey to identify them.

"Jeanie? What happened? Are you hurt? Who's hurt?" Mrs. Tingey's husband hurried down the driveway in his bare feet, making good time.

"Pooooom-pooooom!" Mrs. Tingey held the dog out toward him. "I had to let him out because you fed him cheese." Her voice rose shrilly in accusation.

Mr. Tingey grunted at her hysterics and stepped up next to his wife. "What happened?"

"She's so small, sir. I didn't see her." *And I wasn't looking or paying attention,* he reprimanded himself. It didn't help that Mr. Tingey had taught DJ's senior history class, his worst subject. Mr. Tingey had a stern glare DJ was hard pressed to ever forget.

Right now, Mr. Tingey glared at the dog, though, sparing DJ. "Hmm. Must have hit her square on with one of your tires," he said. Mrs. Tingey wailed louder. If she didn't take it inside soon, someone would call the cops. That would make for a great end to an already too-eventful night.

Now Mr. Tingey directed his gaze to DJ. "I'm going to have to talk with Rob about this," he said, dropping the chief's name.

Hopelessness engulfed DJ while he watched Mrs. Tingey cry. She'd loved that dog like it was one of her children, and he'd taken it away from her with a few seconds of inattention. "I understand." He deserved worse than a lecture from his boss.

"Ohhhhhhh, Pom-pom!" Mrs. Tingey's sobs grew louder.

Mr. Tingey scowled and put an arm over her shoulder. "Better move along." He turned and guided his wife back down the drive. DJ dropped his head and banged it against the side of the truck.

"We'd better go. Highway patrol wasn't far behind us, and they'll wanna know why you're parked in the middle of the highway," Leavitt said, putting a hand on DJ's shoulder. No other cars drove the deserted two-lane road at this time of night.

"Yeah. Why don't you drive the rest of the way?" DJ replied, pulling open the passenger-side door to climb in.

"Sure. No problem."

As they rode silently back to the station, DJ was grateful at least that the guys had enough respect for Mrs. Tingey's loss not to rib him over it. As they piled out of the truck, Leavitt came around and laid a hand on his shoulder again.

"Don't beat yourself up. Even in the middle of the day, if you'd seen the dog, you would've had a hard time getting this truck stopped in time. It's a big sucker."

DJ took a breath. That knowledge didn't help much, but Leavitt trying to relieve his guilt did. "Thanks."

CHAPTER SEVEN

DJ didn't sleep well the rest of the night. When he wasn't sleeping, he replayed the moments before running over the dog, trying to figure out how he could have changed things. In the few hours that he did sleep, his mind tortured him with worse scenarios—seeing the dog and the brakes not working, the dog turning into children from around town, DJ losing control of the truck completely as he came down the mountain.

Usually he was so exhausted that even the summer sun rising early didn't bother him, but the thin strip peeking through the blackout curtains seemed to run right across his face, no matter which way he turned. He'd been drifting in and out of sleep when he heard a voice downstairs. A voice he recognized too quickly for his own good—Chelsea. Careful not to wake his crewmates, he hopped out of bed and headed downstairs. For a few seconds, the heavy weight from the night's events lifted. He couldn't forget the guilt, but with Chelsea here, the idea grew that maybe he could actually be forgiven for the terrible thing he'd done.

She surveyed the room, chewing on her bottom lip. She held Austin's hand in hers, keeping him from climbing up the trucks. And it wasn't the boxes in her hand with the familiar logo that made him call out. "Chelsea?"

He caught his reflection in the mirror of one of the trucks. One side of his hair was smashed flat against his head. Not his most attractive look. When Chelsea's eyes flickered toward him, concern filled her expression.

"I thought that was your voice." He managed a smile for her. *Please stay*, he thought, even rolling his eyes mentally at how desperate that thought sounded. He needed to keep that hope for a little bit longer.

Chelsea bit her lips, embarrassed over showing up. "Oh. Man, I'm sorry. I know you guys were out late last night, and here I am barging in and waking everyone up—"

"You brought a box of something from Wendy's. Immediate forgiveness." DJ waved away her words and reached for one of the boxes.

She handed it to him, keeping the second, which had a couple colorful drinks in it. "Yeah I thought you could use . . ." She looked at her watch. ". . . lunch." She rocked back, her concern increasing with every second she studied him. "We can go so you can get more rest."

He swallowed. Lightened or not, the guilt still rested heavy in his chest. "Haven't had much of that tonight."

"Deej." She came forward, throwing her arms around his waist. "I'm sorry about what happened," she said into his chest.

He wrapped his arms around her, turning so he could breathe her in, feel the softness of her hair against his cheek, find comfort that for this one second, his world was upright again. How could someone be that for him so quickly?

He tightened his hold. The truth was, she *had* been that person once, a shadow of it, as his best friend. Though that friendship had cooled over the years, he still needed it, especially now with his future so uncertain. He'd come to Clay to find a home.

He'd found Chelsea instead.

But . . . what did he do with that knowledge?

Two small arms wrapped around their legs, making Chelsea turn to look down at Austin. "You want to hug DJ too?" She broke their embrace but not before he noticed the flush in her cheeks and the brightness in her eyes that said she might have stood there forever with him. Instead she reached down and swung her son up into her arms.

He cried out, "Dee!" and reached for DJ, propelling Chelsea back against him. He took Austin but kept his gaze on Chelsea. They stared at each other, uncertainty in their eyes.

"Have some? Pease?" Austin squealed, demanding attention from at least one of them. He pointed to the box in DJ's hand.

"That's up to your mom, buddy," DJ said, turning to walk back up the stairs with Chelsea following. His justifications for pursuing her returned, as demanding as Austin was about getting treats. "Brownies? For lunch?" he asked Chelsea over his shoulder as they emerged from the stairs into the firehouse's small, empty kitchen area. Anything to distract his brain.

DJ set the box on the table then carried Austin through to the also-empty living space. Austin squirmed, reaching back for the box DJ had left in the kitchen, which almost made DJ laugh. The kid had a sweet tooth as desperate as his mom's efforts to squash it.

"I thought today might be a brownies-for-lunch type of day." Chelsea sat on the edge of one of the couches. He sighed as he sat on the other couch on the end closest to her, settling Austin in his lap with an Xbox controller.

"What's this?" DJ asked as she handed him a pink drink, the whipped cream on top squished by a lid.

"Italian soda."

They each slipped the paper ends off the straws and took sips. "That's good." DJ glanced at the sticker with the Cutie Pies's logo on the clear plastic cup. "Since when does Wendy have Italian sodas?"

"Yesterday. She added flavored hot chocolate and these to the menu. It was pretty easy—she just had to buy the flavorings. The grocery store had a bunch, and she ordered some other flavors from Amazon—it's practically all I served yesterday." She took another sip.

"Sounds like a great idea."

"It was mine." She smiled and gave a little shrug. "Wendy's worried about staying competitive with Rees' Diner while still being a different type of shop."

"She's lucky to have you." DJ nodded with conviction. Gratitude that she'd come released some of the tension in his neck, and it meant something to him that their renewed relationship had driven her to comfort him.

"Thanks," she said softly. They shared a look again, then sympathy filled her expression.

The fact that she already knew about Mayor Tingey's dog made the guilt settle squarely back on his chest, an ache even Chelsea couldn't fix permanently. "It shouldn't surprise me that you already know. Did they print a special edition of the newspaper for it?" he asked. He wanted to land the joke, lighten the mood rather than weigh Chelsea down with his own problems, but she only gave him a half smile, none of her sympathy disappearing.

"Mrs. Tingey called Wendy to order a special cake for a memorial service she's going to have tomorrow." Chelsea bit her lip.

DJ rubbed at his cheeks with both hands. "She's really going to miss that dog."

Chelsea leaned closer, gripping one of his arms. "It was an accident. A tiny dog in the middle of the night. Wendy says there's no way you could've avoided it—something about the truck being super heavy."

"Leavitt said the same thing, but I should've been paying better attention." He sighed. "I should've done better."

"DJ," she said in a voice that made him meet her gaze. "It was an accident."

Senior year, the football team had lost a close game for the state championship. Both Brady and DJ had come out of the locker room with their heads hanging, discussing everything they should've done to win. Chelsea had taken them both by the hand, leaning closer to Brady, of course, and told them they couldn't change it. Her eyes had even shone with tears. He'd known then that it wasn't because they'd lost the game but because her boys were hurting.

"I wish I could make you feel better with a snap of my fingers," she'd said. Her expression now held the same fierce affection it did then. The urge to reach out and pull her into his arms again, the same way, he realized now, that Brady had that night, rushed over DJ in a wave.

"You're a great guy," she said, moving her hand to his leg. "Don't let this bring you too far down."

He laid his hand over top of hers, interlacing their fingers. "Thanks, Chels."

She stared down at their hands for a long time. "Should we . . ." She paused and took a deep breath then met his gaze. "Should Austin and I go? You need your rest."

He read way more into that question, into her hesitant expression. She probably should go if DJ wanted to keep his sanity. If he wanted to keep his relationship with Brady.

He compromised with himself and released her hand, which she slowly pulled away. "No way." He waved her off. "It's past noon. I've had plenty of sleep. You guys can stay and have . . . lunch." He nodded toward the table and the brownies she'd brought with her. "Unless you'd rather I make Austin a PB and J."

Chelsea eyed DJ, chewing on her lips. He raised his eyebrows. "Do you not feed him peanut butter and jelly?"

"Uh." She forced an uncomfortable laugh. "Not a lot, actually. And he usually eats peanut butter that I make myself. Fewer preservatives. Less sugar. Better for him." Her voice grew smaller with every word as she shrank in on herself, avoiding looking at him.

He'd heard the way Madison talked about the food Chelsea made for Austin, criticism leveled at her for her dedication to making sure he ate the best she could give him. He hoped Chelsea heard the awe in his reply. "You can make your own peanut butter?"

"Uh, sure, if you have a blender powerful enough. And I sweeten it with honey instead of sugar, or worse, high fructose corn syrup. It's sweeter, so you need less of it and . . . it's really good. I like it better than normal peanut butter. You should try it sometime." She still wouldn't look at him.

"I bet it is. We have a nice blender. Some of the guys are very serious about protein smoothies here. Want to show me how to make it?" He stood, setting Austin on the floor and waiting for her to follow him to the kitchen. He'd made strict dietary choices himself when he'd played football. He wouldn't fault a mother for making those choices for her child.

"Won't running the blender wake the other guys up?" she asked.

DJ shrugged. "Maybe. But we weren't out that late, and it's noon. Come on."

"Okay . . . You have peanuts, right? That's kind of a key ingredient."

He held his hand out to the kitchen. "I know I've seen some around. Follow me, Chef Chels." Her gratitude steadied his heart, allowing the guilt to slip into the background for a little while.

DJ gathered the peanuts, honey, and the blender from the half a dozen cabinets in the kitchen. When he finished, he turned to her and held his hand out toward the ingredients on the counter.

"It's your peanut butter." She pointed toward the peanuts. "And I don't want to be the one yelled at when one of those buff fire guys busts out here complaining about the noise."

"Buff?" DJ wiggled his eyebrows and flexed for her.

She giggled and then stifled it with her hand.

"Don't worry," DJ said, already trying to figure out how to make her laugh again. "The guys here will forgive pretty much anything if there's something from Wendy's involved. I just might have to share my brownies."

"Sounds like a big sacrifice." She trailed her fingers through Austin's hair. He'd come to stand next to her for a moment, but a second later he was back in DJ's shadow.

"This peanut butter better be worth it."

"I'm not making any promises, but it's good. Get out about a cup full of the peanuts and dump it in the blender."

"Yes, ma'am." He obeyed before turning to her for the next instruction.

"Turn it on high and watch. You'll know when it's ready. Then you add the honey and mix some more."

He flipped the blender on. Austin covered his ears and yelled,

"Moothie?" at Chelsea, but she shook her head and picked him up while the blender worked. Midway through, Leavitt poked his head through the door of the bunk room, but when he caught sight of Chelsea, he simply nodded a hello to her and shut the door again.

They finished with a few more instructions from Chelsea before DJ scooped it out of the blender and into a container. She acquiesced to using the jam in the fridge since they didn't have time to make any. When DJ finished making the sandwiches, he and Chelsea took seats at the table. Austin sat in DJ's lap, devouring the half-sandwich DJ had given him and smearing peanut butter and jelly across both cheeks.

"So," DJ began after swallowing his first bite, "why this all-natural thing?"

Chelsea bit into her own sandwich and chewed before answering. "Why not?" she responded, still staring down at her plate.

He recognized the frustration brewing in her expression and held up a hand. "I don't see anything wrong with it, Chels. I just wonder why you go to all the extra work. It must be hard when he doesn't . . . love everything you make." He offered a sheepish shrug.

She relaxed but still took a moment to form her answer. "He used to be such an easy baby. Slept great. Ate great. All that. Now he's not, and making sure every bite is as nutritious as I can seems about all I can control right now."

Chelsea might have more support than some single moms out there, but she still had her share of challenges. More than ever, he wanted to be part of that support network. Sitting here with her and Austin made him wish for a more permanent version.

"Well, you're right about the peanut butter in any case. It's a lot better."

Her eyes softened, and her smile built to full-wattage, full of grati-tude. A compliment—that's all it had taken. And it made DJ feel six inches taller.

She broke his gaze too soon, looking down at the table. "If you don't want to go through all the trouble, you can buy natural peanut butter at the store. It's just expensive." She shrugged after she'd said it, her chin dipping in embarrassment. Probably at mentioning her financial situation. He'd caught her tensing when she talked about the cost of the expensive baby food pouches he'd brought over.

A few more bites passed in silence before either spoke again. "So after last night you're probably wishing you'd taken your chances with football, huh?" she said.

He chuckled, but still couldn't hide the tightness in his voice. "I tried that." Yeah, after last night, and every other night in Clay he wished he'd been drafted or even had a team seriously interested in him. DJ had *belonged* on his football team. A football had belonged in his hands. Off the field, he couldn't quite figure out how, or where, he belonged.

"Oh." Chelsea closed her eyes in embarrassment. "I didn't realize . . ."

He waved her concern away. He'd come to terms with it a while ago, shifting his disappointment over the end of his football career into a desire to give back to his community. Last night had only taken more of the wind out of his sails.

"I mean, even playing for an indoor league or something probably would have been better than the stellar career I'm building here. The . . . thing that happened last night isn't going to help," he mumbled the last few words. Another job that wasn't going to work out. Maybe that's what made him feel the most like a failure. He'd wanted something simple—just to find his place in life. That was turning out to be a lot harder than he thought.

"You're a good fireman." She leaned over the table, laid her hand on top of his, and squeezed it. Then her eyebrows furrowed. "They can't fire you or anything over this, can they?" Indignation threaded through her voice.

He shrugged. Truth was, he hadn't thought a lot about that part of it yet. "Any other dog? Probably not . . ." He let the rest of the sentence trail off. He deserved whatever he had coming. He'd proven over and over that something wasn't clicking with this job. He couldn't figure out why.

He let her pull her hand away this time instead of holding onto it, even though he wanted this small connection with her, to dip his toes in the water for another minute, just to see. It didn't have to mean anything. He dated so much in college, charmed and flirted on a constant basis, but Chelsea drew him to her stronger than any other girl before.

Her voice was a bit breathless as she went on, and he smiled at that. "Well, that's ridiculous, so don't let something like this make you question everything."

"Thanks, Chels. I wish I could get the hang of it better though, rather than feeling incompetent half the time."

"It'll come," she said.

A million things ran through his brain. Was this a good idea? Was it wrong? What would Brady think? "So," he said, but then he stalled.

"So . . ." she prompted. She'd dropped her hands into her lap below the table, where he couldn't see them.

He couldn't spill what was really on his mind. "So you're a great mom and I'm a good fireman. Agreed?"

She nodded. She took a bite of her sandwich, not looking at him, and he did the same, both of them chewing and watching Austin make the uneaten half of his sandwich "drive" along the table.

Then Austin patted DJ on the cheek with his peanut butter and jelly streaked hand.

Chelsea let loose a laugh, which made DJ's lips twitch. He calmly reached for the dishtowel hanging on the nearby stove and wiped the mess off. "Wow. Thanks, pal."

Austin held up the last few bites of his sandwich to show DJ how he'd opened it up and picked out the middle. "Mmmmm," Austin said.

"Next time your mom can teach me how to make jam. I can see the glint in her eyes from all the sugar you're getting right now." DJ looked over Austin's head at Chelsea and grinned.

She shook her head and laughed harder. "I'm not that bad," she protested. "How many times over the last few days have you heard me say yes to a treat you're trying to give him?"

"Which means you won't mind if I share my b-r-o-w-n-i-e-s with him, will you?"

"You're evil." She reached across the table for the box and opened it, splitting a brownie in half and handing the smaller piece to Austin. As she took a bite of her half, DJ grinned at her I-can-be-reckless expression.

She made it so difficult for him to consider the serious consequences of falling for her. He leaned over and bit off the top half of her brownie, grinning when her mouth fell open in surprise.

She couldn't fix what had happened the night before, but she'd made his day brighter. That was enough for now.

———

THE FACT that none of the guys on his crew had made an appearance during Chelsea and Austin's visit to the station left DJ wary as he climbed back up the stairs after walking his visitors to the sidewalk half an hour later. It had been a fantastic lunch. He welcomed the idea of spending more time with her.

"So. Chelsea Lewis brought you brownies," Zollinger said as soon as DJ's head was visible coming up the stairs to the kitchen. He'd had already eaten half of a brownie. So had most his crew by the looks of it, but he would trade brownies for almost an hour of uninterrupted time with Chelsea any time.

"Just trying to make me feel better," DJ said. The smile he couldn't contain said a lot more.

"By the looks of it, it worked." Leavitt punched DJ in the arm. "But was it the brownies or the hand-holding that did the trick?"

DJ shook his head. It shouldn't surprise him, but they *were* grown men. "You guys spied on us? What is this, high school? Besides, it's not like that."

"What is it like then?" Leavitt asked.

"Seriously?" He didn't want to answer the question. He liked hanging out with Chelsea, but the guys starting gossip about them wouldn't help matters. How soon before Brady heard something and called him out? Right now, there was nothing to explain and DJ was doing his best to make sure of that, difficult as it was.

"Hey, you put five guys in a room like that for an hour with nothing else to do, we're going to talk," Miles Hansen said, handing a brownie to DJ.

"Thanks," he said dryly.

The fire bell rang, saving him from any more talk. He shrugged at Leavitt and Hansen, stuffed the rest of his brownie in his mouth—a true waste of culinary effort—and beat them to the fire pole.

CHAPTER EIGHT

Chelsea leaned against the counter at Cutie Pies, chewing thoughtfully as she studied the green muffin. She tried to mull over the taste—not too bad. Yeah, okay, not the over-sugared delicacies that Wendy created, but not that bad. Not bad enough for Austin to rip apart and throw over the side of his high chair after one bite.

But her mind wasn't on the unfair judgment her two-year-old made on her healthy-eating masterpiece. Instead, it kept going back to her visit to the fire station and her lunch with DJ. And the walk the day before. The way he drew her to him. How their hug, though it had been a spur-of-the-moment, driven to comfort him kind of thing, had turned her inside out with excitement and hope. She'd convinced herself they were just going back to their old friendship, but that's not how she'd felt when his arms were around her.

She had wanted to reciprocate all the small but meaningful things he'd done for her the last week or so. And she'd wanted to see him. Commiserating over what had happened with the mayor's dog seemed like a good excuse.

But dating him would be *wrong*. Wrong as Austin's ability to taste spinach in this stupid muffin like he was some kind of spinach-finding supervillain. Spinach had no taste. Sure, it had a lot of unfortunate color, but no taste. Austin's no-spinach policy bordered on prejudicial.

Did Brady hate spinach? Did Austin get it from him?

Brady and DJ were like brothers. She cringed at how much she wished she could push that particular thought away. She could see why she was attracted to DJ. He joked and teased the same way Brady had—but not the same. DJ could be serious when situations called for it. That was something Brady had never managed.

Great. So she was trading up. Even more wrong.

Her visit wasn't that big a deal, she told herself as she reached for another muffin. It was service. Really, as a member of the Relief Society presidency, she had a duty to perform compassionate service . . . even if it was in the wrong ward.

And service helped her, too. Bringing DJ brownies, reassuring him, it *had* lifted her spirits. Although he'd turned her act of service around, complimenting and agreeing with her about the strict food choices she made. Having to constantly defend herself for Austin's diet needled her. What was so wrong with giving her child the best food she could? What was so wrong about showing him how to make good food choices and following the Word of Wisdom?

She slapped the counter in her righteous indignation, then smiled when she considered how DJ had reacted. He'd sounded like he almost agreed, like he could support her instead of raise his eyebrows and insist that Austin was a baby and babies would eat what babies would eat.

DJ brightened her day with talk like that. She didn't always feel useless and like a mooch, even though he was usually helping her out. And then there was the fire that had raced through her at being held in his arms. She kneaded her temples.

Her phone rang with a FaceTime call. When she saw Brady's picture, she sighed. The first month or so of their divorce had been awkward for both of them as they contacted each other about raising Austin. Then Chelsea's mom had passed along some advice from a divorced woman in her ward—to always communicate no matter what. And to communicate in a kind, thoughtful way. As adults. If the parents could be friends, she'd told Denise, things would go *a lot* smoother. Chelsea had told that to Brady, and they'd made a commitment to at least do that for Austin. It wasn't always easy but easier than when they'd been married. When they were married, she'd felt so much pressure to try and make him happy and nothing seemed to work. Him admitting that he didn't love her had freed her from that pressure. She didn't need to make him happy, she just had to be his friend.

But it wasn't awkwardness that made her watch the FaceTime call ring and ring until he ended it. Well—at least not *that* awkwardness. More like one where she'd wonder if everything she said would point to how hard she was falling for DJ.

Sorry, she texted. *I'm at work.*

He sent a face-slap emoji. *My bad. I knew that. We'll talk later.*

Anxiety dashed through her chest. *Did* he know about her and DJ hanging out? Had DJ said something? She'd read enough in the tightness of his embrace to know he probably felt at least a little of what she had. She chewed on her lips and looked at the baggie of muffins, which was significantly lighter without her consciously remembering having eaten them. And she hadn't tasted the spinach, so no way Austin could. Her constant failing made the drive for her to best him in this challenge that much greater. She could get him to eat spinach somehow. She could and she *would*.

Of course, in the meantime, she had an entire pan of muffins to eat.

The bell above the door jingled, and Chelsea straightened and hid the muffin behind her back. Nobody coming into Cutie Pies wanted anything green. But it was Wendy coming back from delivering the cake to Mayor Tingey's for the memorial service.

"Thanks for watching the store," she said, rounding the counter as Chelsea took the muffin back out.

"No problem. That's what employees are for." She took the final bite of muffin.

"What was that?" Wendy scrunched her nose.

Chelsea swallowed, and her challenger mentality kicked in. Somebody would like these muffins; not little Miss Sweet Tooth, but someone. "Muffin, and it's not that bad. Don't judge until you try it." She held up the baggie she'd brought, which still held a few muffins.

Wendy shrugged. "Okay, I'm game." She plucked one out and took a bite. In true Wendy fashion, she closed her eyes and chewed slowly, not speaking as she swallowed and took another bite, mulling it over the same way Chelsea had the first. After four similar bites, she finished and opened her eyes. "Not too sweet, sure, but not bad. Not dense—really fluffy actually. The color's kind of off-putting, but for a healthy muffin, it definitely passes."

Having Wendy's approval sent an instant grin to Chelsea's face, the accomplishment warming her almost as much as DJ's compliments had. "Thanks."

Wendy leaned against the counter next to her. "I've had a few people ask about special diet treats—you know, sugar free, dairy free, gluten free, and all that. Want to give it a shot? You know my heart's not in it if I can't pour cupfuls of sugar in."

"Me?" Chelsea turned to face her cousin. "You think I could pull off something like that? I don't know anything about gluten-free food or dairy free or whatever."

"Of course you. Your idea for the hot chocolate and the Italian sodas was a huge hit. Maybe because it's all new, I don't know, but still. Besides, you've got a knack and you like to experiment. These muffins are a prime example. How much sugar?" Wendy asked.

"Actually, none." Admitting it both embarrassed Chelsea and made her proud at the same time, especially since Wendy had already expressed liking them. "I used applesauce instead. Uh, homemade, of course, from some Red Golds. They're the sweetest apple variety."

Wendy raised her eyebrows in triumph. "See? Exactly. I know you could come up with some stuff, and if it works out, it works out. If not," she shrugged, "oh well."

Chelsea had never understood how Wendy could look at life like that—give it a shrug and say, "Oh, well. Better luck next time." "You're awful blasé about my possible failure as a baker."

"They're muffins, Chels." Wendy nudged her with an elbow and headed for the back. Chelsea watched her with envy, as always. Wendy's no-big-deal attitude extended to larger endeavors too. She'd lost a good chunk of her savings a few years before when her attempt to run a cutesy tea-room shop had failed. She'd found a job for a while as a dispatcher, saved up, did stuff on the side, and got back into the entrepreneurial world with Cutie Pies. This time it looked like her attempt had stuck, so maybe Wendy was onto something.

Wendy poked her head out of the kitchen and held up a box. "Hey, mind dropping these off at the fire station on your way home?"

Chelsea shook her head vigorously. "I do mind. Sorry." Her heart thudded at the thought of seeing DJ again, but she couldn't.

Wendy frowned and came back out, her apron dangling, untied, around her waist. "What's the big deal?"

"I don't want people to get ideas." Chelsea's cheeks grew hot thinking about what the citizens of Clay were probably passing around about her and DJ, especially the guys at the fire station. Brady's former next-door neighbor. The life-long friend he grew up with. She escaped around the counter and headed for the door.

"What kind of ideas are people going to get from you dropping off day-old cookies to the firemen?" Wendy held the box in one hand and put the other on her hip, her expression indicating she thought Chelsea had taken a dive into the crazy pool.

But all Chelsea could think was what would have happened if Austin hadn't interrupted that moment? If they hadn't been in as public a place as the fire station?

Kissing? Would they have kissed? And how bad would Chelsea have felt about it?

Wendy's expression merged into a knowing smile. "Chels . . ."

Chelsea looked at the floor as she answered. "That there's something going on with me and DJ."

"Why would people think that?" Her cousin held her breath, on the verge of laughter. Chelsea heard it in her voice.

Chelsea thought her cheeks might burst into flame. "I don't know. I mean, he's close to Patty and Dale and stuff, so him coming to church with them isn't a big deal, but since Dale was subbing on

Sunday for one of the youth classes, DJ sat by Mom, so of course I had to sit by him. And he just babysat for me because he's a good guy, but Allison Rees got it into her head that, you know . . . And I just don't want people to talk about us. If I'm the one that goes to drop off the cookies, it'll fan the flame." She'd had lunch with him the day before, and by all accounts, it had looked like a date, a lunch date that the other firemen suspiciously stayed out of. Who knew what they'd already told their families?

It took Wendy a second to recover from the flood of words that had spilled out of Chelsea, but she didn't hold her laughter at bay long. She came forward and put the box on a chair before placing her hands on Chelsea's shoulders. "Everyone comes into my bakery. *Everyone.* And I haven't heard anyone talking about the possibility that you and DJ have something going on. But, girl, it's all over your face."

"Stop, Wendy. He's helping out. Being nice. You know how he always was with Brady—keeping him out of trouble and watching out for him. He's doing the same for me. That's all."

But with every second Wendy stared at her, the heat in Chelsea's face intensified. Why would Wendy believe her when Chelsea didn't even want to believe herself? Gah! She wanted to take those cookies by. To give DJ another hug . . . to see what might happen.

"Yeah. Okay. Whatever. I'll drop the cookies off." Wendy shrugged. "But only if you spill it. Come on, I'm your best friend. Girl talk, right now."

"It's. Nothing," Chelsea reiterated. "Like I said. He's been helping out and . . . and, I like it, but isn't that terrible of me?"

Wendy stared at her, eyebrows coming down in a slant. "Why would that be terrible? You're divorced. Brady left, and it's okay to be attracted to other guys now. You're going to want to get married again someday."

"But not to DJ!" Chelsea threw her hands up.

"Why not?" Again, Wendy had on the she's-lost-it look.

"Wendy, they grew up like brothers."

"But they're not, so don't worry about it." Wendy pointed a finger at Chelsea, who'd opened her mouth to interrupt. "Chels, nothing even has to come of this at all. Enjoy the feeling if that's all it is right now. Don't sweat the small stuff." She reached out and pulled Chelsea into a one-sided hug.

Chelsea pressed her lips together before replying dryly. "Let me guess. If it works, it works?"

"Exactly." Wendy swept up the box and headed back toward the kitchen. "I'll tell him you said hi," she called over her shoulder, chuckling as the door swung shut behind her.

"Wendy! Come on . . ." Chelsea called after her.

"See you later!" Wendy answered, and Chelsea escaped before she let loose any more ridiculous ideas.

———

THE BUTTERFLIES GOING AROUND and around in Chelsea's stomach when Wendy picked her up that night resembled, too much, first-date type butterflies, which made Chelsea want to gag a little. At some point, she *would* go on a first date again, wouldn't she? She'd never pictured herself single for the rest of her life—she'd just never considered dating again either. Except when it came to DJ, but somehow her mind had bypassed dating right to established relationship. She pictured arriving at the restaurant in his truck, their hands enjoined over the console, chatting and laughing with each other before he got out and hurried to her side of the car to open her door. The thought felt so . . . right.

Still, she banished the idea from her mind. Tonight, she needed to focus on friends and quit worrying about what, if anything, was going to happen with DJ.

"Why are you so nervous?" Wendy asked with a glance at Chelsea's hands in her lap. They were already pulling up in front of the diner. Curse this small town. It never took more than a few minutes to get anywhere. "It's not like DJ's going to be there." Wendy's grin was full on mischievous as she put the car in park.

"Stop it." Chelsea pointed at her cousin, trying not to show her panic. What if Wendy teased her in front of the women inside? That would require explanations that she'd rather not give. And if Wendy had guessed so easily where Chelsea's thoughts were, would the other women know something was up too? Would they pry?

"Chill, sweetie." Wendy laughed and pushed open her door. "You know I'm teasing. I think the fact that you're so worked up about this means you need to take it into serious consideration."

"Let's go inside, okay?" Chelsea pushed her own door open and got out before Wendy could reply. She knew Wendy meant well, but she didn't want to have this conversation again.

She sat down next to Sharae Barber at the tables the staff had pushed together for them. She was the new Relief Society secretary, and her twins were about the same age as Austin. Her sister-in-law, Kelsi, had worked as a dispatcher at the same time as Wendy.

"Hey," Sharae greeted her. "I'm glad you came."

"I really needed to get out," Chelsea confessed as she scooted her seat in. "I used to do this with friends in Salt Lake."

"With better restaurant choices." Gretchen Riggs pulled a frown from where she sat across the table. She'd gone to school in Rexburg before marrying a local guy and moving back to Clay. Chelsea thought about how Gretchen had intimidated her in high school and laughed to herself over how she'd hated that Brady had chosen to take her to prom—until he explained that DJ had suggested Gretchen since they planned on switching dates. And after her evening with DJ after prom, she hadn't given it any more thought except to wonder how she would have felt if Brady had connected with Gretchen the way Chelsea had with DJ that night. Jealous, but the thoughts hadn't consumed her like they had before.

"I do miss the options," Chelsea said. The butterflies did a swift lap around her stomach. It seemed she couldn't get away from thinking about DJ, no matter how hard she tried.

"What's this grumbling I hear?" Allison Rees pretended to look stern when she came up to their table with her notebook in hand.

"How nothing can compare to your food," Gwen Parrish, Gretchen's older sister, said. The women at the table laughed.

Allison began taking orders, her smile turning teasing when she got to Chelsea. "Who's watching Austin for you tonight?"

Chelsea kept her expression calm, ignoring the allusion to the last time she'd seen Allison. She wouldn't let it bother her that Allison hadn't asked that of the other women. Gwen didn't have any kids yet, but she was at least six months along with her first. The other women, besides Wendy, had husbands to watch their kids.

"My mom, of course." Chelsea's tone might have been a bit too sweet. Allison's smile widened, but Chelsea started her order before she could make another comment.

"What was that about?" Sharae asked in a low voice after Allison had left.

Refusing to explain would only raise curiosity, so Chelsea continued to act as though it wasn't a big deal. "DJ Kaiser watched Austin for me the other day, and Allison got it in her head that it meant something. It's kind of embarrassing that she keeps talking about it."

Sharae nodded, and though Chelsea guessed that Sharae was more curious than she let on, she didn't press. "Small towns, right?"

"Yes," Chelsea agreed with a sigh. "I love it though."

"Me too." Sharae nodded again, reaching for her water.

Chelsea joined in conversations that ranged from jobs, to kids, and then, of course, husbands.

Gwen and her husband, Cale, were finishing a house that he and her dad had built outside of town, and she worried about how much needed to get done before she had the baby later that summer.

"Cale's been working late every night after he gets home. Dad feels bad, but with all the new houses being built in that new subdivision in Bellemont, he can't spare any time during the day. Poor guy, Cale just wants to make sure I'm happy," she explained.

Chelsea aww-ed at the sweetness, along with the rest of the women, and even Wendy gave a quiet "Aww." She couldn't think of a time that Brady had sacrificed like that for her, even though they'd been married for far longer than any of the women at the table. She was sure there must have been things she'd forgotten. Brady's intense schooling had taken up so much in their marriage. He hadn't had the time to really sacrifice for her.

The other women chimed in with their own examples, and Chelsea kept her chin up. She forced herself to stay involved in the conversation, commenting about the men she'd known growing up, nodding along. She wouldn't let herself slip into out-of-place pity, even if this wasn't her life anymore. She liked these women, wanted to be around them, and she wouldn't make them feel bad for having happy marriages.

"Did you see that Mercedes is going back to work?" Sharae said after Kelsi had finished talking about the anniversary trip her husband had surprised her with a few months before. Out of the corner of Chelsea's eye, she glanced over at Sharae. The abrupt change left her sure that the woman had done it on purpose out of concern for Chelsea, and probably Wendy.

"How old is her youngest?" Gwen asked, leaning back in her chair. She hadn't eaten much of her meal. Chelsea could remember those days of her pregnancy. She'd taken home food to Brady during those girls' night dinners more often than not.

"Three, I think," Wendy answered. "She always told me she was going back as soon as she could convince Damien."

The others began discussing when and if they would go back to work. "You didn't have to do that," she whispered to Sharae. "I promise I don't have anything against husbands."

Sharae laughed softly. "We come here to get away from them. Though I love Jace to death, I can definitely talk about something other than him."

Chelsea gave her a grateful smile before turning to join the conversation. "Having a few hours away from being a mommy is pretty nice," she said. "After working for so long before I had Austin, it gets to the point where I'm a little lost just being a mom. Luckily I have a great boss."

With laughs, the others asked Wendy if she had jobs for them. Allison came to ask if they wanted dessert, and another laugh went around the table. "We're, uh, stopping somewhere else for that," Kelsi said, grimacing at Allison.

She swatted at Kelsi's shoulder. "Well, if Wendy made you all something good, I'll be sure to come by after I close up."

"We'll be there," Gretchen assured her.

Chelsea sat back in her own seat for a moment before starting to gather up her things, like the women around her. No wonder Wendy had begged her for so long to do this. Some moments she had felt out of place, but for the most part, she'd enjoyed the night out, chatting and eating good food.

"Make sure I come next time," she said to Wendy when she reached down for her purse.

Sharae answered before Wendy could. "We will."

CHAPTER NINE

It didn't surprise DJ to find Chelsea sitting on the front porch of her parents' house Sunday evening, her legs stretched over a couple steps, staring out over the wide, green lawn. Studying the house next door—or other weightier thoughts—apparently engrossed her so much, she didn't notice him approaching.

He'd gone to her ward, claiming again that he'd overslept, so he could hear about her new calling. She'd probably seen right through him since he'd made sure when she had lunch with him at the station that she knew he got off on Friday.

He thought she'd be great in the Relief Society, but he could tell from the plastered smile she gave the congregation when she stood up that she still worried about her ability to serve. That look had brought him on his walk toward her parents' house when he knew he should stay away and avoid the temptation.

"You're gonna do great," he said as he came up the walk.

Her face snapped up at his voice. She pulled her feet up to rest on the wooden step below her, drawing herself in. "You said that already at church."

"You look like you need to hear it again."

She leaned against the railing on the porch. "I'll survive, I guess. I was in the Relief Society before, in Salt Lake. Still, with all the changes since then, I have a lot to learn."

DJ took a seat next to her, wishing he could close the foot or so of space he left between them. DJ almost resented how wide the steps were. If they'd been smaller, more standard sized, it would have forced him to take a seat closer to her.

He thought about how the warmth of satisfaction enveloped him when he helped her. How eating peanut butter sandwiches with her had brightened his day, and even the memory of their afternoon made facing up to the dog incident that much easier. His mind dwelled even longer on how good she'd smelled and how perfect she'd felt in his arms.

"That doesn't explain why you look so scared. Changes or not, this should be old hat," he said. "Plus, you only have half the meetings you did then."

"Back then I had a husband and an eternal family. I was doing everything right then. Now . . . "

DJ scowled. "You're not doing anything wrong now."

"I just feel really underqualified and like anything I teach about families and marriage will sound hypocritical." She turned to him with such a disheartened expression he couldn't help scooting over and reaching up to wrap his arm around her shoulders. She didn't reject his effort. She even leaned her head on his shoulder.

"I think a lot of women probably feel the same way—despite being married and raising good kids. Nobody's perfect, Chels. Besides, there's a lot more you have to give than your experience raising your son or your marriage. How about your healthy-eating techniques? Or how to budget and live within your means? Or how you've helped Austin cope with big changes in his life? Those all seem like good Relief Society lesson topics. And I know there's a lot more about you that I haven't figured out yet." He would definitely like the opportunity to figure out some more things about her. It seemed a shame that they'd grown up in the same town, that he'd spent so many nights with her and Brady, and yet he didn't know her like he thought he did.

She sat up and studied him for a few moments before saying, "I used to think you handled everything with a joke, like Brady, but you always take me seriously—everything. Even when . . . a lot of people think my insistence about Austin's food or doing so much on my own is me being weird and stubborn. But you've never made me feel like that. You make me feel legit."

"Chels." He shook his head slightly, wishing he could find some way to make her see that she wasn't failing. He'd never met a girl he wanted to lift up as badly as he wanted to lift up Chelsea. In Provo, he'd liked making girls laugh by joking with them—flirting and all that. In a house where most of the girls wanted the attention of his old roommate, the great "Rocket" Rogers, he brought a smile to the girls who *didn't* get noticed. Not that Anthony ignored people on purpose, it was just that *a lot* of girls had hung around. Anthony couldn't have paid attention to all of them, as much as he might have wanted to.

So yeah, DJ hadn't been serious about things in Provo. But then, he'd never met a girl with serious trials like Chelsea's . . . or at least he'd never paid enough attention to notice one. That had been more Sean's sort of thing. He was the dependable, reliable roommate. The one who sat back and listened. Sean would have found a way to say the right thing to Chelsea.

"What?" she prodded.

He blinked, coming out of his thoughts and channeling his former roommate for the right thing to say. "You are definitely legit. I'm not saying this to make you feel better. You're going to be great. Trust the bishop. Trust yourself. Trust the Lord."

They sat there, staring at each other for a moment that kept stretching out. Embarrassment crept over her expression, but she didn't look away. He reached up with the hand that wasn't around her shoulder and let his fingers graze over her cheek, feeling the heat there. She took a deep breath, and he had to as well. He wanted to kiss her, to take care of her and help her and . . . be everything for her. He slid his hand around her neck and guided her closer. They stared at each other.

"DJ?" she asked in a soft voice.

He couldn't pull completely away. He swallowed. "What am I doing?" he whispered.

She tipped her head back. "What do you want to do?"

"That's simple," he said with a laugh. "I just . . . we can't do half-measures here, can we?" Brady was a huge obstacle he didn't know how to get over, as much as every moment with Chelsea drew her to him.

"No, we can't," she agreed.

Still, neither of them moved. Neither of them got up and walked away from this tipping point. He fingered a piece of her hair that fell in front of her shoulder. "He's like my brother and I don't know if there's any point where this won't feel like I'm betraying him . . . even . . . even if being with you might be more important."

She settled her hands at his waist, gripping the sides of his T-shirt. "I hate that this has to be so complicated." She tipped her head so that her forehead rested against his shoulder.

He pressed his cheek to the side of her head. "I know." He lifted both of his hands to rest behind her neck and tilted her face back up to him, brushing a thumb along one of her cheeks. "I know." He studied her from inches away, heat spreading through his chest.

Kiss her?

Walk away?

What do I do?

Her expression must mirror back his emotions. Fear. Uncertainty. Longing.

Did he want to take the next step and deal with the consequences? He should make the decision soon, especially if he *wanted* it more than he was *scared* of it. Any moment, he might come to his senses. They both might.

"I want this," she whispered.

That was all it took to make his decision.

———

HE KISSED HER.

Everything inside of her spun. The moments she'd spent with him the last few weeks had been the best in her life, besides the night Austin was born. The kiss was no different. Except it was So. Much. Better. Electricity exploded inside her.

The feeling scared her, but not in the way she thought it would. It scared her how much her lips ached for him. How light the feel of his fingers at the base of her neck made her, how he slipped them into her hair. How his touch made her shoulders melt and turned her legs into pudding. She'd forgotten how intoxicating a first kiss could be, how anticipation mixed with happiness made for such a dangerous cocktail.

When he pulled away, they stared at each other for several moments. She couldn't get enough of staring at him. She wanted to memorize his face and make sure she could remember it for a long, long time.

"Now what?" he asked, not putting any distance between them.

She used her hands at his hips to pull him even closer. She thought about how she might feel if Allison came upon them for some reason, and the nerves on that score had lessened. She thought about how DJ was nothing like Brady, not even the improved version, like she'd worried about. He was just DJ, and that was perfect.

"I don't really know," she said with a smile.

He matched it then leaned in and kissed her forehead, staying there for a moment. "Chocolate?" he said with a laugh in his voice. "Do I smell chocolate on you?"

Her shoulders shook with laughter as she tilted her head to look up at him. "There's the joke," she said. He grinned back, liking the way she kept her head against his arm. "I made some experimental brownies for dessert. Mom made dessert too because Dad didn't trust me. I guess we'll see after dinner."

"Experimental brownies?"

"Wendy wants me to try some stuff for people with diet restrictions. I found a recipe on Pinterest that I'm playing around with." She shifted so that she leaned up against him with his arm around her shoulder.

"And you're not going to tell me what's in them?" He rested his head on top of hers.

"No. It'll prejudice your opinion."

"So I get to try them?" he asked.

"If you're brave enough." She snickered.

"You're talking to a fireman, you know. We're kind of known for bravery."

"Yeah, especially in Clay, right? It's a rough town."

"I saved the Ice Cream Hut from burning down the other day. If that's not true heroism, I don't know what is."

"I heard it was a pile of grass behind the building that someone threw a cigarette into and that it was mostly out by the time you guys got there." She raised an eyebrow.

"Who knows what could've happened? That's all I'm saying."

She shook her head at him, smiling before her expression turned serious. "You're legit too. I mean that."

Doubt crossed his face in a slight frown and she remembered how he'd told her about going to see Mayor Tingey to apologize. How she'd only nodded and he couldn't help but think that she still saw the joking, fun-loving teenager she'd known when he was growing up.

"I'm trying," he said.

"That's all anyone can ask. So . . ." She took a deep breath and eyed him. "Want to stay for dinner?"

"Should I?" he asked.

She reached up, taking his cheeks to pull him down and kiss him again. "Yeah. You should." She stood and held out her hand to him.

He let her pretend to help him stand up, threading his fingers through hers when they were both standing. "Those brownies better be good."

She cast him a smile over her shoulder as she led him inside the house. "They're *experimental*. No promises."

IT WAS close to ten when DJ got home that night, but he tried calling

Brady anyway. Based on what DJ gleaned from social media, his friend kept late hours, either working or playing. But it didn't surprise him when Brady didn't answer. He tried again, but it went to voice mail after a couple rings. DJ massaged his temples as he hung up. This wasn't something he could leave a message about.

His phone dinged with a text from Brady. *Sorry. Had to come into work after church and can't talk. What's up?*

I really need to have a conversation with you, DJ replied. *Not something to talk about over a text message.*

Brady didn't respond right away, so DJ flicked on the TV. Twenty minutes later he got a reply text: *I'll try to get back to you tomorrow.*

DJ sighed. With Brady, that was the best he could hope for. His friend's possible reactions had darted in and out of his thoughts most of the night with Chelsea, especially when Brady had called after dinner. DJ had noted the surprise on Brady's face when he'd caught sight of DJ. He'd given his friend a quick nod of greeting, but Chelsea had gathered up Austin and taken him into the family room so Austin could talk with his dad. From what he heard of the conversation from the kitchen, neither Chelsea nor Brady addressed the fact that DJ was there. Chelsea had returned to the table only a few minutes later.

"Toddlers have short attention spans," she'd explained with a half-laugh. She and her mom shared a quick look of frustration. DJ wasn't sure if the look expressed their frustration about Austin not sitting still or Brady not being more physically present.

Even though the call had added to his worries, he couldn't regret the night or taking this step with Chelsea. Everything clicked into place with her, like a perfect pass or making the first truck to leave the station. It was difficult to give Brady's feelings as much weight as he should—especially since he couldn't get him to answer a phone call. Irritation rose in his thoughts. He'd considered Brady at every step with Chelsea, but Brady couldn't take ten minutes to give him a call? Brady hadn't called him in months, and the last time he did, their conversation had lasted less than five minutes. DJ had argued with himself for weeks over how this would hurt his best friend, but how much of a best friend was Brady these days?

Or was DJ justifying how much happier his life was with Chelsea in it?

He couldn't tell anymore.

He went to bed and put Brady out of his thoughts, focusing instead on how great his future with Chelsea looked.

———

ON WEDNESDAY MORNING, after working his latest three days on, he had planned on sleeping more than a couple hours before he got up to go help Dale Lewis on the farm, but someone ringing his doorbell just after eight ruined that plan. Before Chelsea, he would've ignored it and gone back to sleep. Most the people he knew understood when he didn't answer the door even if his truck was parked in the driveway. Chelsea would too, but he definitely wouldn't mind a visit from her. He could make them all breakfast or something, learn more about the dietary choices she made for herself and Austin. He'd let his own habits slip pretty far away from healthy since he'd stopped playing football. Maybe she'd rub off on him.

When he opened the front door, it wasn't Chelsea. It wasn't anyone. Instead a small fire flickered on the doormat. DJ's first instinct was to stomp it out with his foot, but better sense stopped him. One, his feet were bare since he'd just gotten out of bed. Two, in the second that he paused, he realized what was probably in the burning brown paper bag on his doorstep.

Stepping around it, he glanced up the street in time to see two teenage boys racing down the sidewalk. He recognized one of them as the mayor's son. He sighed and grabbed a shovel he had sitting on the step, using it to tamp out the fire and then carry the mess from the doormat to the dumpster in the backyard. Then he came back and threw away the doormat too.

He tried not to let the incident bother him as he got dressed—no sense in trying to go back to sleep—but it stayed on his mind as he drove out to the Lewis farm. Considering what he'd done to the Tingey dog, he probably deserved a bag of flaming poop on his doorstep; he for sure didn't deserve forgiveness any time soon. Not for the first time, it crossed his mind that maybe he should quit. Give Mayor Tingey the satisfaction of knowing that he wasn't cut out for the fire station, just like she thought. He could find another job in Clay, couldn't he? He had before, when he'd washed out of the police academy and then after a few disastrous weeks as a substitute teacher. He could explore putting to use his exercise science degree and work as a trainer, but if the high school even needed one, he doubted they could pay him enough to live on. Now that he'd taken this step with Chelsea, his desire to stay in Clay increased enormously. But staying meant working.

He parked his truck on the side of a dirt road on Dale's property, along the fence line he'd told DJ he'd be fixing today. Rows and rows of alfalfa stretched out across the field that would serve as the winter range for Dale's cows. Behind the field, dry, sandy hills rose up and blocked DJ's view of Clay.

Fifty feet down the fence line, Dale looked up as DJ approached and then looked down at his watch. "Shouldn't you be sleeping? Patty said you got off this morning."

DJ yanked his gloves on and grabbed some tools from the small toolbox on the back of Dale's four-wheeler. "Told you I'd help. Plenty of time to sleep later."

Dale gave a short grunt before he went back to work removing the barbs around the hole in the fence. "How's work going?" he asked, glancing up at DJ.

DJ sighed and shook his head before he crouched down and handed Dale a sleeve to repair the split wire. At least he wasn't asking about Chelsea. He didn't know how much gossip had reached Dale's ears yet, but that wasn't a conversation he wanted to have with the elder Lewis before he'd spoken to Brady.

"Never better," DJ said. Once Dale had the broken ends of the barbed wire through the sleeve, DJ grabbed the crimping tool and squeezed it closed. "Sometimes I wonder if I'm ever going to figure out the right career. Seems like I'm always pulling my foot out of one mess just to put it in another." *Almost literally this morning*, he added to himself.

"You thinking of quitting again?" Dale raised a brow, clearly not impressed with that suggestion.

DJ didn't answer.

"Give it time. You've been here less than a year and only been a fireman for five months. Can't be the best at everything you do." Dale wrapped up the loose ends then clipped them and stood, walking toward his four-wheeler and swinging his leg over. DJ followed and hopped on the back.

"It wouldn't be awful if I found something I was at least decent at," DJ grunted. "You know Mayor Tingey wants the chief to fire me. I may not have any time to give it."

Dale fired up the four-wheeler before barking a laugh over his shoulder. "Fire you? Over a dog? Rob would never do it."

"Maybe not," DJ yelled back. "But she thinks the incident is 'indicative of my inability to take my responsibilities seriously.' And who can blame her, considering?"

Dale didn't answer until they reached a section of fence farther down and he'd stopped and shut down the four-wheeler. "It was an accident." Dale scowled, gathering his tools back up to repair another line of barbed wire.

DJ shrugged. "I'm sure her insistence has more to do with some of my less-than-serious shenanigans in high school and some of the mishaps that have happened since I moved back to town." He smiled ruefully.

"Told you not to keep that barbeque so close to your house." Dale chuckled and bent over. "Stick it out," he said when he stood back up. He studied DJ. "You can't bail every time things get tricky. I mean it. Work hard and do your best; that's all anyone can ask."

DJ ground his teeth. The last thing he wanted to do was disappoint Dale. "I'm not going to quit," he said, the promise hardening inside him as he did. After all his other failures, he had to prove that he was capable. He couldn't let Mayor Tingey chase him off. He couldn't let this incident lead to failure at one more thing.

He would figure out some way to show Mayor Tingey that it had truly been an accident, that he was sorry for it, and that he took his job as a Clay fireman very seriously. He'd sat in on the last town council meeting—shouldn't that count for something too? Most people didn't bother with the mundane, day-to-day workings of the town government. In any case, Mayor Tingey had some town beautifying project ideas that had fallen on deaf ears. Maybe DJ could find a way to make some of those happen. It might go a long way if she wasn't getting support from anyone else.

DJ loved Clay and was one of the few young citizens who *wanted* to come back and make his life there in the small town. He wanted the same community that had invested in him for his children. If Mayor Tingey got him fired, he wasn't sure what other job opportunities were left.

Which is why he had to make sure he kept this job.

"What's that look for?" Dale asked, interrupting DJ's thoughts as he crouched to start removing barbs for the next repair.

"I've got an idea. About getting back on Mayor Tingey's good side." The optimism inside DJ grew.

"Not sure she has one," Dale said with a chuckle.

"Well, if anything, I need to show her I'm sorry and that I'm invested in this town. She can't say that about many guys my age." He crouched and took off some barbs on his side of the split, his smile growing as the ideas took root and started spreading.

"No, she can't," Dale agreed. "Don't stretch those too tight. You'll pull out the whole thing." He slapped DJ on the back. "I can't imagine how lazy and fat your dad must be getting in Utah without all this work to help me with."

"Mom says he has a pretty big garden. Big as the yard will allow."

"Bet she loves that."

"Said she gave away most of it last year." DJ grinned. "Took my fair share home from a visit. Did my fair share of harvesting too."

"Man, I miss old Greg. If it wasn't for you, I think I'd have to give up on this farm."

DJ glanced over the fields in front of them, a slight breeze ruffling the tops of some of the alfalfa. It hadn't just been his dad helping out here but DJ, Brady, and Charlie too. When they had talked about the future, Brady—and Chelsea, of course—had dreamed about coming back to run the farm. But Brady was a lawyer now. DJ doubted he still wanted to live on the farm. Or even anywhere near it.

He gave Dale a smile. "If it's up to me, you won't ever have to." He wasn't sure how he meant to keep that promise, but he'd figure it out.

CHAPTER TEN

On Wednesday afternoon as Chelsea headed to work, her phone rang. She cringed when she saw Brady's name. They hadn't had a chance to talk since he'd called on Sunday. She'd avoided extending the conversation after Austin got off like she normally did. DJ had told her he planned on calling Brady Sunday night and explain about them so she didn't have to. She braced herself to hear Brady's opinion.

"Hello?" she answered.

"Hey, it's me."

"You'll need to be quick. I'm almost to work. Sorry, I meant to call you later on Sunday night." But of course, she'd gotten distracted with DJ.

"It's okay," Brady said. "I had to go back into work and didn't get home until late." So maybe DJ hadn't been able to get a hold of him. She felt sure that if they'd spoken, Brady would have mentioned something. "If I get Friday afternoon off, can you come down for the weekend?" he went on, pulling her thoughts back.

Chelsea let out a sigh. "It's not a good weekend. I'm behind on the books for Wendy and was going to take some time on Saturday to catch up, and I have a presidency meeting Sunday after church." Not to mention she hoped to spend some time with DJ. She smiled at the thought, tapping her lips, then pulled herself back to the conversation. She remembered her commitment to be honest and went on. "In the last six months, I've been the one to come there every time you've seen Austin."

"I know, I know." He paused. "Chels, I'm sorry, but I'm so busy. The firm just got a big client, and things are crazy around here. I haven't been home before midnight this entire week."

"Your job is important. I'm not discounting that. But so is mine and my life here. We have to compromise." She squeezed her fingers together. As important as it was for them, she never enjoyed conversations like this with Brady, especially after nine years of not ever having them. She swung open the door of Cutie Pies and walked in, waving at Wendy, who was helping someone at the counter.

"I understand. I'll figure something out."

Chelsea tucked the phone between her shoulder and her ear, holding it there while she put the apron on. "Thanks, Brady. Listen, I just got to work, so I need to go." They hung up, and Chelsea joined her cousin at the counter.

"What was that?" Wendy asked as the customers left.

"Brady." Chelsea stuck the phone in her pocket and started to tie her apron in place. "We're trying to schedule a time he can see Austin."

"Asking you to come down again?" Wendy asked, her tone clipped.

"Yes," Chelsea replied and shot her cousin a look. "But he understood when I pointed out that I've been the one to go down the last few times. Cut him some slack, please."

Wendy nodded. "Okay, okay."

Chelsea pulled a Tupperware box from her bag. "Here. Time for you to pass judgement on the brownies."

"Ooooo." Wendy rubbed her hands together and pried the lid off, plucking one out. They walked toward the back, propping open the door between the kitchen and the shop in case a customer came in.

As Chelsea waited, she didn't know if she could handle baking for

Wendy. Her cousin did her slow chewing thing, eyes closed, pondering every bite she took, and for the life of her, Chelsea couldn't figure out if Wendy liked the brownies or not. Bless his heart, DJ had choked down two on Sunday, insisting they weren't too bad. She'd made some changes since then, but Wendy gave no indication if they were for the better. Chelsea gripped the edge of the island a little tighter as she gazed around the kitchen and tried to find something other than Wendy's impossibly slow analysis of the brownies to distract her.

"Come on, Wendy." Chelsea threw her hands up. "Yay or nay?"

Wendy, who sat casually on a stool at the counter, still took her time swallowing the last bite. Chelsea groaned in frustration. Her cousin kept a straight face for a moment longer, tapping a finger against her cheek, before she broke into a smile. "They're good. Reeeeally good. No way they're gluten free. What's in them?"

Like with DJ, Chelsea had refused to divulge the ingredients before Wendy had tasted them. "Black beans," she said as relief doused her.

Wendy picked up another one and tore off a piece before popping it into her mouth. "No kidding. I've heard of the recipe. Never dared try it."

"It took some tinkering. I tried using applesauce to sweeten it again, but no go. None of the test subjects liked that one, not even Austin. You'd think I snuck spinach into it the way he reacted." Giddiness bubbled up in Chelsea's chest as she watched Wendy pick up another brownie. She'd made it with honey and some brown sugar, and even managed to tweak it enough to sub some of the coconut oil for yogurt.

"Test subjects?" Wendy asked.

Chelsea tapped her fingers on the counter and avoided Wendy's questioning gaze, staring instead at the timer on one of the ovens. Judging from the homey, sweet smell drifting through the kitchen, it was a batch of Wendy's famous chocolate chip cookies—a recipe she'd gotten from their other aunt.

"You know," Chelsea said and cleared her throat. "Mom, Dad, Austin . . . anyone who dropped by."

"Like maybe DJ?" Wendy teased.

Chelsea met Wendy's smirk with a frown. "Yeah. Okay. He came by on Sunday so, yeah, he tried a brownie for me." Her face heated, giving her away immediately.

"Chels!" Wendy cried, grabbing her hands. "Tell me, tell me, tell me!"

Chelsea laughed and shook her head. "He kissed me. Everything is so complicated between us, but when he kissed me, I just knew it was all going to work out."

Wendy squealed and squeezed Chelsea's hands some more. Finally settling down, she looked Chelsea in the eye. "*Don't* overthink things." Her expression turned stern. "If you didn't date any of the single guys in this stake because they know Brady, that's a lot of guys. So stop worrying so much."

"It's different with Brady and DJ. You know how close they were." She worried again about what she'd asked DJ to do by encouraging him. This affected him so much more. Her and Brady were done; her decisions were her own now. He didn't have a say in who she moved on with. DJ didn't have the luxury of dismissing it like that.

Wendy let her exasperation out in a sigh before taking another bite. She shook her head at Chelsea while she finished chewing. "Why do you care what Brady thinks? He's not here. Not anywhere near here, Chels, and judging from the last year, not likely to poke his head in the picture much either."

"Stop. I'm not going to talk about him like that." She pulled the plate of brownies toward her and changed the subject. "These brownies aren't strict gluten free. The store didn't have the right oats for it—so that might make them a bit more expensive to make. But even without the gluten-free stamp, these are only three Weight Watchers points."

Chelsea waited for Wendy's response, hoping she'd go with the subject change. She understood her cousin's reasons for her to jump in with DJ without hesitation, but Wendy wasn't the one in Chelsea's shoes.

Wendy raised her eyebrows and finished off her brownie. "No kidding?" she said, showing how impressed she was with a well-done look. At least she'd gone along with the subject change.

"No kidding." Chelsea reached for a brownie of her own. Despite having eaten too many brownies over the past few days, these ones tasted surprisingly rich and chocolatey. "I ordered some certified gluten-free oats from Amazon. They should be here tomorrow."

"Perfect. Come in and make a big batch. We'll see how they do. Got any other ideas in that twisted brain of yours?" Wendy wiped her hands on her apron and grabbed a bowl from the open side of the island before she stood up.

Chelsea beamed, thinking DJ might be right that she could use her healthy-eating quirks for the good of others. This felt like something more than an obsession over what Austin ate—it felt like a talent, like something useful. Like something she might love doing. "Yep. Some dairy-free cookies."

"I'm sure they're going to rock." Wendy grinned, and they both squealed again.

———

DJ LET OUT an enormous yawn as he stood at the edge of the park and surveyed the four, worn garden boxes on the far side of the picnic pavilion. Mayor Tingey had wanted to revive the community garden project. DJ had agreed with the rest of the council that building the community boxes had been a waste to begin with. Everyone in Clay had a garden plot in their backyards. Most of the residents came from farming stock, and many still had acres outside of town where they ran farms, like Dale did. DJ had a huge garden space behind his tiny house. He'd already transplanted his tomatoes and had pretty much everything in the ground. Starting a garden this late in the season might not even produce anything.

But DJ needed to show Mayor Tingey he had changed. His apology seemed to have fallen on deaf ears. He needed to do something to show her he cared, not just about what he'd done to hurt her, but about Clay and the community. He couldn't fail. If she wanted these garden boxes fixed up and the community garden up and running, he'd figure out a way to make it happen. He pushed his tired feet forward to inspect the boxes closer. They all needed a good coat of paint. Two of them had broken sides. They'd need some good soil too. He made a mental list. A trip to the hardware store came first.

An hour later, he had the precut lumber and paint arranged next to the boxes and the proper tools gathered. He set to work removing the broken sides first. He'd gotten the first split plank free when a voice caught his attention. He looked up to Chelsea pushing Austin in a stroller over the grass toward him.

"Seems kind of early for you to be up," she said, unbuckling Austin from his stroller and turning him loose to play in the grass. She came over and sat down next to him. He wouldn't mind a hello kiss, but he'd admitted to her when he came to her house for dinner the night before that he still hadn't gotten a hold of Brady. Neither of them wanted more people than necessary to know before Brady did that she and DJ had started dating. "You had a lot of call-outs last week and not much down time. At least I hope that's why you only called me twice." She smiled up at him and let her hand fall to his knee.

He put his hand over hers and tangled their fingers up. "It's eleven a.m. My mom would say that half the day is gone already," he said, holding out his watch hand.

She brought their fingers to her mouth, quickly kissing them before dropping their enjoined hands back to her knee. He'd only had one night off last week to take her out. They'd spent the evening at his house, her teaching him how to make noodles from scratch for a veggie-filled beef stew. It had been a perfect night.

"Not for someone who probably got less than six hours of sleep in three days," she said, staring at him with a soft smile. "What are you up to?"

DJ didn't know how obvious he should be about his projects for Mayor Tingey. Who knew what the mayor would think of his efforts?

He could trust Chelsea though. "Mayor Tingey mentioned at the last town council meeting that she wanted to get the community garden project up and going again. No one seemed interested, but I thought I'd give it a shot."

Chelsea nodded at him, dropping his hand to grab a hammer from his toolbox. "I see."

"Well, and what are you up to this fine morning?" he asked, coming to kneel beside her.

"Besides ogling you while you fix things?" She whistled a catcall. "Just spent an hour or so making my newest special diet baked goods with Wendy," she said, wedging the claw between one edge of the broken plank and its adjoining side.

With a glance around him, he ran a thumb along her smiling lips and dropped in for a quick kiss. "Can I see you tonight?" he asked when he pulled away.

"I hope so," she said softly. "What do you have in mind?" She sat in the grass, leaning her elbows on her knees as she stared up at him.

"Breaking into the bakery and stealing all the brownies?" He patted his stomach before going back to the garden boxes.

She bumped hips with him as she pushed back up to her knees. "You ate half a pan on Saturday. Wendy told me Madison came by to pick them up and take them to you at the fire station."

"I had to share those."

She laughed, pressing her weight into the hammer, separating the boards a few inches. "You should have texted. I'd gladly make you guys an entire batch you could keep all to yourselves. Free of charge."

DJ grunted with the effort of getting his own board off the box. "I like supporting you and Wendy. What'd you make today?"

"Dairy-free peanut butter cookies. We'll see how they do next to the brownies." She chewed on her lip the way she did when she wasn't sure about something. Austin put his hands on her lap and leaned over her, peering at the hammer as she worked. She bent her head to kiss him on the cheek before adjusting the hammer and putting her weight into it again. The whole scene stole another part of DJ's heart.

He needed to get a hold of Brady as soon as possible. To his frustration, after trying to get a hold of his friend all week, he'd missed a call from Brady on Sunday morning while he was in church. By the time he'd called back a couple hours later, Brady was at work again. DJ supposed he could have jumped in on Brady's call to his son Sunday night when he was at Chelsea's again, but it wasn't exactly a conversation he wanted to have in front of her and her parents. He'd also purposefully stayed out of video range this time. No need to get Brady's defenses up before DJ even approached the subject.

"Those cookies are just as amazing as the brownies," he told Chelsea.

"You're not fooling me. I saw your face last night when you had them. It said, 'These are okay, but I'm not giving up the real deal.'"

He reached over and gently pinched Chelsea's cheeks between his fingers, drawing her close again. "Fine. For someone who can't have the real deal—they're amazing."

She laughed and kissed his nose before pulling away from him. She tilted her head and studied him. "Still haven't talked to Brady?"

DJ let out a sigh and shook his head. "I can't believe how much he works."

"Yeah." She gave a dry laugh, her eyes still worried. "He does answer my calls though and usually gets back to me right away if he misses them. Want me to bring this up?" She twirled her finger between them.

"No. It's okay. We talked about this. You're free to date whoever you want—I only want to talk to him because he's my friend. No need to pull you into it." He raised an eyebrow at her. "Unless you're anxious to let everyone in town know about us."

Nerves darted across her expression, but she smiled them away the next instant. "I don't care who knows about it, but I don't want everyone betting on how long before we get married either. It's fine. I'd just like to take something off your shoulders."

"Funny . . . that's how I feel about you."

"I don't have so much stuff on my shoulders. It's not a big deal." She gave him that soft smile of hers again, the one that had him wondering how Brady hadn't toppled head over heels in love with her multiple times over the last ten years.

"My shoulders are bigger."

"That's true," she said, giggling and reaching over to squeeze a bicep.

"And you have plenty to worry about," he finished. "I'll take care of it."

"Okay." She shrugged and turned back to the boxes. "I can't wait until the zucchini starts coming in," she said, nodding toward the planting boxes. "I've come across some great recipes I think Wendy will like. And we're going to do a Relief Society activity later this summer on healthy cooking. Sister Barber thought it was a great idea."

"Of course it was." DJ yanked away his plank and moved over to give Chelsea's a final push before it fell off too.

"What next?" she asked.

He reached behind him for one of the boards. "Put a new board on." Using her hands, Chelsea swept away the dirt that had spilled from the box when they removed the broken board and held onto the first side while DJ screwed it in then held up the other side while he made sure it was level. Meanwhile, Austin played in the grass behind them. The easy comfort of them working in tandem and the family-like setting sparked a hankering inside him, a hankering for more. His old roommates—the guys he'd played football with and considered his brothers as much as he did Brady—they were all settling down. Rocket was married and expecting a baby in January. David was only months away from his wedding. If Sean didn't marry Victoria, DJ was pretty sure he'd end up with Jane, the girl he was writing on her mission. His friends' happiness made him jealous because he wanted all that too. Even considering the oddness of their situation, things felt right with Chelsea. That had to mean something, something besides him liking the fact that he'd finally figured out how to take care of someone.

As he finished the last screw on the box, Chelsea nudged him. "Hey, look who it is," she said in a low voice. DJ glanced up to where she pointed. Mayor Tingey strolled down the sidewalk toward Town Hall on the other side of the park. Heat swept up his neck. He hadn't counted on the mayor witnessing his good deed. In fact, he hadn't really thought out how she would find out he was responsible. That hadn't seemed to matter when he came up with the plan, though he saw the flaw now.

"Maybe if we sit here quietly she won't notice."

Chelsea eyed him, confusion in her expression. "Won't notice? Isn't the whole point to show her how sorry you are?"

"Uh, yes. Kind of."

Chelsea shook her head at him. "Hello, Mrs. Tingey!" she called and waved at the mayor.

Mayor Tingey smiled and waved at Chelsea, then paused on the sidewalk before walking over to them. Her expression turned stony when she saw DJ.

"Hello, Chelsea. DJ." She glanced around their mini-project site, her lips twitching up a little when her gaze rested on Austin banging a screwdriver against a piece of wood not yet nailed in. But even the shadow of a smile left when she turned back to DJ. "What's going on here?"

"A couple of these boxes were broken. Thought I'd fix them," DJ said.

"Wouldn't that be great if we could get people interested in using them for a community garden?" Chelsea beamed at DJ and turned back to Mayor Tingey, waiting for the woman to heap praise on DJ as well. That wouldn't happen.

He was right. Mayor Tingey remained stone-faced. "I've been told that too many people have their own garden plots to care about a community garden."

"Hmmm." Chelsea pressed her lips together, and a moment later she grinned. "I've got a great idea. The First Ward Relief Society could use it as a project. Then, at harvest, we can talk about canning and preserving and donate the food to needy families."

DJ patted Chelsea enthusiastically on the shoulder. "*That* is a fantastic idea, Chels."

Even Mayor Tingey's face softened. "I agree."

"Good thing DJ is fixing these up then—and volunteering to help me with the project." Chelsea elbowed him and cast him a look that said, *Well, you wanted to get back on her good side . . .*

The edge to Mayor Tingey's expression reappeared when she turned toward him. "Yes. It is good of him. I have a meeting at Town Hall. Have a good afternoon." She waved, mostly to Chelsea, and started off again.

"I see a lot of weeding in my future," DJ said as he watched.

Chelsea chuckled at his side. "You betcha."

"Any excuse to hang out with you is a good one." He nudged her shoulder, though he wanted to take her in his arms.

"Funny," she said. "That's how I feel about it."

He grinned. "Thanks, by the way. For trying with her." He nodded at Mayor Tingey's retreating figure.

"She'll come around." Chelsea reached up and brushed down some hair at the back of his head. When she dropped her hand, he pulled it into his, weaving their fingers together. Excitement at the possibilities between them pounded through him.

"I don't need her to like me," he said in a low voice. Confessing that to her felt as right as taking her hand did. "I just want her to know I *am* sorry. That I take my job seriously. I take Clay seriously."

"I know." She wrapped her arms around his waist, pressing her cheek into his chest. He couldn't resist any longer, even if the whole town was watching. He put his hand at the back of her neck and leaned over, kissing her with only half the intensity he wanted to.

"Mine!" Austin cried, surprising DJ by diving between them, wrapping his arms around Chelsea's legs. They both stared down at him, surprised, until Chelsea started laughing.

"He used to do that to me and Brady," she said, but her eyes lit up. She swung Austin up into her arms and smothered his face with kisses. "His personality is showing again," she said over Austin's shoulder as she grinned at DJ.

"Then I guess I can forgive him," DJ said. The excitement that had pushed him to kiss her pounced on him. Again, the complete, family-like thrill hit him, filling his chest.

She leaned up and gave him a quick peck. "I might be his right now, but tonight I'm all yours."

DJ slipped an arm around her waist as he walked her back to the strollers. "What time did you say he went to bed? Four?"

CHAPTER ELEVEN

"This feels so . . . wrong." Chelsea resisted letting DJ coax her any farther into the dimly lit cultural hall.

He gripped her hand and pulled her forward anyway. "You are a young single adult, whether you like it or not, and this is a good place for you to spend time."

She ran a finger down his arm. "I'm not *so* single anymore," she reminded him. She eyed the couples slowly rotating around the room and then turned back to him. "Let's go back to Mom's house and eat the rest of those dairy-free cookies. I think there's even some frosting we can slather on them. *Aaaand* Mom brought scones back from work today, the good ones with Wendy's almond icing . . ." Chelsea tugged against his grip on her hand, managing to keep them by the door.

Dating DJ was one thing. Since Brady definitely seemed to be dodging DJ's calls for whatever reason, they still kept things quiet, which meant date nights were usually at his house or her mom's. She couldn't imagine the gossip they'd ignite after dancing together at a church dance.

DJ put his hands on her shoulders and faced her. He even tried out an intimidating glare, though Chelsea wouldn't ever be able to take that expression seriously. Brady had told her plenty about his and DJ's mischievous childhood. Poor guy. No wonder DJ wanted so badly to change Mayor Tingey's opinion of him.

"That look won't work on me," she said.

He laughed. "Your son is at your house. This is your night off, and don't argue about it because even married moms get date night."

"Fine. We'll go to your house."

DJ hesitated, and she thought she might have won him over until he shook his head. "No. You're getting a date night *out*. Everything we've done together these past couple weeks have been married-couple dates. And our relationship has a ways to go before cuddling on the couch and watching TV counts as a date." He winked at her, but the joking tone didn't stop the tap dancing that started up in her stomach.

She pressed a finger into his chest. "You've been counting it plenty. Otherwise we're not dating at all. We're just kissing."

He pulled her closer. "That's exactly why we should stay. My mother would never approve of me not taking you on dates."

She laughed but shook her head. And even though he wasn't letting her out of it, she still liked the tingles that spread through her shoulders where he touched her. "Have you been away from Provo too long? You know what walking out there hand in hand is going to be like, the kind of territory you're going to stake. The kind of talk there'll be." She hoped that struck enough fear into him to keep them out of the cultural hall.

But to her surprise, he studied her with confusion. He led her back outside to the steps that led up to the church. Still standing near, he looked down at her with worry. "Are you . . . are you worried about talk, Chels?"

She didn't get to enjoy the electricity racing up and down her spine—that wonderful expectation that spilled into every minute she spent with DJ—for nearly a long enough time with him so concerned. "I'm not worried about talk," she assured him. "I'm worried about you. About what Brady will say to you if he finds out from someone else. About how it's going to damage a lifelong friendship."

He leaned over, resting his head on top of hers. They stood there for a long time, DJ running his hands up and down her arms.

"DJ?" she asked softly.

"Do you want to date me?" he asked. "Do you want this to be more than hanging out?"

"And kissing," she reminded him, a smile starting.

His chest rumbled lightly with a laugh. "And kissing," he added. "Is that what you want?"

She tilted her head back to stare at him. His expression was questioning, hopeful, serious. Still uncertain. "Yes. For sure."

Everything inside of her spun at that look. She really wanted to be dating him. From their first flirtatious moments, she'd suspected she had wanted DJ all along. Their first kiss and every one since then, every date confirmed that she'd wanted this between them for a long time. Whenever he put his arms around her, it made her nervous in a good way, and working beside him on the garden boxes had been the best few days she could remember in a while.

She'd loved Brady's humor, but he handled too many things with jokes. She'd thought that about DJ too—most people thought that about DJ—but she'd been wrong. He knew when to joke, but he knew when to comfort. He didn't seem afraid of tears. He wasn't afraid to ask her a question that might have an answer he didn't like. He wasn't afraid to talk to her about anything.

"What about you?" she asked. "Do you want this to be more than just hanging out . . . and kissing?" She quirked an eyebrow at him, eliciting another laugh. Maybe she'd learned that from Brady, to joke when she was afraid of what the real answer might be. That DJ might not think she was worth losing Brady over.

He let out a huff of a laugh. He'd leaned closer to her so it washed over her face. He smelled like peppermint and . . . maybe chocolate. Did he really like her brownies that much? Sure, it could've been Wendy's Over the Top brownies, but . . . it could've been one of Chelsea's.

"I do. Way more than I should. Enough to not care what Brady says or if he's mad or if he never talks to me again."

She had to press one hand against her heart, to somehow muffle the thudding it had started when he declared she was more important. "Wow," she whispered, wishing he knew how much that meant. She'd been around him and Brady enough to know what kind of relationship DJ was giving up when he didn't even know if things would work out in the long run for them.

He lifted both his hands to rest behind her neck and brushed a thumb along one of her cheeks, leaving a trail of heat behind. "I know," he said. He studied her from mere inches away as every nerve inside her went on the fritz. When his lips met hers, the intense warmth that blasted through her was surprising. It felt like another declaration.

When he pulled away, he took her hand and led her down the steps toward the parking lot and to his pickup. Without letting go, he pulled down the tailgate and helped her up into the bed of the truck. Then he hopped up and sat with his back against the cab, patting the spot next to him. She sat without hesitation and leaned against his shoulder, laying her head on it. The night held the slightly muggy warmth of a perfect summer evening and not even the trademark Wyoming wind to mess it up. Above them, stars twinkled in the cloudless sky. Bliss.

"Better than the dance," she said, unable to keep the triumph from her voice. She peeked at DJ out of the corner of her eyes.

"I never doubted that." He squeezed her hand then wrapped his arm around her shoulders, pulling her back into his chest. "It just feels like we skipped things, doesn't it? Nervous first dates. Worrying if I should hold your hand or not—if I should kiss you or not?" He kissed the top of her head.

"I don't think there's anything wrong with that," she said.

He murmured his agreement, and then they sat quietly, staring at the sky, breathing each other in. The night they had sat and talked in his car after prom had been a night Chelsea tried hard not to think about over the years. How comfortable she had been talking to DJ, how easy it had been to tell him things, things she'd never really talked about with Brady. Now it fit just like another piece of the puzzle that made up them. A picture they could keep adding to, piece by piece.

"You're not worried what Brady's going to say?" he asked, breaking the silence. Her heart skipped. She'd be lying if she didn't admit that the fact that he still worried about it worried her. Until the two spoke, that wouldn't feel resolved.

She shifted back to sit at his side instead of leaning against him and turned her head so she could look at him. "No. I don't think I care what Brady thinks." She smiled ruefully. "I did care that *other* people would think I was trading Brady in for someone better. I wouldn't want people to believe that. And I know you have to think about it differently."

DJ moved his hand so that it closed over hers. Warm. Rough. Nice. "Setting that aside for right now, since things didn't work out for you guys, I would hope, as your friend, that someday you do find someone better for you." Then his lips twitched. A joke was coming, but she didn't mind. "Unfortunately, I'm pretty sure that someone is me." He gave a mock grimace, one that covered up a true dilemma for him.

"Confident, huh?"

"After being around my old roommates, it's become a survival trait," he said.

She chuckled. "I bet you were fine."

"Yeah, I was."

"Do you miss living with them?" she asked.

"Those guys? No way." He moved his hand to slip it around her shoulder and hold her next to him. He rested his head on top of hers, and she knew what *she* missed most about living with someone—with a partner. Someone to share everything with. Someone to hug her. Her parents could do all that, but it wasn't the same. Doing it all alone, with Brady trying to parent via FaceTime, left her with a lonely ache.

"I do miss how easy things were back then. Play football, go to school. I never failed at any of that," he said.

"Date a bunch of girls," she teased.

"Maybe." He hugged her closer. "Sometimes I'm not quite sure what I'm doing here in Clay."

"Sometimes I wonder why I'm here too, besides the obvious, you know. I came here after Brady left and never questioned if it was the right thing to do. At the time, it was the only thing to do." She sighed and relaxed into his side. Everything was quiet except for the sound of music coming from the church behind them. One thing she knew, she liked the smallness, the quietness of this. "But then you came home."

His lips moved softly through the hair at her temple, and she closed her eyes. She shouldn't compare him to Brady; it wasn't fair. But Brady hadn't done a lot of small things. If she made comments about him making more of an effort with little gestures like a kiss on the cheek or flowers just because, he'd say, "You know I love you."

But she'd never known that, not even when they'd gotten married. It was all so wrapped up in the fact that they *had* to. Of course, she saw now that there had been other choices—but the mere idea of not having Austin, a consequence of not making any of those other choices, made her panic inside. She regretted making the mistakes she did, but she would never regret Austin.

Maybe it wasn't fair to compare, but the small ways DJ showed his affection mattered: a quick squeeze of her hand, a light kiss on her forehead, bringing over pouches of food to see if Austin would like eating them. The small things mattered *a lot*.

"I'm glad you're here in Clay, even if you don't know why," she said.

"Me too."

CHAPTER TWELVE

Chelsea adjusted her cardigan as she watched the sisters file into the Relief Society room. She smiled the best she could at each of them. She pressed her hands into her knees to stop the nervous bouncing. Sister Barber was conducting—Chelsea wouldn't have to for another two months. She wasn't even giving the lesson. Sister Barber just wanted her to spend a minute or two introducing herself. Nothing big.

When Allison Rees stopped before walking into the room, Chelsea's stomach sank. DJ had showed up for sacrament meeting again that day. He'd sat with Chelsea instead of Patty and Dale but hadn't done anything else to make the change in their relationship obvious. Another week had gone by with Brady avoiding DJ, though neither she nor DJ expected to keep their relationship totally quiet. But DJ had tried. It was all on Brady at that point.

"Hello, Chelsea," Allison said, beaming as she leaned in to give her a light hug.

"Hello, Sister Rees. Welcome to Relief Society." Chelsea fought to keep a smile on her face as she waited for Allison's comments.

"DJ's certainly been coming to our ward a lot lately." Allison chuckled a light, fake laugh and laid a hand lightly on Chelsea's arm. "Did he move and I didn't realize it?"

Chelsea bit back an exasperated sigh. Why did she have to be so nosy about the whole thing? Couldn't she let two people interested in each other just let their relationship happen?

"Not that I know of." Chelsea responded with the same fake laugh.

"Austin seems to love him," Allison went on, digging further in an attempt to get at the truth. "Must be spending a lot of time with him."

"DJ has spent time around Austin since he was a baby. He's always been close to our family." She hated reminding this gossipy woman, of all people, about DJ and Brady's relationship, but there was no other way to answer her except to tell Allison that she was dating DJ. And that wasn't going to happen.

"I think it's sweet of him to want to help." Allison had donned that knowing smile.

"It is." Chelsea nodded, hoping Allison would get the hint that Chelsea was not going to confide in her. Chelsea looked around, wishing Sister Barber would call her over and give her something—anything—to do. She wanted to enjoy the beginnings of this relationship with DJ before the whole town had them married off.

More sisters came in, and Chelsea snagged the opportunity to turn and greet them, asking about their week and making conversation until Allison moved away. Once the newcomers sat down, Chelsea made a beeline for the four chairs behind the podium and sat. She could use the time to go over what she'd written down to say about herself. That had been challenge enough, figuring out how to talk about moving back to Clay without alluding too much to her divorce.

The meeting began a few minutes later, and the song and prayer went uneventfully. Sister Barber got up and took a few minutes to introduce herself and then asked the first counselor, Sister Grant, to come to the podium. Chelsea missed everything the thirty-something mom of five said, and before she knew it, Sister Barber nudged her to go up. Fingering the card in her hands, she prayed for the courage to do this. It shouldn't be hard. She had talents that could benefit these sisters. The Lord had called her to this position for a reason. She had to remember that.

"Good afternoon, sisters," she began, scanning the room. She made a point not to make eye contact with anyone, and she completely avoided the front row on the left, where Allison sat. "I'm sure many of you remember me since I grew up in this ward. In case you don't, I'm Chelsea Lewis. I moved back to Clay last year. Right now, I work part-time at Cutie Pies and part-time as a free-lance accountant and spend most of the rest of my time with my two-year-old, Austin. I'm looking forward to getting to know you sisters better." She hurried back to her seat and let out a relieved sigh. She hadn't said everything she meant to, but it didn't matter. Sister Barber gave her a quick pat and a reassuring smile before turning her attention to the secretary, Sister Barber's daughter-in-law, Sharae.

Sharae talked about how excited she was to get to know the sisters who had known her husband growing up and how she was sure to learn even more from them than they from her, especially where it concerned her eighteen-month-old twins. She sounded so much more self-assured than Chelsea. Did all of that come from having a husband to support her? Chelsea had been just as confident in her motherhood —or at least in her ability to learn—not very long ago. Why had she let Brady take all that from her?

Sister Barber got back up to give a shortened lesson, but Chelsea's mind caught on Brady and getting divorced, like a knot you couldn't quite loosen enough to untie. What would she have done if Austin went through his no sleeping, no eating stages *before* Brady left?

She would have never driven him around to get him to sleep. She wouldn't have worried too much about him keeping her and Brady up —or even about the off-chance that he'd keep up their neighbors. She'd kept a strict sleep schedule for him. They would've toughed their way through a couple weeks of rough nights, and eventually, Austin would have gotten over it. Chelsea had enabled him because of the guilt. Guilt that he didn't have Brady anymore. Guilt that Austin was waking up her parents. Guilt that she couldn't hack it as a single mother.

But she could. She knew she could, and she needed to step up. Getting Brady to be involved in Austin's life was out of her hands. But there were things she *could* manage. If she wanted to stay home, even part-time with Austin, then she had to live with her parents for the time being. That much couldn't change. But no more driving Austin around at bedtime. Sleeping in her bed was one thing—they both could use the comfort and she didn't mind spoiling him in that small way—but it had to be on her terms. She needed her confidence back— a reconnection to the knowledge that she was a great mom or, at the very least, that she had the ability to become one.

———

WHEN HE HEARD the garage door open, DJ jerked awake, sitting up just as Chelsea walked through the door that separated the garage from the kitchen at her parents' house. "Some babysitter," she teased, coming over to sit next to him on the couch.

"Your parents got back about half an hour ago," he excused.

She leaned closer, kissing him quickly, but DJ slid an arm around her waist before she slipped away, lingering over their kiss. "I know," she said. "I noticed their car in the garage. Which makes me wonder why you aren't home sleeping."

"I was waiting for a chance to see you," he murmured, pulling her back to him again.

When they pulled away a few minutes later, she smiled happily at him. "You're really going above and beyond in the boyfriend depart-ment," she said with a contented sigh. "First watching Austin so I could make girls' night, then sticking around to see me when I know how busy your week was at the station."

DJ's heart sped up, and he grinned. Her boyfriend. It had been a pretty long time since a girl had attached *that* to his name. He liked it best coming from her lips. "Gotta catch every moment," he said, giving her a grimace. "The guys tell me the next two weeks will be worse, and probably even after that. Fireworks fever." Though fireworks were only legal to set off on the day of the fourth in town, outside of town, residents could shoot them off as they pleased.

She snuggled up next to him. "Mmmm. I'll take what I can get then."

He leaned back against the couch and ran his fingers through her hair, closing his eyes and enjoying the moment. He hadn't even had time to call her during his last three-day shift. They'd traded hit and miss texts before he dropped into bed between calls, and it definitely wasn't enough. Not for the first time, he thought about how inconvenient it was that they lived in separate houses, that when he came home at the end of a shift, he didn't automatically get to see her. He didn't want to rush their relationship, but as they'd mentioned to each other more than once, they'd skipped over some parts and settled right into established relationship. Didn't that mean he could think about marrying her sooner? He smiled to himself . . .

"DJ?"

He jolted, startled, and turned to her. She stared up at him, her grin growing wider by the second. "You should go home," she whispered. "I should've skipped tonight so we could hang out."

"No." He shook his head and sat up. "You enjoy those girls' nights, and I'm glad I could help you out so you could go. What did you ladies gossip about tonight?"

"Jobs, actually," she said, cringing. She normally shied away from talking about careers with him since she knew it often left him discouraged about his own. "Gwen Parrish said that her dad and Cale are looking for someone to do their books. Gwen doesn't want to do it after the baby's born, like she thought she would, and her mom says she's retired. I might pick up their account to work from home—but it would be more than I'm used to. I guess Gwen does a lot of their other paperwork too, not just the numbers." She chewed on her lip.

"That sounds like a big deal and a big client," he said. "What's worrying you?"

"I don't think I could keep working at Cutie Pies. I could still do her books, but I couldn't work the counter in the afternoons. I'd need the time for the M&P account—but if Mom worked those shifts, I wouldn't have anyone to babysit Austin so I'd have to shift when I could work anyway. It's just a lot to think about."

"I wish I could watch him for you whenever you needed." He rubbed her shoulders. "Maybe I could open up a daycare when I get fired."

Chelsea scowled. "Is she still on that? Really?"

"Hansen overheard the chief talking to her on the phone earlier this week." DJ sighed and shrugged. "I don't know what else to do. I mean, I have gone several days without any serious mistakes." He gave her a half smile.

"DJ," she said, her tone bordering on stern. She leaned forward and took his cheeks in her hands. Before she could lecture him further about believing in himself, he closed the distance and kissed her again. She chuckled softly, knowing his game. "What will you do?" she asked when she'd settled back again. "If she gets you fired?"

He let out a long sigh. It had been on his mind so much. "I don't know. I could go back to school, I guess. Go into physical therapy. I think I always sort of had that as my backup plan if football didn't work out—but I don't think I ever actually considered football not working out. And now I'm here . . . and school doesn't sound that appealing."

She took his hand in both of hers, threading their fingers together and holding tight. "What do you *want* to do?" she asked.

He smiled crookedly at her. "That's simple," he replied, the same answer he'd given her the night he first kissed her. "Be here with you if I can."

She tilted her head, staring at him and smiling the way she did when something had gone just right—like when she'd finally gotten her brownies right or when she'd taught Austin to sing "I Am a Child of God," and he'd sung along with her.

"Even when you should be sleeping?" she admonished.

He untangled their hands so he could reach up and nudge her closer, kissing the side of her head. "Even then."

Firefighting had to work out. He had to find a way to be here with her—always.

———————

CHELSEA STILL COULDN'T GET over how happy DJ made her.

She felt it in the smile she'd sported since he'd first kissed her. Even though the last two weeks had been so busy for him that she'd hardly seen him. Even all through church the last few Sundays, and even when Allison made more pointed insinuations about DJ coming to their ward and sitting in her row with her family.

Chelsea didn't care about those insinuations anymore. That's how she knew things were so good. The morning felt full of possibilities. Maybe she would go check out their garden boxes, make sure the park's sprinkler system watered them well. Sister Barber had praised the garden idea for the Relief Society project. She'd beamed at Chelsea and sounded so enthusiastic. DJ was back at work, but maybe she and Austin would drop by the fire station and see if he had a minute to steal a little time with her.

"Hey, little man. Let's go for a walk," she said as she swooped him up into her arms and smothered him with kisses on his chubby cheeks. Austin giggled and tried to wriggle out of her arms.

She grabbed the stroller but let Austin walk at first as they headed out of the neighborhood on the quiet streets. Austin ran ahead as fast as his little legs would carry him and then stopped to pick up a rock from the middle of the sidewalk, clutching it tightly in his little fist.

"Morning, Chelsea, Austin." Sister Barber came down the sidewalk from her house as they passed by, carrying a small ball of fluff.

"Morning, Sister Barber." Chelsea grabbed Austin's hand to hold him while they stopped and talked to her. "What do you have?"

"A puppy. Mind if Austin pets it?" Sister Barber grinned as she showed Chelsea the small black dog with a brown spot on its forehead.

"Oh, it's adorable!" she cried. "Austin, want to see the puppy?"

Austin scooted closer to Chelsea's leg, but his eyes widened when Sister Barber crouched down and held the puppy out a bit to entice him forward. Austin didn't need much more prodding to reach out and bury his hand in the fur. Chelsea couldn't help stroking it either. It was soft and silky.

"I didn't know you'd gotten a new puppy," she said.

Sister Barber shook her head. "We didn't. This poor thing was abandoned out on the Lewis farm. She's a mutt, but DJ thought of Jeanie Tingey when he found it." Sister Barber chuckled. "He thought it might go over better if I talked to her about it."

Chelsea chuckled along with Sister Barber. "He's sure going to have a hard time convincing Mayor Tingey how sorry he is if he doesn't own up to all the thoughtful things he's doing for her."

"He's a good kid. Roger Tingey ought to remember *that* and not all the goofing off those high school boys did," Sister Barber said, her voice going a bit defensive.

"DJ loves this town," Chelsea agreed warmly. He was so worried about failing again. She prayed that Mrs. Tingey wouldn't make that happen just because she couldn't forgive him. DJ deserved to know what a good man he was.

Sister Barber met her gaze. "Of course he does." She reached over and squeezed Chelsea's shoulder. "So, if Jeanie says no, shall I bring this doll over to you, Austin?"

"Grammie might oppose that plan," Chelsea said with a sigh. Austin snuggled the puppy in his lap now, and he looked like he was in heaven.

"Grammie Denise is a party-pooper." Sister Barber laughed. They spent a few more minutes playing with the dog before Sister Barber left and they continued on their walk. Austin tired quickly, so he didn't fight her when she asked him to get into the stroller once they reached the slightly busier Main Street of Clay.

At the station, she didn't have to look far for DJ. He worked in the driveway, washing down one of the trucks.

"Dee!" Austin called happily when they reached him, squirming to get out of the stroller buckles. "Dee!"

Chelsea unbuckled him and let him run up to DJ, who scooped him up and walked back to Chelsea. "Hey, there. What are you two up to?" He stepped close to her.

"Wanted to see you," she said leaning toward him. "Is it okay that we dropped by? You look a little busy."

He rolled his eyes. "Rookie stuff. It's always okay when you stop by." And even though he had Austin in one arm, he used the other to tilt her chin up and kiss her, both of them smiling when someone wolf-whistled from inside the open garage door. DJ scooped his hand around her back and gave her a slight dip—well, as best he could with Austin in his arms—as he finished the kiss.

"Good to see you too," Chelsea said, her smile breaking her face. Austin clapped his hands and leaned over toward her, planting his own sloppy kiss on Chelsea's lips.

"Hey, now." DJ pretended to be stern with him as he whirled him away from Chelsea in a quick half-circle. "Mine," he said playfully.

"Mine!" Austin shouted.

"Want to see the fire trucks?" DJ reached behind him and grabbed for Chelsea's hand as he led them closer to the truck he'd been washing.

"Up," Austin bounced, pointing to the ladder.

"Not only is that against regulations, I'm pretty sure your mom wouldn't allow it either. Want to drive instead?" He walked Austin around the front, pulling Chelsea along right next to them. "How's your day?" he asked.

"Perfect." She leaned into his shoulder. "You?"

He hesitated enough that her curiosity piqued, but then he answered, "Mine too, now." She made a note to ask him later. He let go of her hand to reach up and open the cab door then climbed in and set Austin on his lap. Chelsea grabbed her phone and took a quick snapshot. Austin threw his hands up in the air with a loud squeal. He stood in DJ's lap and gripped the big steering wheel with both hands, trying to twist it back and forth. DJ added to the fun by making a soft, siren noise. Austin's grin was so big Chelsea's smile mirrored it. She'd spent so much time worrying about her son's diet and sleeping schedule, she hadn't thought a lot about fun for him. Maybe getting out more herself and spending time with friends would benefit not just her, but Austin too.

No time like the present. She pulled up her messages and texted Sharae. They'd been texting on and off since the dinner. It had started out with Relief Society business but ended up being more about mom stuff. Her twins and Austin would have a great time together. During their presidency meetings, she'd come to like Sharae more and more.

DJ and Austin climbed down. She reached for her son after she'd sent the text, but DJ walked past her with a smirk. She followed them into the station, listening as DJ told Austin about the weight room, the chief's truck, and helped him slide up and down the pole.

"Can he have some juice?" DJ asked as they headed toward the soda fountain in the back.

"Juice?" Chelsea said with a raised eyebrow.

"Well, lemonade. Unless you prefer he drink root beer." He pulled a cup from the stack next to the fountain.

She didn't have the heart to tell him that the lemonade was just as full of sugar. She shrugged, pretending nonchalance. "Either one."

Beaming, DJ filled up a few swallows of the root beer and handed it to Austin, who lifted it to his lips, dribbling some down his shirt. "I expect a big thank you from you. Your mom's so nice now that she's dating me," DJ said in a stage whisper. Chelsea laughed and nudged him with her elbow.

The fire whistle rang through the station, startling Austin, especially when DJ handed him off before rushing for his gear. She stepped back against the wall so they wouldn't be in the way then took Austin's cup and set it aside so he could cover his ears against the sounds. As DJ pulled out a few minutes later in the truck already parked outside, she lifted Austin's hand to wave at the departing firemen. He didn't notice, intent on the job before him, but that didn't bother Chelsea. She had a certain amount of pride watching him race off—and some fear for the first time. Seeing him in action made it more real, what he did every day.

"Be careful," she said to herself as the last of the trucks sped off down the street, lights flashing. Even with the new worry, she and Austin set off for her parents' house with big smiles. So simple. Just hanging out with him for a few minutes had made her day.

Yep, this was a very good thing.

———

"Sorry I had to rush off," DJ said when he called her later that night.

"You should be, but only because it ruined our visit with you," she replied.

"I'll let people in town know that fires are not acceptable when we're together." They laughed, and then he asked, "Is Austin in bed? Do you have a minute to talk?"

"Yeah. Do you?" she teased.

"I'm posting on Facebook now for everyone to hold off on fires until I hang up."

Chelsea kicked up the footrest on her dad's recliner and leaned back. Her parents had gone on a walk as she put Austin down and hadn't returned yet. "So," she asked. "What was up today?"

"What was up?" Confusion filled his voice. "When you came by? Nothing."

"You hesitated when I asked you how your day was."

"Oh." He paused. "Brady is still dodging my calls, and it's obvious now that it's on purpose. Do you think he might know . . . about us?"

"He hasn't said anything to me." She chewed on her lip, sad that DJ had to continue to worry about this. Maybe next time Brady called she'd mention something about trying harder to get back to DJ— although that might give it away, and DJ had admitted worrying about putting Brady on the defensive right off.

"I don't know what to think," DJ said. "If my friendship with Brady had stayed the same over the last year, I don't know if I would've considered letting a romantic relationship happen between you and me." Chelsea ignored the little tumble her stomach gave at that thought. Guilt filled her. It was a traitorous thought, but she was glad they had grown apart. She was just as glad DJ wasn't there to see those emotions play across her face. "But he's been pulling away for so long," DJ continued, bringing Chelsea back to their conversation.

"And even though part of me feels wrong for thinking it, the other part of me keeps wondering why *I* shouldn't get you in the divorce?"

She chuckled at his joke. "Seems only fair." They sat quietly for a moment before she went on. "If you want to not see me until you've talked to him, I understand." It made her insides twist to think of avoiding DJ, but she had to consider the position this put him in.

"That could be a while." He sighed. "It sounds miserable. I don't want you to avoid me."

Her stomach unclenched. "Good. I don't want to avoid you either."

They chatted for a little bit, their conversation turning to lighter topics, until DJ admitted that he should try and get some rest even though it was only eight. It surprised Chelsea that when she hung up, worry over Brady's reaction didn't remain with her. She'd done her share of praying over how to proceed with DJ, and so far, not a single stray thought warned her away. In the days, weeks, and months surrounding her divorce, she'd grown close to the Spirit and allowed it to guide her. She trusted the decisions she'd made, knowing the Lord would stop her if she chose the wrong path. Over the last month, she'd grown more sure with every date, every stolen minute, that this was right for both of them.

Soften Brady's heart, she prayed, but that was more for DJ's sake than hers. She settled further into the recliner, reaching over to flip on the TV and enjoy a few moments of daydreaming like a giddy young woman.

CHAPTER THIRTEEN

Chelsea hummed to herself as she scraped a batch of black-bean brownies out of the batter bowl in Wendy's kitchen. She'd been coming in early a few mornings a week while Austin slept to bake some of the items she'd come up with for the bakery. Her brownies were selling out every day, which was a huge accomplishment for her. Today, the Fourth of July, she'd gotten up extra early to help Wendy get a jump on baking. The town parade would start at ten, and Wendy wanted help making sure things were ready for the influx of people on Main Street that day—which hopefully meant an influx of customers.

Her phone vibrated on the counter next to her. Her heart jumped, thinking it might be DJ. It was maybe a futile hope. She hadn't heard from him at all last night, which meant he must have been out pretty late on fire calls. Which meant that at seven a.m., he was unlikely to be up. When she saw the name on the caller ID, though, her heart skittered for a different reason.

Brady.

Her mind immediately jumped to the idea that DJ must have finally gotten a hold of him, and now Brady was calling to chew her out. For a second, she was back in her marriage, worried about how he would react to something she'd said or done.

She shook herself out of it with a gulp. She and Brady had come so far in the last year. Even if he did say something unkind, she knew how to handle it now.

She stared at the phone, wiping her hands absently. If he'd found out about her and DJ, would he call her first? She hated the way that even the thought of talking to him about it made her thoughts spiral down from the giddy high they'd maintained since she'd started dating DJ.

The phone buzzed again, this time with a text message from Brady. *Are you at your mom's? I'm in town. Can I come by?*

In town? Just like that? He hadn't even let her know he planned on coming. She put the brownies in the oven before she answered. She didn't want Brady to think she'd ignored his call on purpose—and she hadn't. It had stopped ringing before she realized she *should* answer.

Austin is sleeping, so I'm helping Wendy at the bakery, she replied a few minutes later. At least she hoped he was. Her mom hadn't texted her to let her know he was up. He hadn't slept well the night before, and she hoped he'd made up for that by sleeping in. After she made the goal not to drive him around, they'd had some rough nights, especially that first week, but he *was* getting better about sleeping, little by little.

Okay, Brady answered. *Can we talk? In person?*

Her eyebrows jumped up and curiosity bloomed inside her. He'd been really busy at work—at least he used that excuse for ignoring DJ —and his calls to Austin the last couple weeks had been short, just him touching base. She hadn't broached the subject of him making more of an effort again, but maybe he'd finally realized that he needed to change something.

Sure. I'll meet you at my mom's in ten minutes, she replied. She poked her head out front, where Wendy had finished serving an early-morning customer some doughnuts. "I've got to run home. Timer's on the oven. Need me to come back?" she asked.

Wendy shook her head. "No, I've got a good plan for getting stuff ready this morning. I made up a bunch of doughs and batters last night. Just come sit in front for the parade so you can help me with customers."

"Will do," Chelsea promised and headed back to her mom's. Austin wasn't up when she got back, and the house was quiet. Her mom was probably enjoying the chance to sleep in. She often got up around six to help Wendy open the shop.

Chelsea dropped onto the couch in the front room and distracted herself with a recipe magazine her mom had bought at the local grocery store. She was engrossed in a section on cooking with garden vegetables when a soft knock sounded.

As she got up to open the door, her brain scanned through all the possibilities of why Brady wanted to talk in person, the most obvious being her relationship with DJ. There was no way Brady didn't know about it at this point. She and DJ had been dating for over a month now. Someone in Brady's family was bound to know, no matter how low-key they'd kept things.

"Hey," she said in a hoarse voice, nervousness jittering through her —but not the same kind that had accompanied him asking her out for the first time when they were in high school. Not the same nerves she had felt anticipating her first kiss with DJ or on the evening they'd spent sitting in the back of his truck. These were wholly different and unwelcome. Would he expect an explanation from her? What would she say? What if she messed up whatever DJ had planned on saying?

"Hi." Brady rocked forward and put his arms around her, pressing her toward him. Even the way he had to bend—like he'd always had to —felt foreign, like he was a cousin she'd met a few times but never really gotten to know.

She froze in his arms. What was he doing? The last time they'd seen each other it had been different, for sure, but awkwardness hadn't filled the room the way it did now. She took a quick step back, trying to think of something to say to cover the wrongness of their embrace. His dark hair was cut shorter around his ears but longer than he'd usually kept it on top. It also looked styled—messily so—but with gel nonetheless. It was a different look than when he FaceTimed her and Austin from work, but more put together than the last time she'd seen him dressed down, nice-looking jeans and new-looking tennis shoes. The only thing about him that seemed like the old Brady was his T-shirt, but even it looked nicer than his worn-in Clay Football T-shirts or BYU T-shirts that had been a staple in his closet when they were married. This one was thicker, maybe better quality, and she almost wanted to comment on it. Which was stupid. He sent the checks he needed to, and she wouldn't be the ex-wife that complained about what he spent his money on. He was a lawyer now. He could afford to update his wardrobe.

She shut the door behind him and faced it for a few seconds to take a deep breath and reorient herself. Brady's enthusiastic greeting had thrown her off. Her heart thumped at an odd rhythm, not in any way she liked. They'd been communicating fine for months. What was making him so nervous?

"So, what's up?" She turned around and found him standing in front of the couch, hands still in his pockets. They might as well get the truth out right away.

"I miss Austin. I made a lot of mistakes with him, and I need to fix that. I need to be in his life. I want you to move back to Salt Lake." He shifted side to side, staring at the thick, gray carpet.

"I . . . what?" She narrowed her eyes at Brady. They'd had this discussion ten months ago. She'd gone back to Clay after they split, needing to regroup and make decisions for her and Austin. He called and wanted them to come back to Salt Lake to keep Austin near him. She'd told him she couldn't. She didn't have the money, and she didn't want to anyway. Everything fell apart in Salt Lake. And now, more than ever, Clay was where things had started to come back together. "I . . . can't."

"You *could*," Brady argued. "If you went back to work. I can ask around."

She took a deep breath even though her immediate reaction was to let anger take over her thoughts at his demand. At him asking her to leave the support network she had here in Clay because he wanted to change things. "I'm open to revisiting this discussion, Brady, but this is kind of sudden."

His expression turned desperate, which again, caught her off guard. "We can figure out something to make it work. Listen, if I could move back to Clay, I would, but that's not an option right now. I need this job to support Austin. You know that."

She sat down, taking a minute to recover. Brady wouldn't have dropped this on her to upend her on purpose. She could tell by the way he clenched and unclenched his fists that he was upset.

"Austin and I have a life here, Brady. I'm not saying I won't consider this, but . . ."

"DJ might be disappointed?" His jaw had gone hard, but that was the only indication that he wasn't happy with her response.

She stood back up. "Have you finally answered his calls?"

Brady shook his head and looked away. "Maddi heard a rumor."

"You need to talk to DJ instead of listening to rumors." She folded her arms.

Now he sat, leaning forward so his elbows rested on his knees as he stared up at her. "Is that what's keeping you here?"

She sat too so she wouldn't look like she was lecturing him. "Part of it. And my family, working for Wendy, which I really like. It's all part of my life. But I'll always do what's best for Austin."

"You'd move?" His expression turned hopeful and alert.

Would she move? Disappointment was arcing through her at how difficult this would make her relationship with DJ, especially since it was just beginning. But she could figure out a way to work part-time and probably get quite a few more freelance clients. She could talk to Cale Parrish and Gwen's dad and see how they would feel about her not being in town. She'd talked to Gwen more the other day, and it sounded like she did all the work from home anyway.

Brady scooted forward. "I'll make you a promise. Move back to Salt Lake, and when I can, I'll start a firm in Clay and move back here."

Her jaw dropped. When they had first gotten married, they had talked about moving back to Clay someday, but all that talk stopped just before he graduated and went to law school. Every time she'd asked, he became more and more resistant to the idea. He could never be successful in a small town. Didn't they want their future children to have more opportunities than they'd had? He could provide them with all that in a bigger town with a better job.

"Are you serious?" she finally asked.

"If this is where you want to be, where you want Austin to grow up, yes. We both have to make compromises. We both have to give if we want it to work." He met her gaze and held it steadily. "Please, Chels. I can't let my son grow up without me."

Tears pricked at her eyes. "I'll see what I can do."

This time when he crossed the room to hug her, it didn't feel as strange as it had before. He only held her briefly, full of gratitude. "Thanks," he said, his voice cracking with emotion she had so rarely seen. "This means a lot, even you just saying you'll try."

She blinked at him, but before she could ask what had made him come to these decisions, Austin called out "Mama" from upstairs.

Chelsea scowled. It was only seven thirty, and he'd been up so late. She moved to go upstairs, but Brady stopped her by putting a hand on her shoulder. "I'll go get him." He didn't wait for her to agree before he disappeared up the stairs. She strained to hear Austin's greeting.

Her son looked confused when Brady brought him back into the living room. As soon as he caught sight of Chelsea, he stretched his arms out toward her, calling "Mama" again.

"It's okay," she soothed.

"Daddy has you," Brady added. But Austin began to wail. Brady cast her a confused look.

"He hasn't seen you in two months. That's a long time for a two-year-old." Her arguments against going back to Salt Lake stretched thinner. After what he'd promised? How could she say no?

She watched Brady rock him as he swayed around the room, whispering into the baby's ear the same way he used to at bedtime. Austin's wails calmed to whimpers and then to the occasional sniff.

Brady turned to look at her, hurt in his eyes even though Austin had given in and nestled against him. "He's so little, Chels," Brady said. "I'm missing everything, and I can't keep doing that."

She nodded. "I know." Brady closed his eyes and rested his head against Austin's. Emotion choked her. What had changed? She ached to ask him, but she didn't want to interrupt his moment with his son. Not when he'd finally figured everything out, however the realization had come.

"So, do you have big plans with him today?" Brady asked, his expression hesitant.

"Nothing specific." Her stomach clenched at the idea, but she offered anyway. "You want to hang with him today?"

"If that's okay, yeah. I thought I could take him on the Dash," he said, speaking of the local town race that took place that morning. "It starts at eight thirty, right?" He glanced down at his watch.

"As far as I know. We'll be sitting by the bakery if you want to come over there, but I think Dale and Maddi were planning on sitting on the lawn in front of the church so Patty could sit in the shade." Brady nodded along, and Chelsea moved toward the stairs. "I'll go get him ready."

Brady shook his head. "I can figure it out. I know I took you away from helping Wendy, so why don't you head back to the bakery?" She raised her eyebrows, and he laughed. "We'll be fine. Maybe run upstairs and warn your mom?"

She laughed. "Okay, fine. Stroller is in the garage, and his seat is in my car. There are some food pouches in the fridge you can feed him for breakfast." A gift that DJ insisted on dropping by every week because he got a discount at the store.

"Got it."

She dashed up the stairs and let her mom know the plan. Denise was already dressed anyway, so she joined Chelsea when she came downstairs, heading over to the bakery with her.

Chelsea forced herself not to worry as they walked toward the bakery. Brady's two-year-old babysitting skills were probably rusty, but Maddison was likely to be along for the day. She always ran in the Dash with her husband and kids. She'd probably love telling her older brother what to do when it came to Austin. And *love* feeding Austin whatever she wanted. Chelsea pushed the bitter thoughts from her mind. If Brady was serious about sharing custody, she'd have to get over stuff like that. Now was as good time as any to start.

The air around them was already pretty warm, at least mid-seventies, even though it wasn't quite eight. Today would be hot. Denise was quiet as they walked, giving Chelsea time with her thoughts, but the ten-minute walk to Cutie Pies didn't give Chelsea any epiphanies or ground-breaking spiritual guidance. Only random thoughts flitted through her brain. She could call her old boss and see if she had any connections to get her a part-time job or help her start her search for clients. She had enough savings for a deposit on an apartment, even though she cringed at giving up some of what she'd saved to buy a house.

But she would miss her friends in Clay.

She would really *really* miss DJ.

What would happen? What would he think?

By the time they reached Main Street, she only knew that Brady's proposal at least deserved some serious thought.

"Okay," Denise said as they approached the front door of Cutie Pies. "Give me the quick version of what Brady is doing home."

"He finally realized how much he's missing," Chelsea said. They had a lot to talk about, but Chelsea wanted more advice than her mom could give in a few minutes, and she didn't want to discuss it in front of Wendy.

"That's good," Denise said, but she frowned at Chelsea's expression.

Chelsea gave her a one-sided hug as they went in, the smell of the brownies enveloping them both.

"What are you doing back here?" Wendy asked when she came through the door to the kitchen. Her gaze was pointed at Chelsea, and she had that nervous look on her face she got when Chelsea accidentally mentioned how much time she'd spent doing work at home. "Where's Austin?" Her voice took on an almost accusing edge.

Chelsea nearly laughed. "Brady is home, so he took him to run in the race."

"Brady is here?" Wendy's eyebrows shot up the same way Denise's had when Chelsea told her it was Brady downstairs and not DJ, whom she'd grown accustomed to seeing at strange, non-normal dating hours, thanks to his job.

"Yes. So you don't need any help?"

Wendy shook her head. "Not really. I did so much pre-baking last night that I've got things in hand. Rees' Diner was serving chicken noodle soup yesterday. I had a lot of free time."

Things had been slow enough the afternoon before that Wendy had sent Chelsea home. They'd both grimaced over Allison taking advantage of the visitors in town for the holiday by serving her local favorite. Wendy had once tried to convince Allison to sell the soup and rolls at Cutie Pies, but Allison had argued that the soup and bread drew people to the diner, and why would they come if they could get it any time at Wendy's bakery? Wendy had experimented, trying to come up with an equally delicious soup recipe, but her calling was baked goods, pure and simple.

"You just need something better," Chelsea said.

Wendy pressed her lips together. "No . . . I don't need something better, I need something *different*. We need a low-calorie version or dairy-free version or some kind of diet version so that the people who *can't* eat Sister Rees's soup can eat mine."

Chelsea grinned, but the warmth behind it died before it spread through her. What if she went back to Salt Lake? What would happen to her helping Wendy and coming up with new recipes? It wasn't her area of expertise, but she liked the creative side of baking she'd discovered.

"That is a good idea," Chelsea said. She tried to keep up her enthusiasm. She didn't want to discuss it with Wendy. She knew her cousin's vehement opinion on everything Brady-related. She might march over to Madison's house and tell Brady it was insane and inconsiderate to even suggest that Chelsea move back to Salt Lake.

Chelsea's phone buzzed in her pocket, and thinking it might be Brady, she almost ignored it. She didn't think he'd pressure her, but in any case, she wasn't ready to face him. Things were too jumbled in her mind. But she had to answer, even if it was him, in case he had a question about Austin. She pulled her phone out and was relieved to see it was from DJ.

Your brownies still hot?

Some of the tension fell away as her muscles relaxed. *Yep,* she wrote back.

What would it take for you to bring some by?

Nothing at all, she thought to herself. In fact, it was exactly what she needed. He could at least calm the tempest inside her and give her some much-needed advice, though already the answer was worming its way inside her.

Austin needed his dad.

How often had she told Brady that?

I'll be right there, she answered DJ. "Good thing you don't need my help," Chelsea said, pocketing her phone and then ringing up a few brownies—and a couple of Wendy's—for herself. She might need them later.

She hurried to the fire station, arriving in less than twenty minutes. She'd barely walked through the front door when DJ came bounding down the stairs, a box under his arm. He set it on a table before rushing to greet her.

"The brownies aren't *that* good," she teased. Seeing him had settled a few of the scattered pieces inside her.

He circled an arm around her waist then slid his hand to her neck, drawing her closer for a brief, sweet kiss. "That is," he said when he pulled away. She hated the idea of giving *this* up every day, the sweetness of DJ and the relationship they had kindled. "And I never know how long I'm going to have with you, especially today."

She buried her face in his shoulder for a moment, unwilling to show him yet how true that might be in a way he *wasn't* thinking.

"I have a surprise for you," he said. Sliding his hand into hers, he pulled her toward the table where he'd dropped the box. Then he stopped, studying her for a moment before narrowing his eyes. "What's wrong?"

She shook her head, bringing a smile to her lips more easily than she thought she could. But then, DJ had a way of infusing her with a dose of everything-will-be-okay. Wendy may be able to see the bright side without much effort, but Chelsea needed DJ for that. He completed her that way.

For a few more minutes, she wanted to pretend that nothing was going to change. That she might tell Brady no. "Surprise first." She let the warmth of his hand in hers blast its way through her, wishing it would take her worries away.

DJ shot her a concerned look before picking up the box and handing it to her. "Open it."

She slid her fingernail along the tape and popped open the top of the box, revealing a mint-green container that looked like a bottle. She looked up at him questioningly.

"It's a refillable squeeze bottle like the ones that baby food comes in. And there's these too." He pulled out another, smaller box. "They're the same kind of disposable pouches, only you fill them yourself. I thought we could try them both and see what Austin likes better."

Something stuck inside of Chelsea's throat and kept her from answering. Yes, she'd missed having a partner—but she'd never had a partner like DJ. But Brady did say he wanted to try. To fix things. Maybe if she gave him the chance, he could be more like DJ when it came to Austin. The thought of leaving and having to make a long-distance relationship with DJ work made her stomach churn. But Austin had a father who wanted to be a part of his life. She couldn't ignore that.

"Well, what do you think?" DJ asked after she'd stared at him in silence for too long.

"I think you're really awesome," she said, her voice catching as she reached for his hand.

"That's nothing new." His teasing tone was gentle, and a moment later he'd laced his fingers through hers and used his grip to pull her closer. "What's wrong, honey?"

Oh, merciful heavens. The softness in his eyes and the slight downturn of his lips—the obvious concern—threatened to turn her *into* honey. The sound of that word on his lips made her crazy in the best way.

"Brady," she breathed when she remembered to answer him. "He's here. In town."

His eyebrows slanted down in confusion. "What did he do? Did he say something to you about us?"

She shook her head. "He's heard rumors, and he admitted he's avoiding getting back to you—but it's not that. He asked me to move back to Salt Lake."

The slant changed to an angry one. "Just like that?" DJ asked, not moving away, for which Chelsea was thankful.

She nodded. "He doesn't like being so far from Austin, and I don't blame him. But there's nothing he can do right now. He can't come to Clay. I understand that. I just don't know what to do." That might have been a lie. Options had already started piling up in her head, which she feared was the answer about whether she should move or not. That scared her the most, that after only an hour, the answer stared her in the face. It seemed unfair that when she'd struggled through single parenting, answers seemed to take their time, but now that she wouldn't mind telling Brady she needed time to think, the answer came all too soon.

She continued, reluctance heavy in her voice. "He deserves to be with Austin. If I can help him be closer, maybe that's what I need to do." She lowered her head onto his shoulder, hoping he would come up with some kind of answer that would solve everything, then her cheeks heated as she thought of what that solution would be. She couldn't expect DJ to marry her after only a month, but how else could she convince him to follow her to Salt Lake for a few years? His job was here. The life he was trying so hard to succeed at was here. If he left now, it would be like giving up—and in his mind, that would equate to failing again. And that was all beside the point because marrying someone after a month was too soon.

DJ's body stiffened, and she pulled her head back up to see that his expression had gone from angry to blank.

"Do you want to go?" His tone had turned careful and hesitant.

She took a deep breath and thought about it. "I don't want to take Austin away from him. It would kill me if *he* tried to do something like that. But what about everything here? Working with Wendy, the Relief Society project? You?"

"I see where I rank," he teased, but it sounded hollow.

She squeezed his hand that much harder. "I can get a better job in Salt Lake, maybe even more freelance clients. Enough that maybe I could work from home. Or even find a job where I worked evenings, when Brady could be home with him . . . there are just so many more options *and* Austin could be near his dad. It would be nice to have more of Brady's help." The act of saying her reasons out loud convinced her even more than her own thoughts.

Her heart sank.

Moving meant leaving DJ.

He shook his head slowly, taking a step back. She nudged him closer with their still enjoined hands, but he resisted. His smile relaxed at least, but it looked more sad than anything else. He must realize it too, what her decision would mean, although she hoped he wouldn't pull completely away.

"You'll think about it and pray about it. And you'll figure out what's best for Austin and for you."

Despite his hesitance, she leaned forward, wrapping her arms around his chest and resting her face against it. He remained stiff for a moment but then relaxed and put his arms around her.

"Thank you, DJ." She barely managed to keep the break from her voice. "We'll figure this out." She hoped that moving back to Salt Lake didn't mean losing DJ. She didn't know if she could bear it if it did.

CHAPTER FOURTEEN

DJ half-heartedly spread his homemade peanut butter over his piece of toast. Not the best dinner considering that, as a fireman, he never knew what a night would hold, especially *this* night. His crew would cover the fireworks show, and they were likely to be up most of the night responding to calls.

But Chelsea had been right that the homemade peanut butter tasted far better than the store-bought stuff. There was nothing like eating it on a hot piece of toast with a tall glass of milk. Except maybe her black bean brownies. That had pleasantly surprised him after his first experience with them. Now he didn't buy a dozen every other morning just to support her; the other firemen couldn't get enough either.

He sat his pitiful dinner on the wobbly wooden table in the firehouse kitchen and slumped into an equally wobbly chair. He hadn't been a fireman long enough to know if the worn furniture had come that way or had simply weathered meals from too many firemen for too long. Thinking about Chelsea's healthy baking talents depressed him. Ever since she'd left the fire station that morning, he'd gone around and around the situation in his mind.

If Brady was avoiding his calls, it meant he wasn't happy about their relationship. *And* he wanted Chelsea to move back. Even though she'd been emotional when she spoke to him about it, he could see she knew what she should do. With so many obstacles in their way, how could he and Chelsea possibly make things work? What did their future hold? Brady would always want to be near his son, and Chelsea seemed willing to make sure that happened.

Which led to another thought gnawing at him. Chelsea had told him about the relief, and guilt, she'd felt when she realized that she and Brady didn't love each other. But she'd also told him how well their relationship worked now, how much they'd grown in the past year to be able to communicate in a way they hadn't when they'd been married.

Brady had asked her that morning to move back to Salt Lake, and she'd all but decided within a matter of hours. How long before they realized they'd been wrong? That they did love each other? That they could make it work now.

Austin was sealed to them. The guilt at stepping between that piled on every time he thought about it.

So that was his answer, then, to whether or not he should pursue a future with Chelsea. It was a bit of a slap in the face, and later than he expected, given the happy weeks they'd had together, but he should have expected it. Just because he'd convinced himself that the deterioration of his friendship with Brady made dating Chelsea okay didn't make it true. He couldn't help but wonder why he'd been led down this road only to have it come to an abrupt halt. Maybe so he could see clearly why things wouldn't work out?

He stared at his half-eaten piece of toast still sitting on the table, uninterested in finishing. He only had one argument against his guilt: Chelsea deserved more than Brady. DJ loved Brady. He didn't know the inside of their marriage, but it was no small thing that Brady had left in the first place. It was no small thing that he'd said he didn't love her.

Ever since DJ started spending time with her, things in his life had figured themselves out. Like the reason he came to Clay. It wasn't because he loved the town he grew up in and wanted to serve there, but because of Chelsea. He'd helped her. And maybe it was selfish to think about how his service to her had helped him so much, but it had. If he gave up Chelsea, all he'd be left with was a mediocre career as a small-town fireman. Depressing. It hadn't bothered him before to think about Rocket playing in the NFL and David playing major-league baseball. Sean might not love the way his job was going right now either, but at least he was good at it.

He pulled out his phone to text Sean. *What do you have going on next week? I've got a couple days. I should come down.* Maybe hanging out with the old crowd would help. Anthony and Ty were around too. It would be fun. Chelsea would love them—

Life sucked.

Thought you were trying to spend every minute with your girl. You bringing her down? Sean had read his mind, no surprise there. DJ had told him about his relationship with Chelsea and that despite the lingering guilt, he'd felt good about where they were going.

Actually, I could use a distraction. Things with the girl went . . . a little south.

You talked your glory days up too much, and she found out the truth. That I was the real star.

DJ had to chuckle, which brightened his mood. Sean was giving him a distraction, trying to cheer him up. In the old days, maybe even a few weeks ago, he would've gone with it. But not anymore.

More like . . . Brady asked her to move back to Salt Lake and I think she's going to go. I don't know what it means for us, but I don't think it's good. I thought it was the right thing, pursuing something with her. I should've known better.

It took a while for Sean to answer. The reply was a GIF of a woman with her mouth dropped open in shock. DJ laughed again. He should buy Sean's niece a cookie or something because the GIFs never ceased to crack him up, and today he could use that.

That's . . . well, no words. That really sucks.

No advice? DJ asked hopefully.

His phone rang, Sean's picture announcing that it was him. "You prayed about it?" he asked when DJ picked up.

"Yeah. Of course."

"And?"

DJ pushed his chair away from the table and headed back to the bunks. "I care a lot about her, and I want her in my life, but, ultimately? The decision is up to her, and I can't—I shouldn't do anything to sway that." He didn't like how the thoughts spilled out of him, putting words to his worry. His words made it definite. Like he couldn't argue with it.

He clenched a fist as he dropped onto his bed, thankful the bunks were all empty. He couldn't get around it. He couldn't encourage a relationship between him and Chelsea when there might be a chance for her marriage to Brady to work again.

"Have some faith," Sean said with a sigh. "Maybe for now let someone else take control."

"Yeah," was all DJ could answer. "Yeah, I guess."

———

BRADY TOOK Austin on Saturday too, which freed up way too much of Chelsea's time. She wasn't used to not having him with her nearly every hour of his waking day, and she didn't really like it. But it did give her the opportunity to make a list of things that would need to be arranged for her and Austin to move, just so she could get a picture of what it all meant. She needed that in order to give Brady any sort of answer about whether she *could* move, even if her brain had already decided it was going to work out. When she'd thought of every tiny detail, she went back through the list and wrote down how she could arrange for that detail. Most of the spaces were filled, which made her heart race.

That night, after Brady brought Austin home and put him to bed, she called her old boss in Salt Lake. "Chelsea!" Helen cried happily. "How are you?"

"I'm good. I'm wondering if you might know of anyone looking for an accountant." She hoped her voice didn't shake with the anxiety she felt. If Helen didn't know of anything, Chelsea would have to search and put off the move. She didn't hate that idea either.

"Me," Helen said, matter-of-factly. "At least temporarily. Megan and Karen are both going on maternity leave in a couple of weeks. They're both *planning* on coming back, so I was going to tough it out. Please tell me you can help me instead."

"Uh . . ." The comment left Chelsea speechless. She *had* been praying, off and on, and consistently she'd felt good about moving back—until her mind would catch on leaving DJ. But things were falling into place too quickly. "I'm definitely interested, but I haven't made a final decision about moving back to Salt Lake just yet."

"I could really use you, Chels," Helen pleaded. "To not have to struggle through those months without someone. And on the off chance one of them doesn't come back, the job would be yours."

Chelsea thought she might hyperventilate. One of the biggest things to consider had been her employment. She'd figured it would take her a couple of weeks to find something, at least, and then she'd have that time to work out with DJ what they wanted to do. But this was fast. And so easy. They chatted for a few more minutes about people at the office before hanging up, but not before Helen had pleaded her case one more time. Chelsea stared at the phone for a long time after they'd hung up, terrified of what it meant that a job had all but fallen into place, but also awestruck.

She hoped all that night for a call from DJ so they could discuss things, but he had warned her that the weekend around the Fourth would be busy. She hated not having him as a sounding board.

He didn't show up for church on Sunday either, even though she knew he'd gotten off early that morning. It was the first time since they'd started dating that he hadn't come to her ward—except for the one time his shift had fallen over a full Sunday. She didn't want Austin racing up and down the aisle to sit between her and his dad, so she and her parents sat in the row behind, and she tried not to think about what Allison Reese thought about Brady being back in town and DJ's mysterious absence.

The lesson in Sunday school focused on tithing, and Chelsea surprised herself by sharing openly about the blessings paying her tithing had brought when she was first divorced and bringing in a meager income. It led to several other women around her jumping in to discuss difficult times in their life. One sister couldn't pay tithing for several years because of the arguments it caused with her non-member husband; another sister, who Chelsea figured obeyed every commandment to the letter, talked about the struggle to continue paying when her husband retired and their income was drastically reduced.

The discussion put DJ in her mind yet again, how he had assured her that everyone had difficulties to overcome and no one felt perfect.

It wasn't until Sunday afternoon, during Austin's regular nap time, that DJ called.

"Hey, I've been just sitting around waiting for a call from you," she said when she answered. "Busy few days?"

His return laugh was forced. "Busy enough, sure. I was thinking a lot, you know."

"Of course." Her heart rate sped up at his awkward tone.

"I don't want our relationship to add to the weight of what you have to decide," he said. "Or to confuse you when we haven't really had enough time to know what this is."

"Okay . . ." she drew out the word, a sort of panic dancing through her chest. He was letting her down. Had he talked to Brady finally? What had they said to each other? DJ had declared that he was willing to risk his relationship with Brady because she was important enough —what had Brady said to change his mind?

"I'm sorry, Chelsea, if I hurt you by moving forward when I probably shouldn't have."

Her heart dropped into her feet. She blinked, realizing that tears stung in her eyes. "I . . . it's okay."

"I'll see you around." He didn't wait for her to respond before he hung up, and she was left staring at the phone.

CHAPTER FIFTEEN

When DJ pulled down the dirt drive of the Lewis farm on Thursday evening, it surprised him to see both Chelsea's Honda and Brady's two-door Toyota pickup. He'd driven the same vehicle since high school, though the thing had to be on its last legs. Why hadn't he bought a new one with that fancy job of his? With all the hours he worked, he had to make enough for something at least a little newer. The fact that Chelsea was there would make dinner awkward; the fact that Brady was back in town for the second weekend in a row meant he was serious about his relationship with Austin—and probably with Chelsea, too.

When DJ had called Chelsea Sunday afternoon to tell her he thought they should keep their distance so he didn't muddy up her decision making, he'd heard the reluctance and indecision in her tone. It made it harder for him to do the right thing, but the fact that she'd let it happen meant he had to stick to his decision. He couldn't be the thing that stood between her already existing family.

Given the fact that he'd just gotten off an hour before, that it had been yet another grueling shift, he should've begged off. He could now—flip his car around and call Dale on his way home to tell him he needed the sleep. That wasn't a lie. He put his truck in reverse, ready to back out of the driveway, when Madison came up the path from the garden with a shirt-front full of green beans. She waved at him with her free hand. Turning back now would make things even more awkward. Reluctantly, he put the truck in park, pushed open his door, and got out.

"Better be making those with bacon," he said as he joined her heading into the house.

She raised an eyebrow. "Chels won't let Austin eat them if I do," she countered with a smirk.

DJ shook his head. Though Madison was three years younger than he, Brady, and Chelsea, her oldest child was almost five, and she had three more. Her belief that she knew better than Chelsea how to raise a child showed in the advice she gave her, the way she talked about Chelsea's mothering, even if she never said it in words.

"Guess I'll sacrifice for Austin then," he said.

When he and Madison entered through the kitchen door, he found Chelsea setting plates around the table with Dale. Her eyes widened with surprise when she saw him, but she didn't react beyond that, casting a glance at Madison before giving him a stiff smile.

"Hi," she said, pink rising in her cheeks. She nodded to the doorway that led into the living room. "Boys are in there," she said. "Well, Austin and Brady anyway." She turned her smile to Dale, who laid out forks next to the plates she already had on the table.

"Thanks." It took everything in him to keep his hands in his pockets and walk through the doorway, leaving her to finish up dinner preparations with Madison and Dale. He wanted to grab Chelsea's hand and drag her outside, let her know it would be a mistake to go back to Brady—but that would be the selfish thing to do.

He was disappointed that Patty wasn't in the living room with Brady and Austin. Likely she was in her room, sleeping so she could join them for dinner. It would have kept him from an awkward conversation with Brady. He'd been reluctant to accept the invitation all along, but he didn't want Brady making a bigger deal out of his relationship with Chelsea than he might have, based on the "rumors" he'd heard from his sister.

"Hey, Kaiser." Brady looked up from where he sat on the couch, watching a cartoon with Austin. He slid Austin off his lap to stand and shake DJ's hand then pat him on the back.

"How's it going?" DJ asked, recognizing how stiff both their greetings had become since they'd last seen each other. The fact that they behaved more like distant relatives might've once strengthened his argument that he could date Chelsea without ruffling too many feathers. Too bad it didn't matter anymore. Either way, this new relationship was better in the long run. How long would it take before DJ and Chelsea could attend family functions like this without awkwardness? Long enough that DJ might consider not coming anymore. He wasn't actually Brady's brother, and although he wouldn't set aside Patty and Dale's friendship, he didn't have to show up. He could find excuses to stay away whenever Brady and Chelsea were around.

He and Brady sat back on the couch, and the movement made Austin turn to see DJ. "Dee!" he cried, hopping over Brady to plop in DJ's lap.

"I've helped Chelsea out with babysitting a couple times," DJ explained when Brady gave him a questioning look. That was the easy answer. Still, Brady's lips pressed into a thin line.

"So, sorry I didn't get back to you," Brady said, leaning over to rest his elbows on his knees. "Work has been crazy." His eyes darted around the room, and DJ wished he hadn't brought it up. What was the use talking about it now?

"No problem." DJ watched Austin play with his keys instead of meeting Brady's gaze. It was probably part true about working so much, but a couple pictures on Brady's Instagram feed said he'd at least had some time for a soccer game that week. And Chelsea had told him Brady had purposefully been avoiding his calls.

"So, what's up?" Brady asked, the words coming reluctantly.

DJ couldn't help that his gaze flicked toward the kitchen. Man, he wanted to just get up and walk out. Forget all of this had happened.

Anything to get rid of the ache in his heart and the awkwardness in the room.

"Oh, well . . ." He didn't even know how to word it. He'd practiced stuff in his head before trying to get a hold of Brady, but that had been before, when he planned on persuading his friend to give his blessing, per se. "Uh . . . I mean, I know you've heard that Chels and I went out a few times. You know, small town and . . . but now . . ." He shrugged, meeting Brady's eye for a few seconds before turning it back to Austin. He stopped himself from saying anymore, especially since he didn't want to risk accidentally admitting that he was pretty much in love with her.

"Yeah. Uh, Maddi mentioned something about it."

It was such a non-answer, giving away nothing about how he might feel, although DJ could guess from the tension in Brady's jaw. "Well, there are only so many single girls around here." DJ hoped the joke would make it so they could move on.

Brady chuckled, forced. Still full of tension. "That's true."

"Yeah." There were so many things DJ should say. The old DJ would've encouraged him to get back together with Chelsea, maybe given him a few tips on how to make things work. But considering any advice he might give came from his short dating experience with her, he kept his mouth shut. "How are you liking your job?" he asked instead.

Brady relaxed considerably—both of them did now that the dreaded conversation was out of the way. "Besides the fact that I barely have a life outside of it, it's good." Brady reached for Austin, pulling him back into his lap as he leaned against the couch. "What about you? I've heard you've had some trouble settling in?" His eyes twinkled with his usual mirth. Jokes about DJ's failures were a given in their relationship in the past, the same way DJ would've ribbed Brady about his. But in the past, they also would've shared frustrations, triumphs, and everything else in real conversations, something they hadn't done since before Brady's divorce. So the jab stung.

"It's been rough," he said, managing to keep the bitterness out of his voice. Brady's eyebrows pulled together anyway, saying that he'd caught on that DJ wasn't going to joke about it.

"Let's eat," Dale said from the doorway.

DJ sprang out of his seat, not caring that it was obvious that Dale had saved him. "You need help bringing Patty in?" he asked.

"That would be great," Dale said, leading DJ down the hallway toward her bedroom. DJ caught Brady's stare as they moved past him, but he didn't dwell on it. One thing DJ knew—he wasn't a part of this family the way he used to be.

———

CHELSEA LEANED her head against the lawn chair, watching in silence as Austin rebounded off every surface of the trampoline—even the safety net surrounding it—and giggled nonstop. A smile slipped onto her face, the first all night. Dinner with Brady's family had been awkward, to say the least. DJ had been invited. If Chelsea had known that, she would've just dropped Austin off with Brady.

DJ and Brady's interactions were stiff, an act on both sides, pretending their relationship was the same. She didn't know what they'd talked about in the living room before Dale called them in to eat. Dale and Madison had been discussing various meal preparations, leaving no room for Chelsea to eavesdrop. DJ had intended to talk to Brady about dating Chelsea. Had they talked about it beforehand? What had they said?

Her phone dinged, startling her out of her reverie. *Wendy says you're not coming tonight?* It was from Sharae Barber. They had another girls' night planned.

She cringed. She should've skipped the dinner in favor of the girls' night. It certainly would have been less awkward. *I have a family thing. Maybe I'll come over to the bakery if it's not too late.*

Do it! Sharae responded. *We want to see you.*

I could use some chocolate! I'll try.

See you later then. :)

Wendy had made a rich, moist chocolate cake with a chocolate-chip-cookie-dough-flavored frosting for the girls night. It was tempting, though Chelsea would need to eat the whole thing by herself if she had any hope of fixing her emotional state.

At dinner, her heart had twisted every time she met DJ's gaze. He acted as friendly as ever, of course, but it ended at that. He hadn't tried to talk to her since their phone call on Sunday. Did he really think that stepping back would make her choices more clear? With everything else already falling into place, DJ was the only thing she could think about.

He'd left something missing inside of her. His comforting friendship had filled all the little corners of her heart. Had *she* been wrong to let things happen between them?

Austin jumped up and down and side to side on the trampoline, rolling off the net with shouts of excitement and laughter. Though Chelsea kept her eyes on him, her thoughts spun through many other things.

She remembered first starting to date Brady; the excitement that someone so popular liked her, the pounding of her heart the first time they'd held hands and kissed, the glowing pride of walking down the halls of her high school with his arm around her or wearing his extra jersey at a football game. She wondered if, when she'd thought it was love, it was just familiarity. The truth was, she hadn't been deliriously happy when they'd gotten married. They both knew he'd only asked because she'd wound up pregnant. It hadn't been romantic. It had been terrifying.

"He's having fun."

Chelsea's head snapped up at the sound of Brady's voice behind her. She turned to see him approaching—alone. Of course. DJ had left right after dinner, saying his shift had been tough and he needed sleep. The bags under his eyes had said he could probably use a few days' sleep, at least.

"He's always loved your mom's tramp," Chelsea said to Brady, turning back to Austin. Brady wore an older pair of jeans today, a few rips here and there, and a familiar, worn CHS football T-shirt. He looked more like the Brady she used to know. She had asked herself so many times since the divorce: had she ever actually loved him? Or had it all been a high school crush that she'd ended up stuck in?

"We should get him one," Brady said.

"I haven't seen any apartments with living rooms big enough. Not that I can afford, anyway," she teased.

His expression lit up. She hadn't told him yet for sure about moving to Salt Lake. She still wasn't one hundred percent sure herself, but everything was leading her in that direction.

"You'll move?" he asked, a grin stretching across his face.

"I talked to Helen the other night. She has a job for me for at least a couple months, filling in for some girls on maternity leave. And I can keep the freelance clients I already have, maybe get some more . . ." She shrugged.

"So, yes," he prodded, giving her a puppy-dog look she'd always laughed at before. She did the same now.

"Maybe. Maybe yes." She still couldn't cut one more string, but she didn't want to talk about that with Brady.

He sat down in a lawn chair next to her, watching Austin. "I kinda already looked around and found a house I can afford; it has a finished basement apartment. I was thinking you could rent it from me. Is that weird?"

"Weird? A little," she said. "But convenient for both of us."

Brady chuckled nervously. "I want him to have a yard, like this one. I don't want to take away the good things you've given him here."

She turned to him, narrowing her eyes. "What happened, Brady?" She couldn't help asking. "A month ago, I was begging you to make more time to see him. Now you're telling me in a few years you'll turn everything you've worked on upside down for him."

He turned to stare at her. "You've always turned things upside down for him," he pointed out. "Like moving to Salt Lake just because I asked."

"Because you make a good argument. I wonder if you could turn that into some kind of a career?" She tapped her chin in mock thought, and Brady laughed.

He turned back to Austin. "I guess I just figured it out."

There was more, but Chelsea didn't push. "The house thing is a good idea."

"It makes sense. I know I'll have a solid renter that I can trust, and I'll have my son close."

They sat in silence for a while longer, and then she couldn't help asking another question. "Did you talk to DJ?"

"Uh . . . yeah. A little." He tapped his fingers on the arm of the chair, his gaze zeroed in on Austin in a way that said he wasn't just enjoying watching his son play but was avoiding looking back at her.

She waited for more.

He didn't offer it.

Ugh. So on the one thing she really wanted to push, he'd reverted to the old days, making her drag information out of him. "And . . . ?" she questioned.

Still nothing.

"Are you guys good?" As well as they got along, she couldn't frame this the way she wanted too—it would be too uncomfortable. *So, did you tell him to stay away from me? Is that why he won't talk to me or even discuss having a long-distance relationship?*

"We're okay," he said.

She was ready to pull her hair out. What did that mean? Okay? He wouldn't tell her without more pushing, and she couldn't bring herself to go there. She stood up. "Wendy invited me to a girls' night thing tonight. You want to keep Austin here for a bit?"

"Yeah, please," he said.

She couldn't help studying his expression, soft and content as he watched his son. He'd certainly figured something out.

"Can you make sure he's home and in bed by eight?" she asked.

He turned to her. "Maddi has a pack and play at her house. How would you feel about him spending the night with me?"

It was a wonder her body was in one piece the way it split in two so much lately. Her stomach dropped with panic the same time her heart soared at Brady asking for even more time with Austin. "Sure," she said.

Brady bit back a smile. He couldn't have missed the tension in her tone. "If you're not okay with it—"

She cut him off. "No, it's fine. You're his dad, and I can handle him staying with you. It's just new. I'll get over it." She hadn't actually spent a night away from him since he'd been born, but she had to make adjustments. Brady wanted a bigger part—she wanted him to take a bigger part—and this was something she'd get used to . . . eventually.

"Thanks, Chels."

"There should be enough diapers to get you through the night in the diaper bag. If not, I think one of Maddi's kids is in the same size . . . or close enough." She waved her hand around like none of this bothered her. "I guess I'll stay out all night or something."

She could still hear him laughing as she walked across the lawn.

———

CHELSEA ARRIVED in time to meet the girls at Wendy's. They all sat around stools at the counter in the back, digging into Wendy's decadent cake. Sharae patted an empty stool next to her when Chelsea came in.

"Everything okay?" she asked, furrowing her eyebrows.

Chelsea had to laugh, wondering how much worry had been written into her expression. "Brady's in town, and Austin's spending the night with him," she said in a low voice. "It's just . . . the first time I've been away from him all night."

"Ahhh," Sharae said, forking a piece of her cake. Chelsea didn't waste another minute before cutting herself a piece. Wendy cast her a look from across the counter where she sat with Kelsi, but Chelsea shook her head. She didn't mind talking with her or Sharae, but she didn't want to discuss everything with the group.

"Jace's mom took the twins so we could spend the night in Billings a couple of months ago, and I made Jace drive us home at ten that night instead of using the hotel room because I couldn't take it." Sharae laughed at herself.

"Well, I just left Austin about ten minutes ago, so the night is still young." She shook her head at herself as she dug in. "I really want Brady's help and for him to be in Austin's life as much as possible, but sometimes the tradeoff for that sucks."

"I know." Sharae reached over and squeezed Chelsea's hand, letting Chelsea take the conversation where she wanted instead of pushing her to discuss it more.

Chelsea let the company and the food distract her for the next hour so. When she walked out with Sharae, she stumbled to a stop as she caught sight of DJ running down the block across the street from them. He lifted his hand to wave but ran on by, not really looking her in the eye. If things hadn't crashed and burned with him, she could picture herself stopping him, teasing him. *I thought you said you were going home to sleep.* As it was, she worried about him *not* going right home to sleep, at the fact that he needed to burn off energy with a run. She held in a sigh.

She glanced down at the flip-flops she wore and wondered if she could catch up. But he was already disappearing down the street, far from her.

"It's none of my business," Sharae said from beside her, "but I thought you two . . ."

Chelsea took a deep breath, ignoring the fact that watching him run away from her had shaken her more than leaving Austin with Brady—left her more scared. Brady would take care of his son, and wherever he might fall short because of lack of experience, Maddi and her husband could make up for. Maddi certainly let Chelsea know how well she could mother.

But she didn't know what was happening with DJ or if she could fix it. The only thing that made sense was that Brady must have told him to step back, and DJ had decided to honor that, for whatever reason.

"I think Brady might have said something to him." Chelsea tried to shrug off her answer to Sharae. She wished it was darker because she was afraid her friend might notice the tears brimming in her eyes.

"Oh." Sharae bit her lip.

Inside, Chelsea almost wanted to laugh. Uncertainty crossed Sharae's face as she tried to come up with an answer. "It's okay," Chelsea said. "There's no easy to fix, and I brought it on myself for leaping in head first with someone Brady grew up with. I just thought . . ." She shook her head, wishing that would shake out all the disappointment welling up inside her. "I'll be okay. It's probably better." And she shrugged again because she didn't know what else to do. Sharae simply reached over and hugged her before they separated for their cars.

Her mom was sitting in a chair, reading a book, when Chelsea came in. She took one look at her daughter and stood up, coming over to envelop her in a hug. Denise smelled sweet, like the bakery—chocolate, almond, and vanilla.

"Rough day?" she asked softly.

Chelsea's shoulders shook with a mixture of laughing and crying. "Do you know what's bothering me the most? Not that Brady has Austin for the first time overnight—the first of many to come—or that I'm about to uproot my life again."

"DJ?" Denise guessed with a sad smile. Chelsea nodded, and her mom pulled her back into the hug. She spilled out all the worries she'd had about what Brady might have said or why DJ was pushing her away, feeling the release of confiding to someone. DJ had played that part for her for a few weeks, and she missed it. She missed him, even after only a couple of days.

She was in love with him.

She had known it was possible all those years ago when it had been so easy to talk to him, to be around him. But for better or worse, when she married Brady, she'd promised fidelity. She'd come through on that. But connecting with DJ again had brought her right back to the tipping point, and it hadn't taken much to make her fall.

And just like all those years ago, Brady was taking it away again. She fought against the bitter, unfair feelings. She'd made choices that had led her down that road too.

"What should I do?" she asked Denise as they sat on the couch, Denise's arms around her.

"Pray. You already know that moving to Salt Lake is the right thing to do. The Lord must have a plan for you and for DJ, so trust Him and hope that it's the plan you want."

Chelsea nodded. It was the obvious answer, one she already knew, but perhaps she needed to hear it again. And again. She gave her mom another tight hug and went up to bed.

She did pray before she slept, expressing her frustration and begging the Lord to do something about it. She prayed for clarity. Her mom was right. It hadn't taken long for her to realize that she should move—things fell into place too quickly. But she hoped for answers about what lay ahead after she did. And why it had to mean leaving DJ behind. Though the praying brought a measure of peace, she didn't get immediate answers. It took too long to get to sleep, her brain working to come up with something, anything.

When she finally drifted off, she slept fitfully and woke up a few hours later, blinking into the darkness, trying to recall the dream that had her reaching across the bed again. It surprised her when she grasped enough of the pieces of the dream to realize she hadn't been grasping for Brady—but for DJ.

It took hours to get back to sleep again, and she cursed herself for losing sleep on the one night she could have slept without interruption. She tried to remember the dream, but the most she could come up with was DJ's arms wrapped around her, his head against hers as she leaned into him and breathed him in. Security. Hope. Thoughtfulness. Comfort. Friendship. All those things swirled around inside with him next to her.

She lay awake with that image in her head, hoping the relief it brought would calm her through the night. It did, and eventually, those feelings banished her confusion and allowed her to fall back asleep.

———

BRADY HAD to leave Clay Sunday afternoon to go back to work. He'd kept Austin after church and brought him home that afternoon, promising to see him soon. Chelsea hadn't finalized any plans for when she would move yet, but she probably wouldn't delay long. If she took Helen up on the job, her former boss wanted her to start as soon as she could so they could catch up on any changes before Megan and Karen left.

"So . . ." Brady said, his hand on the door as he got ready to leave. "Should I look into that house some more?"

She swallowed and gave him a smile. "Yeah. You should."

CHAPTER SIXTEEN

On Monday morning, Sharae came by with her twins in the double jogging stroller Chelsea had seen her use around town. Sharae held up a Ziploc bag with a golden-brown loaf of bread inside, its top speckled with nuts and seeds.

"I know you're into healthy stuff, and I thought you could use a little treat." She held the bag out to Chelsea. "A friend from college used to make this. It's healthy *and* pretty darn good."

Chelsea took it, smiling at the thoughtful gesture. "That was really nice of you. Are you out for a walk?"

Sharae nodded. "Easiest way to entertain these hooligans. Want to come?"

"I'd love to." It only took a few minutes to grab her own stroller and ready Austin. Chelsea loved that about summer—grabbing a pair of sandals for each of them and heading out without too much fuss.

They chatted about Relief Society business for a while. Chelsea surprised herself with how little it intimidated her to discuss the sisters who needed help and with how quickly she came up with suggestions for helping them. Perhaps she was getting the hang of things after all.

"I don't want to be nosy, especially since I know you have Wendy for confiding in, but I'm here to talk if you ever need to," Sharae said in a lull in the conversation.

"I don't talk to Wendy about Brady." Chelsea sighed and shook her head. "She has a prejudice. I've tried to show her how us getting a divorce was for the best, but she can't get past him 'walking out.' Which, yeah, he did. But we both knew it was the right thing for him to do. I never would have been brave enough to tell him I was unhappy or that I didn't think I loved him." Sharae *mmm-hmmm*-ed and they walked in silence for a moment. "Moving back is a good idea, but she thinks I'm letting Brady talk me into something again because of a baby." Her cheeks colored. She'd never really brought up her first pregnancy to people. She'd lost that baby so soon that no one in their ward in Rexburg even knew about it, and if people in Clay suspected about their hasty wedding, they never got to see the fruits of that speculation.

"After what you've been through, I can see why she'd get overprotective. But you're a smart woman." One of the twins squealed, and Sharae reached into the basket of her stroller to pull out some crackers. "Does Austin want one?"

Chelsea nearly said no but stopped herself. A couple crackers on a walk wasn't the worst thing. It was okay for her to worry about his eating. She wouldn't let guilt burrow inside her over that, but she had to loosen up a little and let life happen. "Yeah. Thanks."

"Honestly," Sharae said after she'd distributed the treats, "I'm just good for an ear. I feel out of my depth trying to help, but I'm sorry you have to go through it all. I think it's great that you want to keep a good relationship with Brady and that you're compromising to help Austin stay close. I had an aunt and uncle who got divorced—after their kids were all grown—but any time they were at a family function for their kids or grandkids, they could barely be civil. It was the worst."

"It helps that we can talk like friends now and not have to battle each other." Chelsea rolled her eyes. "That's not to say that I won't still eat that whole loaf of bread slathered in butter. So much stress."

"And you'll only have to feel half as guilty." Sharae laughed. "It *is* still bread. But hey, nobody's perfect."

"You're pretty close," Chelsea said. "Beautiful kids, great husband, gorgeous house . . ."

Sharae's laughter increased. "Chelsea. Have you never heard the saying that we're all a hot mess, but some of us are better at hiding it?"

"Yeah. Maybe." But Chelsea couldn't imagine anything in Sharae's life being messy. She even dressed fabulously.

"It's definitely true for me too." She didn't elaborate, and Chelsea didn't push her. She thought back again to what DJ had said after Chelsea was called into the Relief Society presidency, how every woman there felt like a failure at something. Just because hers were different, he'd been saying, didn't make her any less able to serve.

As they continued on in quiet again, Chelsea wondered if maybe it made her *more* able to serve. "I'm glad you stopped by," she said.

"Wait until you taste the bread."

———

TUESDAY MORNING, Chelsea stood in the kitchen, straining to see out the window and down the street to the park where the garden boxes were. Maybe Brady showing back up had killed any romantic future for her and DJ and muddled things up in her mind, but her dream about him had weighed on her mind since early Sunday morning.

She had second-guessed herself too. Had it been Brady's face in the dream and she had put DJ's face in its place when she struggled to remember? She sighed as she stood on her tiptoes and tried to see farther down the street. But DJ could walk to the park from so many places, she might not see him—if he came at all. He'd only gotten off that morning, so he definitely wouldn't show up at nine in the morning. No, he'd be at home sleeping.

She couldn't stand there in the kitchen all day watching for him. She'd already gone in early to the bakery to mix up her brownie batter, so she couldn't use that to distract herself either. She tapped her fingers against the edge of the sink, still wishing DJ would come to check on the garden boxes. Maybe she could start figuring out a chicken noodle soup recipe for Wendy. She'd said she would the week before and hadn't even thought about it again. The situation with Brady and the *lack* of a situation with DJ had taken over everything.

She walked across the kitchen, scooping Austin up from where he sat playing on the floor. She crossed into the family room and went to the computer to search for a basic recipe to start with, reading through several of the top hits while Austin played in her lap with a toy Brady had given him Saturday night. Still, her mind kept wandering toward her dreams and the decisions she was faced with. She sat Austin down next to the computer and went back into the kitchen, getting a drink of water and staring toward the park.

She forced herself to sit at the table with a piece of paper. Allison used cream in her recipe to make it so rich. How could Chelsea get the same flavors? She *could* make her own cream of chicken soup using skim milk instead of heavy cream. If she got the seasonings right, she could downplay the difference in taste. Everything else would come easy after that. Low-sodium broth. Plenty of carrots, celery, and —*turkey*! Yes, turkey instead of chicken. Inside a flavorful soup, it wouldn't stand out that much. It was worth a try for sure. It wouldn't be a rich, creamy soup like Allison's, but like Wendy said, they needed something different anyway.

Working out the rest of the recipe and coming up with a grocery list took up another hour. She couldn't take waiting around anymore, so she got Austin into his stroller to walk to Cutie Pies and show Wendy the recipe to see what she thought. When she started out, she finally saw DJ walking toward the park, and she decided to take the long way to Main Street so he would see her. She had to talk to him and at least let him know that she'd decided to move. She didn't know what else to say, but maybe seeing him would be enough.

It would have been nice if he hadn't noticed her right away so there wasn't so much awkwardness in the time it took her to walk down the sidewalk toward him. Of course, with Austin pointing and laughing at everything around him, it was kind of hard for people not to notice her. Though her heart did wild laps inside her chest as she anticipated how DJ might act, Chelsea hoped that, at least on the outside, she looked calm.

When she pulled even with DJ, he was kneeling next to the garden boxes, carefully pulling weeds from among the tiny plants starting to come through the rich dirt he'd brought in. He'd glanced at her approaching over his shoulder a few times, and she didn't miss the tension he held in every muscle increasing the closer she got. Maybe she should just say "hi" and walk on by. She paused on the sidewalk despite her insecure thoughts. Her feet stopped of their own accord. The need to see him multiplied with him so close.

"Heading to Cutie Pies?" he asked, sitting back in the grass to look at her. He wore his characteristic smile, but it didn't crinkle his eyes or even reach too far into his cheeks like usual. Did having their brief, wonderful beginning snatched away bother him as much as it did her?

"Yeah." Chelsea looked toward Main Street. The two-block-long park faced the backsides of a few of the businesses, including Rees' Diner. Cutie Pies was another block south. "I came up with a new recipe I want to go over with Wendy." She swallowed more insecurity and asked, "Can we help you weed?"

DJ's eyes widened before he nodded. "Uh . . . yeah."

She unbuckled Austin from his stroller and moved it off the sidewalk and out of the way before she came to kneel at the same box as DJ. Austin took a few steps and then sat down in the grass, ripping chunks up and examining them in his hand before ripping up more.

"How was your shift this week?" she asked, picking at a few small clovers that had popped up in their neat rows.

"Uh . . ." DJ didn't look at her, concentrating solely on the weeds. "It was fine. Things slowed down a little."

He sounded anything but fine, and her heart lifted with hope that it came from them being apart. Chelsea went for honesty. "It's been a hard week for me too."

He gave her a small smile, so thin and so sad. "That's under-standable."

She should get right to the point, but she couldn't help that she liked being with him, even in this awkward moment. She looked over her shoulder at him. "Has Mrs. Tingey forgiven you yet?"

"I got the young men in our ward to help me repaint the park benches, so I think she may be warming—or thinking I'm a brown-noser. Which I am." He moved to the next box, and Chelsea went with him since they'd cleared the first box of weeds. Austin stood up from the grass he'd been playing in and headed for the boxes, trying to climb inside one.

"No, no, Austin." Chelsea shook her head at him and then stood to get him out when he didn't listen. She set him down next to her and started weeding again, but Austin hopped up and planted himself in DJ's lap, singing, "Dee, dee, dee," to himself. Chelsea tried not to react or stare as surprise and then tenderness crossed DJ's expression.

"Are your brownies still selling out?" he asked after several moments of silence.

Her chest warmed with pride. "Yes. I think that's why Wendy asked me to try and do a healthier version of Allison Rees's chicken noodle soup. That's what I've been working on this morning. I think I may be able to do it and make it pretty good still."

"Of course you can." Now his smile did reach into his eyes. It made her want to run her fingers along his cheek and over the stubble on his chin. He probably wouldn't shave for the two days he had off work, and she liked that look on him. She liked any look on him.

"So." She closed her eyes and took a deep breath, abandoning her weeding and sitting back in the grass. "I've decided to move back to Salt Lake. It makes the most sense right now for Brady."

Instead of turning to face her like she'd hoped, he kept weeding. The tension that had loosened slightly in the last few minutes returned. "I understand," he said, his voice strained.

She reached forward and put a hand on his arm, stilling him. "What is that going to mean for us?" she asked in a soft, hopeful voice.

He slowly turned to look at her. He stared at her for several seconds before he answered. "Maybe eventually we can feel comfortable being friends again."

Her throat closed up. "DJ . . ." It was a plea. Friends was not enough.

He shifted out of reach and the hand she'd laid on his arm dropped to her side. "I think that's for the best," he said.

She didn't agree. Something had made DJ change his mind about their relationship and that something had to be Brady. How could she argue against DJ's loyalty, even if she disagreed?

"Okay." She stood up, gathering Austin in her arms. "Thank you for all your help. You've been a really great friend." She shouldn't have stressed the word like she did. It made her sound insincere even though she wasn't. But friends? They could never be friends again. Both of them knew it. "I should get over to Cutie Pies before the lunch rush starts." She hurried across the grass, back to the stroller, knowing she had to get away before she started crying.

As she'd prayed to know what the plan was and how she should proceed, theoretically she knew that "not be with DJ" was a possible answer. She just didn't think that was the answer she'd get. It was like a punch in the gut to see their ending so clearly. Something she still couldn't quite believe was real.

DJ had changed so much about her life since they'd reconnected. She'd changed things because being with him made her believe in herself again. Life had bumped back on track.

Could she keep things on course without him?

CHAPTER SEVENTEEN

Since the night he killed the mayor's dog, DJ had been extra attentive any time he drove one of the trucks. He'd put a lot of work into the garden boxes and the park benches. He didn't want to ruin his efforts with another stupid mistake. He was holding on to this job, and any chance of career success in Clay, by a thread. One more incident and he could chalk up firefighting as another failed career. Mayor Tingey would make sure of it.

But the fact of the matter was that he wasn't sleeping well, on or off the job, and he'd just started a shift at the firehouse. Maybe DJ should take some personal days, head down to Provo to spend time with Sean like they'd texted about, and figure out what he wanted out of his life in Clay if Chelsea couldn't be in it.

When the fire call came at two a.m. Saturday morning, DJ was already awake, so he reached the fire truck first by over two minutes. He hopped up into the driver's seat, only having to wait a couple more minutes for Zollinger and a couple other guys to join him before he pulled out of the garage and headed north of town where an old farmhouse a couple miles out was on fire.

He tried not to let his thoughts wander to Chelsea as they drove. That had been what led to the debacle with the dog. But not thinking of her was, of course, impossible. He hadn't spoken to Brady since dinner the Friday before, but they'd texted a few times. Their relationship would never be the same. Given the way DJ had acted at dinner, Brady probably suspected there had been more to DJ's admission about the dates he'd taken Chelsea on. He couldn't continue spending time with any of the Lewises without thinking about their connection to Chelsea. Picturing how he'd kissed her on the front steps of her house. The way the lost look had slipped out of her eyes. How she'd held her hands to her chest when he'd pulled her closer.

He pinched his leg hard before he let himself go too far down that rabbit hole. They passed Rees' Diner. DJ refused to think about the chicken noodle soup Chelsea wanted to copy. It would probably be almost as good as Allison's.

Curse this stupid small town. Everything in it would remind him of Chelsea in some way.

The men piled out when they arrived, prepping the truck while they waited for Zollinger to analyze the scene and call out a plan. A few minutes later, a second truck joined them and then the ambulance, the scene coming alive with first responders. DJ worked alongside them automatically.

"Kaiser!" Zollinger's voice snapped him out of his mindless, one-foot-in-front-of-the-other mode of working. "None of the controls on truck five are working. Did you remember to engage fifth gear when you parked?"

"Of course," DJ answered. Mentally he went back through parking the truck. He'd driven the structure truck before. He knew you had to engage the fifth gear when you parked. He remembered doing it . . . didn't he?

"Well, double check. Something's not working, and I sure hope it's that, rather than something else," Zollinger hollered.

"Yes, sir." DJ hurried around the truck to the driver's seat, pulling up on the handle but to no avail. It was locked.

Locked? Why in the world would his door be locked? He shifted sideways, trying the back door, but discovered the same thing. His heart sinking, he hurried to the passenger side doors; both of them were locked as well.

"Kaiser?" Zollinger stalked toward him now, impatience written in the clip in his step. "What's going on?"

"Truck's locked. I have no idea how." DJ ground his teeth together.

"You didn't engage the fifth gear *and* you locked us out of the truck?" Zollinger snapped.

"No! I didn't lock us out of the truck. Why would I lock the doors? I never do that."

Zollinger let out a sigh and shook his head. "You've been off all week, and we all know it. Go radio the station and have them send someone out with the keys ASAP. We need this truck." He stalked away without another word, but DJ didn't need a lecture to know this was big. The delay could cause them to lose the farmhouse. Luckily nobody lived in it right now, but that didn't lighten the weight in his chest by much.

As DJ worked to do what he could while they waited, every set of eyes on the scene bore into him. How had he locked them out of the truck? He never locked the fire truck doors. Nobody did. And he *had* engaged the fifth gear—he was ninety nine point nine percent certain of it. Of course, that tiny inkling of doubt bloomed inside him, merging with his worries that he wasn't cut out to be a fireman, growing alongside all the mistakes he'd made since becoming one. All the mistakes and failures that had piled up since he moved back to Clay. He'd thought that hitting the mayor's dog was the pinnacle of his mistakes, but painting park benches and working in a garden plot wouldn't make up for this.

* * *

The sun was rising by the time they got back to the firehouse, and Chief Tallant met them there. He beckoned for Zollinger and DJ to join him in his office. DJ shed his gear as quickly as his tired limbs allowed and hurried in, Zollinger right behind him.

"What happened tonight, Kaiser?" Chief Tallant asked.

DJ sat in one of the uncomfortable office chairs he guessed were at least thirty years old and rubbed his hands along the light oak arms before dropping them in his lap. He couldn't meet the chief's gaze or Zollinger's.

"I can't explain it, sir," he said. "Like I told Zollinger, I remember engaging fifth gear."

Chief Tallant chewed on the inside of his cheek before answering. "Will says it wasn't engaged when you got into the truck."

"No. It wasn't," DJ confirmed. "But I promise I didn't lock those doors. It's stupid. Why would I do that? Nobody locks the truck doors." He raised his gaze, pleading with the chief to believe him.

The middle-aged man sighed and shook his head. "Will also says you've been pretty distracted with . . . with some other things going on in your life."

DJ ground his teeth together. He didn't blame Zollinger for confiding in the chief about his concerns. It was his responsibility to make sure his crew performed in top shape. They had demanding jobs, and it required one hundred percent, one hundred percent of the time.

"I didn't lock the truck doors," he repeated. He wouldn't go back on that. Distracted or not, he'd been on auto-pilot, and his auto-pilot didn't include tasks he never did. That wasn't to say he didn't understand Chief Tallant's position. He'd stood up for DJ when Mayor Tingey wanted DJ fired, but this? If DJ couldn't explain it, neither could Chief Tallant.

DJ sighed. He'd tried so hard not to fail at another thing, but at some point he should just give up and walk away. Leave firefighting behind him. Move on. It seemed like no matter how hard he tried, he couldn't be who he wanted to be. And when he was, when he did something unselfish like giving up Chelsea so she and Brady had a chance at making their family work, it only led to more trouble.

"Will? Give me a minute?" Chief Tallant asked. Zollinger exited the room, glancing at DJ sympathetically before he went. DJ couldn't tell if that meant he believed him or not.

Chief Tallant stood, his cowboy boots clicking against the linoleum floor as he rounded the desk and leaned on the front of it.

"I'm sorry, Chief," DJ said. "I know how it sounds. I know how it looks, and I know I don't have the best track record. But I swear—"

Chief Tallant held up a hand and then folded his arms across his chest. He was built like Zollinger—made sense because they were cousins or something—shorter, stockier than DJ. He was nearing fifty, if not there already, but he was as muscled as any other guy on the crew and in as good of shape.

"You're tired. I'm sorry, Kaiser. I don't know any other way those doors could've gotten locked."

DJ nodded slowly. The chief had him there. DJ didn't know that either. "I know." He dropped his gaze back into his lap.

"I want you to take a few days off."

DJ swallowed and nodded again, this time not trusting his voice. He'd considered it himself anyway. But having the chief ask him to do it instead of DJ making the decision himself changed everything.

Chief Tallant remained silent for a long moment before he rapped his knuckles on the top of the desk and took a step away, coming to stand a few feet from DJ, though DJ didn't look up.

The chief lowered his voice. "I know you've got good intentions, DJ, and I know you're here to serve Clay. You did that stuff for Mrs. Tingey because you wanted to make up for what you did and prove how sorry you are, and I think you're a fine young man for it. I do. But maybe . . . maybe firefighting isn't the job for you."

"Maybe not," DJ muttered. Disappointment settled over him. Being a fireman hadn't been something he dreamed about since he was small. He'd just wanted to come home to Clay and do some good. And not fail at yet another thing since leaving football. Half-heartedly he thought that maybe he ought to try being an EMT—but he'd already failed in two sectors of emergency response; he couldn't bring himself to face everyone in another department. He knew them all. By lunchtime, they'd all have heard about how he locked the fireman out of their structure fire truck and had nearly caused them to lose a house.

He'd only been good at one thing in his life: football. But so far, he hadn't been able to make a career out of that either. What did he do

now? Go back to school? Become a PT? Maybe it was the disheartened mood he was already in, but that didn't inspire even a little
enthusiasm in him.

"Good night, Kaiser." Chief Tallant moved to the door and opened
it. "Go home and get some rest."

"Yes, sir." DJ stood and left the office. He didn't bother going
upstairs for any of his stuff. He would come back for it later. He didn't
want to face his crew. Maybe they'd laugh over this. Things *had*
turned out better than they'd expected considering the time it had
taken to get back into truck five.

But he didn't want to deal with pity *or* ribbing. Not today.

CHAPTER EIGHTEEN

Chelsea mentally prepared herself for Brady visiting for the third weekend in a row. She'd been Austin's sole caregiver since the divorce, and giving him up to stay with his dad for hours on end made her edgy in a way that would take a while to overcome.

Chelsea's insides twisted when she watched through the big picture window on Saturday morning as Brady buckled Austin into his car seat to spend the day with him—*away* from her. She rubbed her hands together, wishing the ache away and not succeeding at all. Their custody arrangement since the divorce had been loose. She and Brady had both agreed on her going back to Clay to get back on her feet and figure out the future, and it made sense for Austin to go with her. There'd never been a restriction on when Brady could visit, and since he couldn't come very often, it didn't seem necessary to make specific arrangements for when he could. She told herself that this was getting her ready for when she moved to Salt Lake, for when Brady would take Austin for a few hours every day if he could.

Brady waved at her as he hopped into his truck, which she'd told him he needed to upgrade to something with a back seat if he was going to have Austin more, and she rolled her eyes at his knowing grin. She walked away from the window, resisting the urge to watch them drive away. She could busy herself packing up the last of her things. On Monday morning, she and her parents would follow Brady to Salt Lake, where she'd stay in a small, one-bedroom apartment near Brady's place in Sugar House, until he closed on the house he'd made an offer on the week before. She smiled to herself as she thought of the texts she'd gotten from him last week. He'd managed to get off at a decent hour every evening and spent every single one of them looking at the houses he'd found online before offering on one in Sandy.

The next couple weeks would hold so much change. Starting back at her old job, where, even though she loved her boss almost as much as Wendy, she wouldn't get as much leeway. Moving away from her family and having to put Austin in day care. She didn't let herself think of DJ, because really that wasn't a change. Their relationship was a blip on the record of her life.

She worked most of the day at Cutie Pies, hoping it would distract her from missing Austin.

It didn't work.

"How you doing, sweetie?" Denise asked when Chelsea came home around four. Wendy had shooed her away because not enough customers had come in that afternoon to justify Chelsea working. Denise rubbed at the tightness in Chelsea's shoulders.

"It's not easy, but I'm okay. Pretty soon sharing him will be old hat, right? I'll look forward to the nights or days he's not with me as time I can finally have to myself." She arched a questioning brow at her mother.

Denise smiled with her and squeezed her shoulder. "I don't know. Maybe? I certainly looked forward to moments by myself when you and the boys were little, but that's different."

Later that night, as Chelsea sat out on the back deck with her parents and the bishop and his wife, who'd come over for dinner, she couldn't help but think how unfair it was that she couldn't snuggle with either Austin or DJ. She longed to lay her head down on DJ's shoulder. To hear his comfort and support that she was doing the right thing. To have his arm around her—maybe both arms around her—while she sat and cried about how hard it was to share Austin. Would it be awkward if he knew those tears were also because he'd told her he thought they should just be friends? Calling him might help, but according to her calculations, he was in the middle of his shift. What did they have left to say anyway? They couldn't actually be friends. She kept the emotion at bay, but only by a thread.

"You nailed this soup, Chels," her dad said and dipped his spoon into his bowl for another bite. She'd made a batch after work to occupy the rest of her afternoon.

"Thanks." Chelsea kept her voice even.

"It's not just like Allison's, but it's still perfect. You don't want to compete with her anyway," Denise said. She turned back to Sister Howell to praise the soup some more. "People are going to love it. It's hearty and still creamy. I'm dying that this is only 250 calories."

"Thanks." Her compliments and the way the Howells echoed them warmed Chelsea as much as her own bowl of soup had—but still not enough.

Brady brought Austin home at eight like Chelsea had asked, giving her a reprieve and not taking him for the whole night. Chelsea had to thank him for that.

"Mama!" Austin lunged toward her, almost out of his dad's arms. Brady laughed and gave his son up but not without bestowing a kiss on his head and rubbing it affectionately. Chelsea reveled in the comfort of Austin's tiny arms around her neck. She melted at the way he squished his cheeks against her shoulders. Another swell of emotion pitched high inside her, but she struggled against it and contained it. She used to hide emotion from Brady to avoid confrontations. She wouldn't mind if he knew that being away from Austin had been difficult—he'd already guessed anyway. She just didn't want to confide in him.

"Do you mind if I put him to bed?" Brady asked.

"Nope." Her stomach flipped, but Chelsea ignored it. It was one bedtime out of hundreds she'd gotten all to herself in the past year, even if Austin had been gone all day. "That's fine."

"Come see Daddy?" Brady said, holding his arms back out to

Austin. Austin clung to Chelsea a second longer, and she squeezed him right back, trying to tamp down the longing that wouldn't allow her to unwind her arms. Finally, Austin squirmed to turn around, and his excitement propelled him right back into Brady's arms. The happiness in Brady's eyes as he headed upstairs helped slow down the roller coaster inside her. A little.

"Austin back?" Denise poked her head in from the kitchen.

"Yeah. Brady took him up to bed," Chelsea said. Denise scowled, and Chelsea laughed. "He sleeps good this way. I'm not going to complain. There's one good thing about all this upheaval. Ever since Brady came back and started doing the bedtime routine again, it's worked magic on Austin's sleeping. I look forward to lots of full nights of sleep in Salt Lake." She winked at her mom.

"Well, fine then. I guess I won't get my evening snuggle in. Which is too bad since I'm going to miss out on a lot of future ones." She gave a light huff, downplaying how difficult it was for her to watch Chelsea and Austin move away.

She reached out to give her mom a hug. "Come visit a lot, okay?"

Denise patted her back and squeezed her shoulders in the same desperate way Chelsea had held Austin a moment before. So this sort of thing didn't go away when they got older. "I promise, sweetie."

Brady came back downstairs, and Denise waved at him as she headed back for the kitchen.

"Mind if I take Austin again tomorrow?" Brady asked.

"I do mind. It's so lonely." She grinned at the surprised look on his face. "But of course you can."

"I promise not to hog all his time when we're in Salt Lake." Even now his face lit up with excitement. "Just every evening."

Chelsea narrowed her eyes at him jokingly. "Did you get a new job and not tell me about it?"

He laughed. "No. But I did talk to my boss about my family, which I hadn't done before. He wants me to make sure I put the time in that I need to, without it affecting my professional goals. He's supportive. I didn't know that. I should've talked to him a lot sooner." He gave a shrug, a sort of I'm-still-learning look. "I'll see you tomorrow."

"Good night, Brady." Her heart swelled with a motherly sort of pride as she watched him head back out to his truck. He was learning and, thankfully for her son, learning fast.

CHAPTER NINETEEN

DJ sat bolt upright in bed, blinking against the early Sunday morning light coming through the cracks in his curtains. He looked around, trying to figure out what had woken him. The persistent ringing of his phone on the dresser next to his bed answered that. He looked over, noting Zollinger's number, and answered. "Hello?"

"Sheesh, I've called like ten times, Kaiser. Why don't you answer?"

"Sleeping," he said dryly. He'd figured everyone on his crew knew why he hadn't come back to work all that week. "What do you need?" he asked and cringed at the edge to his voice.

"Get dressed and come down to the police station. You were right about not locking us out of the structure truck."

"What do you mean?" DJ swung his legs off the bed and reached for a pair of nearby jeans.

Zollinger chuckled. "This you've got to see to believe."

DJ paused, realizing he was trying to put his jeans on over a pair of basketball shorts. "Oh, come on. What's going on?"

"I'll see you there," Zollinger said and hung up.

DJ didn't waste any time getting dressed and running the four blocks from his house to the police station. He'd tried to fill his time off working out on the farm with Dale. They didn't bring up the topic of Chelsea and Brady, and that kept things from getting awkward. He couldn't quite bring himself to go down to Provo. That felt like admitting failure, and though he was close to throwing in the towel, he wasn't there yet.

Chief Tallant and Zollinger were waiting for him along with the police chief, Pam Cutter, as he came in the door.

"So," DJ asked, taking a gulp of breath. "Anyone going to explain this to me?"

Chief Tallant pointed across the room. DJ could see through the windows separating the conference room from the bullpen that held the police officer's desks. Seated at the long table next to her son was Mayor Tingey. A policeman sat opposite them, writing something—probably a statement.

"Uh . . ." DJ looked between Chief Tallant, Zollinger, and Chief Cutter. "Ace Tingey locked us out of the truck?"

Chief Cutter held out a phone to DJ. "Sent this video to one of his friends. Deleted it from the phone but forgot to delete the text message. Jeanie found it last night and sent it to me and Rob. Ace says you should've been fired for killing his mom's dog. He was looking for a way to make you look bad to make sure it happened."

DJ rubbed his hand down his face and shook his head as the police chief played the video. Ace had been holding the phone as he snuck up to the truck while the firemen were distracted. He climbed into the truck, laughing and whispering how he would get DJ Kaiser back. When the video showed his knee hitting the gearshift and knocking it out of fifth, DJ and Chief Tallant shared a look.

"Go ahead and say you told us so," the chief said in a low voice as they watched the rest of the video play out—Ace hitting the lock button and shutting the door before sneaking behind some trees.

DJ shook his head, his eyes narrowing as Ace trained the camera on him and laughed when Zollinger yelled at DJ about locking them out of the truck.

"Claims he didn't know we wouldn't be able to use the controls," Chief Tallant said when the video ended. "Doesn't seem very remorseful to me though."

DJ scrubbed a hand through his hair, which was probably a mess anyway since he hadn't looked at it before rushing out of the house. "It was two a.m. How did he even know?"

"Mrs. Tingey said he admitted to sneaking out and following the trucks when you went on calls, hoping to catch you doing something dumb. When he couldn't, he made it happen," Zollinger said.

DJ sighed and slumped against the wall. He knew why the chief and Zollinger wanted him down here—so he could feel vindicated. But knowing that the mayor's son had done it to avenge his mother's dog didn't comfort DJ either.

"If he'd waited longer, he would have caught me in some dumb mistake of my own," he said.

Zollinger shook his head and slapped DJ on the shoulder. "We all made mistakes when we were rookies."

"How many of you caught your own house on fire because you barbecued too close to it?" DJ asked wryly.

He thought he might have heard Chief Cutter start a laugh that turned into a snort when she tried to cover it. Both Chief Tallant and Zollinger cracked smiles.

"Okay," Zollinger admitted, leaving his hand on DJ's shoulder this time. "You can keep that honor all to yourself, but a few mistakes don't make you a bad fireman."

DJ shrugged. "Thanks." His "few" mistakes still drilled against his brain.

Mayor Tingey came out of the conference room. DJ straightened as she approached, but when she caught sight of him, her steps slowed and she avoided his eyes.

"I'm sure we can work something out, Mayor. It was just a prank," DJ offered.

Mayor Tingey's chin snapped up. "Oh, no. Don't you brownnose me, DJ Kaiser. That was not a prank. What if someone had been living in that house?" She pressed her lips together and let out a huff. "I acted ridiculously, I know. It's not my place to judge if your remorse is real or not. I shouldn't have said the things I did, especially in front of my son."

"It's okay," DJ said, his face heating. He didn't want to hear this apology, mostly because he didn't want to think about the things she shouldn't have said in front of her son.

"It's not. And letting Ace off will teach him to disrespect people he should hold in high regard—people I should as well." She took another deep breath and wouldn't look at him. "The things you've done to improve Clay are very telling about your character, and if I'm honest with myself, I should have known that about you." She huffed out another sigh, sounding annoyed. DJ found a smile threatening. He battled it courageously. The last thing he needed was to ruin Mayor Tingey's reluctant apology. "You were a bit . . . fun-loving in high school, according to Roger." She squared her shoulders and met his gaze. He made extra sure to keep a straight face. "But we were all very proud to see you go to BYU, and I know very well what kind of discipline it takes be a collegiate athlete."

"Um, thank you." DJ didn't know if that was the right response to her half-censure, half-praise, but Mayor Tingey accepted it with a tight nod. "I *am* sorry, ma'am," he said.

"I know," she said, then gave him a light pat on the elbow and walked back toward the conference room.

Zollinger let out a suppressed laugh, subdued since the conference room wasn't sound proof. "Considering you ran over the woman's dog, that was a very touching apology."

DJ chuckled with him. "I suppose so." He glanced up at the chief, studying his expression. Last week he'd said he didn't think DJ was cut out to be a fireman. Did Mayor Tingey's opinion change any of that? Did it change DJ's own opinion? Finding out that Ace had locked them out of the truck didn't change the fact that DJ had been on the verge of killing his career quite nicely by himself. Starting a fire at his own house, backing into the chief's truck, running over the mayor's dog, not to mention not being able to hack it at police academy and then letting a room full of freshman run amuck when he tried to substitute teach. He held back his own disappointed sigh. Maybe Mayor Tingey believed in him again, and while it meant the world to him, it didn't brighten his outlook on the future by much.

Chief Tallant put his hands in the pockets of his Wranglers. "Sorry I didn't trust you, son," he said. He chewed on his bottom lip, making his thick mustache shift back and forth. "You've made some mistakes but never given me a reason not to believe you. I think I let *you* down."

It felt like everyone thought better of him than he did. "Thank you, sir."

He nodded sharply. "Go home and get some rest. We'll see you Monday morning with the rest of your crew."

"Sure thing, Chief." DJ waved at Zollinger as he walked toward the door and out into the beautiful summer afternoon, his hands in his pockets. He had been sleeping better the last few days, thanks to some self-hypnosis tips and homeopathic remedies he'd found. It showed Chelsea's influence, though, that he'd looked up the natural solutions online instead of taking a couple of Tylenol PMs.

It shouldn't surprise him. When he was awake, she dominated his thoughts. He knew Brady had come back to town again. He hadn't been around for months, so spending this many weekends in a row in Clay must mean he was serious about fixing things with Chelsea. And although it killed him, DJ couldn't step between them. Even if he suspected she still had feelings for him. And he did; he'd seen something in her eyes the day she came and helped at the garden. He blew out a long breath.

He'd never doubted his decision to move to Clay last year, so why had everything fallen so utterly apart? He rubbed his forehead. Despite his apology, maybe Chief Tallant was right. Maybe fighting fires wasn't for him, but maybe it went further than even that.

Maybe Clay wasn't for him.

CHAPTER TWENTY

Chelsea skimmed down the list of online job ads, tapping her fingers against the kitchen table where she'd set up her laptop for the evening. Though she had a job for now, she couldn't count on either of the girls she was working for not coming back after they had their babies. She needed to keep looking for something after this temporary job was done.

Brady had gotten off at five that afternoon, coming over immediately to get Austin. In the two weeks since she'd moved back to Salt Lake, they'd settled into a rhythm. Chelsea spent the mornings with Austin and went to work in the afternoons, dropping him off at the day care of a woman in Chelsea's ward, where he could take his afternoon nap and then spend a few hours playing before either Chelsea or Brady came to pick him up. Already, Brady had gotten off early twice so he could pick Austin up. Twice more, Chelsea had needed to work later to catch up with things and had relied on Brady to adjust his own schedule so he could be there for Austin. Whenever Brady got him from daycare, he dropped him off around seven-thirty or eight so Chelsea could put Austin to bed. She was slowly getting used to dividing up her time with Austin, and since his eating and sleeping had improved vastly, she desperately tried to see the blessings in not being with him all the time. In a few days, she and Brady would meet with a mediator to help formalize their new custody arrangement, just in case. Neither knew what the future held for them, and they wanted to be prepared. It would take time, but Chelsea had the peace of knowing she'd eventually get used to this new normal.

The job ads couldn't hold her attention. Even though her days had been busy, when her mind wasn't completely focused, her thoughts turned back to DJ. For the past three nights she'd told herself she'd brave the awkwardness and ask Brady why he had asked DJ to stay away. If he had a good reason, if he convinced her, maybe she could respect his request as much as DJ had. It would just help to understand.

She pulled up the accounts for a new client she'd just acquired. The owner of the small clothing boutique was in the singles ward Brady went to; he'd helped her out with some of the legal work then suggested she hire Chelsea if she needed help with the accounting. Along with the Malone & Parish account she'd taken on for Gwen Parish's dad and husband, it made for a full schedule. Full enough that, with a few more clients, she might be able to work almost completely from home when her temp job was over. Focusing on the numbers might help her shut DJ out of her mind so she could get some things done.

It worked for about forty-five minutes, and then she couldn't help watching the clock, waiting for Brady to bring Austin back. She hopped out of her chair the minute she heard footsteps on the stairs. Brady was always punctual about making sure Austin was back home before eight, even when he got home later in the evenings and she knew he wished he had more time. She threw open the door before Brady could even knock and held out her arms for her baby.

Austin squeezed her as soon as she took him, Brady's phone bumping into her head as Austin held her.

"Can I do bedtime?" Brady asked, his fake pout saying *pretty-please*.

She smothered Austin's face with kisses, making him giggle, and gave Brady a mock, long-suffering sigh. "Sure. But I get tomorrow night."

"You know you love it when I do it," Brady said, reaching to take his son back and absently handing her his phone. "He sleeps like a . . . well, baby!" His voice echoed from the bedroom where Austin's crib was shoved in next to Chelsea's full-sized bed. The basement apartment at Brady's new house had two bedrooms—tiny—but at least there were two. Just another week before Brady closed and they could move.

She laughed and glanced down at his phone in her hands, noticing a message. She set it on the table, not wanting to pry in Brady's life, but then she saw the contact said The Kaiser, the way Brady had always identified DJ's number.

How are things going with Chelsea? the message read.

It was sweet of him to think about her and Austin—but why hadn't the message asked about Austin too? Why just her? Why hadn't he texted Chelsea himself? Maybe he was trying to keep his distance, but he'd also said they'd try to be friends.

Chelsea lowered herself back down to her laptop as she listened to Brady read to Austin, each page taking four hundred years to finish. Finally, Brady reemerged.

Chelsea stood and held out his phone to him. "What does DJ mean by how are things going with me?" she blurted. The words had rolled through her mind for all of the excruciating time it had taken Brady to put Austin to bed.

Brady's gaze shifted over the room. "Um. I think he might be under the impression that you moved back here so I could have a chance at working things out with you." With each word, the color in his face rose.

"Working things out?" Chelsea repeated, a sort of panic jumping through her. "Like us getting back together? What did you say to him? Is that what you told him?"

Brady held up his hands. "No. Of course not."

"Then what *did* you say? I thought you guys had talked about . . ." She waved a hand through the air. "You said you guys were okay."

"There wasn't really all that much to say." Brady cringed.

"Did you tell him not to pursue a relationship with me?" She squeezed the back of the chair, waiting for his confession and wondering how she'd react. Her relationship with Brady was important. They were raising a son together. She couldn't disregard his feelings on her falling for DJ—but she could certainly try to argue him out of them.

"No," Brady said.

She scowled. "Why does he think that we're working things out? We're not working things out, Brady. You weren't hoping that's what this was . . ." That panic came back. The things he had said he was willing to do. His feelings hadn't somehow changed, had they? Her brain charged ahead. Was *that* what Brady had figured out that led to him working so hard to build his relationship back up with Austin?

"No, no, no." Brady held his hands up again, taking a step forward. "No, I didn't tell him that. I just didn't . . . correct him when I thought maybe that's what he was thinking."

Her mouth dropped open. "What?"

"Listen, I know we have a great relationship, and I'm glad. It makes this way easier than it could be, but does that mean that *this*—you and him—needs to be okay too?" Now he turned, his hands out at his sides, as if pleading for her to understand.

She blinked. Tears stung in her eyes that all along, in a way, Brady *had* taken DJ away from her. "You care that much?" she asked in a soft voice.

Brady's eyes widened. "I . . . I didn't realize you did." He stepped backward and dropped onto the couch. "DJ made it sound like a couple of dates, Chels. Like you guys had gone out and had fun but it was no big deal—but it's more than that, isn't it?"

She nodded, folding her arms across her stomach and turning away to stare out the window in the kitchen. A family played in the pool in the courtyard. "Could you be okay with it?" she asked.

"Chels?" His tender voice made her turn back around to look at him, leaning forward with his elbows on his knees. "If he makes you happy? Yes." He stood up, coming toward her and shoving his hands in his pockets. "I may not love you the way we would need to make each other happy, but you're the mother of my son. That's a special person to be. Someone I need. I'm sorry I made a selfish decision and forgot that."

She swallowed, more emotion crowding around her at such an admission. "It's okay," she said when she could make her voice even. She let out a laugh and rolled her eyes. "At least you weren't as dumb as DJ."

———

DJ SLOWED his pace as his house came into view. He hadn't meant to get up early to run, but once he'd woken up at five that morning, there was no getting back to sleep. Brady hadn't answered his text from the night before, which wasn't a new thing, but DJ's brain couldn't help harping on it. He shouldn't get nosy about what Brady did to reestablish his relationship with Chelsea, but he felt compelled to check on him and ease the guilt in his conscience for hoping that things blew up.

His phone rang from the running belt at his hip, and DJ pulled it out, curious about who would call at this hour. Brady's picture filled the screen, a selfie of him and Austin that Brady had sent the other day.

"Hey," DJ answered, already figuring out in his mind how he could get information without arousing suspicion. Maybe he shouldn't totally give up on the police work stuff. A few more years to practice shooting, and he might bring his abilities up to par.

"I'm on my way into work so I have a few minutes, and I wanted to talk to you about something," Brady said, his voice tinny and distant through the speakerphone he was using.

"Kind of an early start." DJ laughed, but he was glad Brady had used the time to get a hold of him.

"Trying to work on this end of the clock so I can stop working so late. Did I wake you up?"

"No, I just got back from a run. What's up?" Though the tone of the conversation held the same relaxed vibe from before his divorce, he sensed nerves in Brady's voice. It must be something important to get him to call after months of sporadic text messaging as a means of communication.

"You in love with Chelsea?" Brady asked.

Once, in their backyard when they were kids, Brady had tackled DJ in a pickup game of football. He'd nailed DJ right in the stomach, rolling them both to the ground and taking DJ's breath away for several long seconds. That same feeling came back to him now. When he finally let it out, his words came out in a sigh.

"Things have been really different for you and me since the divorce. I'm sorry. I thought . . . I'll keep my distance."

To his surprise, Brady started laughing. "Never thought you were one who needed your self-esteem boosted with this sort of thing, but I guess things are pretty rough with your job."

DJ ignored the jab, stopping at the gate outside his house. "What?"

"She's in love with you," Brady said. "And I didn't ask her to move so we could work things out. She told me that she told you about why we got divorced and how we both felt about each other. That hasn't changed. She came because I promised to move back to Clay in a few years and she wants Austin to have his dad near him. She believes in me, that I can be better, but she doesn't love me. Not like that."

DJ dropped onto the steps of his porch. Brady had never been so open with his feelings in his life. Guess Chelsea was right that he'd started to open up more after their divorce.

"Are you serious?" he said. "You let me think—"

"I did. I'm sorry. I didn't really realize what I was stepping in the middle of. You're the one that acted like it wasn't a big deal, Kaiser."

DJ rubbed his temples, trying not to laugh. Seems Chelsea and Brady had figured out the importance of communication, but he'd fallen behind. "Things were weird enough. So . . ." He rolled his eyes at himself. "I have your blessing?"

"Do I have to call it that?" Brady chuckled, and the tension that had filled DJ since he'd last seen Chelsea at the community garden started draining away. "Whatever. Yes. Listen, I'm pulling into work, but I'm sure I'll see you soon."

"Yeah, probably." DJ stood back up to head inside his house. It would take some arranging, but maybe he could get a couple extra days off. He'd have to find someone to cover his shift, and he didn't know anyone extra-willing considering the chief had had to call someone in to cover for him just a couple of weeks before. "Thanks."

"Yeah, yeah. See you."

DJ laughed and said his own good-bye. As he headed for his bathroom and a shower, his laugh grew deeper, more genuine. Hearing that Ace had set out to ruin DJ's career had given him a measure of satisfaction but only in the notion that maybe he *could* be a firefighter if he still wanted to be.

But this? It changed everything.

CHAPTER TWENTY-ONE

"**C**utie Pies delivery!"

DJ jumped at the familiar voice coming through his open screen door. After spending the morning promising favors to the other firemen, he'd finally found someone to cover for his shift that weekend so he could go properly apologize to Chelsea. But when he looked up, she stood at the door, holding a bag with the bakery's logo emblazoned on the front.

"You gonna open this door?" she asked, folding her arms. "Because you have a lot of explaining to do."

He took three steps across the room, throwing open the door and pulling her into his arms. "What are you doing here?"

She leaned back, smiling up at him. "I had some business in town: giving Wendy the final recipe for the new soup, collecting payment for the brownies she sells from my recipe, and lecturing a certain fireman about telling girls that are in love with him that they should just be friends."

His grin grew, but he tried to control it into something more contrite. "I'm sorry about that misunderstanding."

Her lips thinned out, and she glared at him, full of real fierceness.

"How could you possibly believe I'd get back together with Brady, after everything I told you about us? How I, specifically, did not love him?" She pressed a finger hard into his chest.

"It's Brady's fault!" he cried, hoping for quick forgiveness. "He let me think that's what was going on."

"You let him think I was just some girl you took out a couple of times." She pinned him with another look, this one more vulnerable. "Am I just some girl?"

"No way." He followed this with what he'd been wanting to do since he saw her at the door. He lowered his face and kissed her, the best kind of relief spreading through him as she melted into the kiss and into him. She put her hands on his chest, fingers rolling over his T-shirt and working up to interlock behind his neck. She reminded him of comfort. The taste of Wendy's brownies when he'd had a long shift, the last two steps into the end zone for a touchdown. The doubts he'd harbored about keeping his job and staying in Clay took a back seat with her there, right where they both belonged. Together. Ten seconds of holding her and he didn't care at all what happened with his job. He rested his head on top of hers.

"I'm sorry," he said again. "I love you."

She pressed her hands to his cheeks and pulled him down to her again, kissing him with more intensity. "I love you." Then her shoulders sagged. "But what are we going to do? I live in Salt Lake now. Brady would probably be willing to take Austin on weekends so I could come visit. And you could come down there when you're off sometimes." She cringed. The drive was long, close to eight hours. She must have left not long after Brady had called him to be there now.

The best solution presented itself, surprising him with how much it didn't surprise him, like he'd known it was the right thing all along. "I'll move down there."

She jerked back, but only enough to stare at him, bewildered. "You have a job here. You love Clay. I can't take that away from you."

He wrapped his arms tighter around her, staring down at her and praying his sincerity was written on his face as he spoke. "I love you more than I'll ever love Clay." The truth of those words wove through him and strengthened him, lifted him above any doubt about what he should do. Making his failures insignificant. He leaned over and kissed her. It grounded him fully and completely. As his relationship with Chelsea had grown, he'd grasped at pieces of the knowledge that fell into place in that moment. That every time he did something for her, it cemented his purpose in life. The misunderstanding with Brady had shaken him up, left him confused, but she'd handed that understanding back to him, this time whole and complete.

"I've watched my friends do really successful things—personally and otherwise," he said. "I've watched and tried to figure out what great thing I'm meant to do. I know one thing that I'm good at—one thing I could be happy doing the rest of my life. One thing, that if I do right, will make me more accomplished than I ever imagined I would be, and that is loving you."

He brushed his thumbs over her cheeks as she watched him. She didn't say anything for a long time. He would spend his life measuring up to the kind of sacrifices she was willing to make for her family, for him even. Considering the way he'd always just wanted to help her, it shouldn't surprise him that this is what it felt like to love her. He lowered his lips and kissed her again, sealing his words and then some.

"You are so wonderful," she said against his lips.

"I've been known to have my moments." He slid his hands down her arms and threaded their fingers together. "I want you to have everything you want, Chels. I want to do everything I can to help you every day of your life."

She tilted her head at him. "Are you asking me to marry you?"

He took a moment to consider that. She deserved him to be serious about what he said. "I think I am."

Laughter escaped. "Think?"

"Only if you're going to say yes. If not, I guess I'm just asking to follow you around until you will." He pulled away so they could study each other. "I understand we haven't had a lot of time together. I'm willing to be there and support you until you're ready to say yes."

Her face shone as her laughter turned into pure joy. "I love you."

She paused dramatically. "And I'm ready to say yes." She let go of his hands to throw her arms around his chest, resting her cheek against him.

She was his sure place. She always would be.

CHAPTER TWENTY-TWO

C helsea leaned back against the wooden bleachers, trying to get more comfortable. Really, it gave her an excuse to look around to see if Brady had shown up. Even after six months, having him take Austin after he got off work still left her nervous sometimes. She tapped her hands on her thighs and eyed the basketball court where DJ warmed up with the rest of his city-league team. He looked at the clock above the scoreboard, likely sensing her unease. She shrugged at him. He grinned and winked. When she looked back toward the door, Brady galloped through with Austin bouncing in his arms. A huge smile lit Brady's face, and Austin giggled at the funny gait his dad had assumed. They stopped in front of Chelsea, and Brady swung Austin up into her arms.

"Sorry," he said, tossing his own bag onto the bleachers in front of her, next to DJ's bag. "He didn't want to leave the playground."

"Playground?" Chelsea's eyebrows shot up. She pressed her cheeks against Austin's and found them cold. "It's January, Brady."

"Don't worry. It was only about fifteen minutes, and he was bundled up. And it's well over forty. Gorgeous day." He sat down and started pulling on his basketball shoes.

Chelsea screwed up her lips but couldn't think of anything wrong with Brady's summary. It shouldn't surprise her anymore that Brady could be a good, responsible dad. He'd proven in the last few months that he meant his promises to do better.

"I'm sure he had a blast. Did you love the park, Austin?" she asked, pulling him toward her and forcing a hug out of him. He'd gotten so busy and uncuddly. Why did her baby insist on growing up?

Austin pointed to the court as Brady hopped up and went to join his teammates. DJ had talked him into joining their team, an effort to untangle their now awkward relationship. Chelsea wanted their friendship closer to what it had been before her and Brady's divorce. Being on the team had fixed things more than Chelsea expected, which boded well for her and DJ's wedding next month.

"Are Daddy and DJ playing basketball?" she asked Austin, pulling him to sit in her lap as she leaned over to watch.

"Ball, Mama, ball," Austin said and strained to get off her lap.

"You can't go on the court, sweetie." She kissed his cheeks and that irresistible space on his neck, making him giggle and push away. The distraction worked, and Austin started playing his favorite game—trying to kiss her while she pulled away and pretended to be surprised when he still landed a slobbery kiss on her cheek or chin or forehead or eyebrow.

"I thought there was a no-kissing rule at the games," DJ said, leaning up next to them. Since the game hadn't gotten underway yet, he still smelled fabulous, like fresh deodorant and the tea tree and lemon oil laundry detergent she made for him. Whenever she smelled it, it reminded her of how proud he always was when she came up with a new recipe for the bakery, which she still worked on from time to time to stretch her creativity. She smiled at his teasing. She and DJ had discussed how to act around Brady before the season started. They didn't need any more weirdness, so around Brady, they kept displays of affection low-key.

But Brady just shook his head and laughed at DJ's sideways glance, especially when DJ bent over and snagged a kiss from Chelsea before standing back up. Things would never be normal between him and DJ again and never truly comfortable either, but it worked for now, and that was all that mattered.

"Ball!" Austin squealed and pointed at the basketballs the guys set down between the bleachers as the refs whistled for the players to come on the court.

"Here," Brady said, jabbing his hand into the backpack he'd dropped next to Chelsea. He pulled out a blue-and-white fabric basketball and handed it to Austin. He turned and jogged after DJ, leaning toward him to say something as they took their places on the court. Watching them made Chelsea warm all over at the leap of faith that led her here, a place she'd never expected to be. She kissed Austin on top of the head.

She'd take it.

The End

ALSO BY RANEÉ S. CLARK

Playing for Keeps Series

PLAYING FOR KEEPS

(Anthony & Ty)

DOUBLE PLAY

(David & Sophie)

LOVE, JANE

(Sean & Jane)

MEANT FOR YOU

(DJ & Chelsea)

ALSO BY RANEÉ S. CLARK

Historical

BENEATH THE BELLEMONT SKY

———

Novellas

GOODNIGHT KISS

WOULDN'T IT BE NICE

LAST KISS

A LADY AND A SPY

ABOUT THE AUTHOR

During her early years of reading, Raneé S. Clark devoured fantasy books, which continued into her adulthood—since she often believes that a well-written romance novel is a delightful fantasy. Though raising three boys can sometimes hamper both romance with her own Mr. Charming and her writing, she tries to get a little of both in every day. And most of the time she succeeds.

Raneé is the author of three contemporary romances and one historical novel, *Beneath the Bellemont Sky*.

Photo credit: © 2018 Brekke Felt